HELL IN A HAND BASKET

A DEVILISH DEBUTANTE'S BOOK

ANNABELLE ANDERS

ANNABELLE
ANDERS

Sophia tugged at the leading string to draw Peaches closer to the hem of her dress. She must keep her precious companion as close as possible.

The dog, small in stature, had very short legs and a long body.

Not that Peaches was strong enough to drag Sophia into the melee of pedestrians. But the passing humans concerned her. The crowded sidewalks bustled with activity today and busy passersby were not always mindful of twelve-inch-tall canines.

Sophia would not wish for Peaches to be accidentally kicked, or worse! She would take no chances with her beloved pet.

Peaches was her baby.

She — the dog, mind you — had short reddish hair with a brown streak that stood up whenever she was provoked or frightened.

In that moment, the streak stood out boldly.

And, as Sophia glanced up, she supposed that if she herself had a streak, it would be standing on end as well.

For rambling down the busy London street appeared a most unusual sight. In a line of tall wagons, all constructed with vertical bars, a caravan of vehicles transported a variety of exotic animals. Were they part of a traveling circus? Perhaps they were new additions to the Tower Menagerie in Regent's Park.

She'd been once, to the menagerie, and although fascinated by the novelty of viewing the magnificent beasts, she'd sensed a wrongness to it all. A similar sensation swept through her today, as the carts rolled past with the animals caged behind bars.

Other onlookers had stopped to stare at the impromptu exhibition as well. A most unusual sight!

Not to go unnoticed by her dog.

For Peaches' tail now curled between her hind legs and a low growl rumbled in her throat.

Oh, no.

Sophia glanced futilely toward the storefront where her friend, Rhoda, had disappeared a few minutes before. The doorway stood empty. Sophia and Peaches were no longer welcome inside of the fashionable milliner's establishment. Well, Peaches wasn't anyhow. Upon their last visit, a particularly lifelike bluebird set in one of the hats on display had appeared to Peaches as somewhat of a mortal threat. Peaches had attacked and subdued the bird.

The store's owner had banned her for life.

And so, Sophia and Peaches would await Rhoda outside

— *"Just for a minute,"* Rhoda had stressed — while she fetched the bonnet she'd ordered earlier that week.

As the train of animals rambled past, Sophia crouched to the ground, petting and soothing the trembling dog. "It's all right, Peaches. Be a good dog now. That's a good girl."

But Peaches had other ideas and let out one sharp *woof*, quickly followed by a string of high-pitched barks.

The horses pulling the nearest wagon cage did not appreciate being taunted by such a ridiculously impertinent animal. In their nervousness, they began dancing and then — oh heavens — bucking!

"Shush, Peaches, Hush now!" Sophia tried infusing authority into her voice, but Peaches had by now worked herself into a frenzy.

"Woof, woof, ark, ark, ark!"

The horses' agitation increased. In an effort to calm them, the driver had now risen to his feet and was tugging at the reins and yelling at them ineffectually. He brought a whip down sharply, hitting the ground near the sidewalk where Sophia stood. "Shut that bloody little bastard up!" he shouted in Sophia's direction.

Suddenly the situation had become most unpleasant indeed. Feeling more than a smidgeon of fear, Sophia gathered Peaches into her arms and backed away from the roadway into a narrow opening between the hatmaker's storefront and a neighboring jeweler.

But Peaches continued barking, and the driver lost control of his team completely.

One horse attempted to bolt while the other continued

bucking. This combination created an unbalancing of the wagon as it rolled past Sophia.

Except that it did not roll past at all.

It listed toward her, and inside sat none other than a large golden lion with glinting eyes and a magnificent mane encircling his face.

Reacting to Peaches' vicious snarls, the lion narrowed said eyes and emitted a growl of his own. As he did so, he slid along the bottom of the cage, toward the bars.

Toward Sophia!

He seemed to forget about Peaches for a moment and scratched and clawed at the floor in futility.

Sophia pressed backwards but was impeded by a brick wall. This was not an alleyway at all, but a cavity between the buildings, about three feet wide and three feet deep.

The cage continued tilting forward and Sophia huddled down, her body wrapped around Peaches.

She prepared to be crushed.

CAPTAIN DEVLIN BROOKES was in a better mood than usual today. Just that morning he'd signed papers finalizing the purchase of a property near Surrey that he'd coveted for most of his adult life. Which was considerable, he grimaced to himself, at the near-ancient age of nine and twenty.

But he felt older than his actual years — military life did that to a man.

Yesterday, he'd sold off his commission. He was a civilian now.

The incident last month with the Earl of Nottingham had given him the nudge he'd needed to sell out. The poor bastard had taken a sword to the bollocks, damndest thing he'd ever seen. The tragic wound had not even happened on the battlefield.

Witnessing it, however, seeing the man's life change in an instant, had stirred something inside of Dev.

He'd seen enough violence for ten lifetimes.

As nephew to a duke and no title to inherit, military service had been expected of him. He'd served for eleven years and felt he'd done his duty to both country and family. He was wont to pursue something of a peaceful existence. The estate near Surrey, Dartmouth Place, would allow him to do just that.

He might even marry.

But he needn't rush. He could pop up to London for a Season sometime in the future, after he'd settled. Perhaps by then he would feel compelled to take on a wife. Or conceivably he would meet a young lady who already resided in the country.

Yes, that might be for the best, a country lass.

No hurry, though. He hunched his shoulders and stretched his back. The hours he'd spent with the solicitors that morning had left him feeling stiff. In addition to that, the civilian clothing he'd donned this morning felt unnatural. Since selling his commission, he'd no longer wear a uniform.

Just as he began considering the conversation he must have with his uncle and father, a loud clamoring commotion — Was that barking? And screaming, yes screaming —

interrupted his contemplative stroll.

The sight that met him around the corner presented more than a hint of Bedlam.

Were those circus wagons? Oh, hell, a caravan of exotic animals. And one of them had tipped over onto the side of two buildings.

The situation would not be dire, really, except for the fact that the toppled wagon contained a full-grown lion.

Ferocious sounds arose from within the vehicle. And from behind it, barking. What in the world? Through the cracks between building and vehicle, he spied a hint of blond ringlets and pastels and lace, the ominous indication that a debutante was in the vicinity.

Yet another girl, with darker hair, cautiously crouched a few feet from the vehicle. "Sophia, are you all right? Are you hurt? Can you answer me, Sophia?"

A few shabbily dressed men paced about.

It was the driver, Dev presumed, doing all of the cursing and yelling at the current state of his conveyance.

Dev assessed the situation and sprang into action.

The chaos would continue, most assuredly, if allowed to go on unabated. Approaching the scene, he ordered the driver to discontinue his volatile language. The driver cowered at Dev's command and obediently shut his mouth. Dev then approached the lady hunkered beside the tipped-over wagon and crouched beside her.

"Your friend, madam? She is trapped behind the cage?"

She turned clear and steady eyes on him. "With her dog."

Of course, except the barking had ceased along with the driver's barrage of colorful language.

"I'm all right!" a surprisingly steady voice called out from the rubble. "But the lion is none too happy right now... and he is... so very close to me."

"What is your name? Madam?"

"Sophia," she answered.

"Miss Babineaux," her friend corrected.

The condition of the lion and the strength of the cage concerned him. "Miss Babineaux, does the cage appear to be intact from that side?"

A moment passed and then a tentative "I think so. But the bars are not as close together as I would prefer. And one of his paws is caught between two of the them."

Dev rose and examined what he could see of the wagon. Made of a solid wood, probably oak, it kept the animal in check with iron bars.

It must weigh nearly a ton.

A few of the caravan's laborers could be heard discussing how one might go about righting it. They apparently had less concern for the girl trapped behind it than for the condition of the lion. One of them suggested a chain be located and another unhitched the horses. Very good. Some activity. Dev, however, did not like the angle in which the cage listed.

If the wheels were to slip, the girl could be injured. Or worse.

Glancing about, he spied exactly what he needed stacked upon another cart parked nearby in the resulting gridlock. As Devlin approached it, this driver, more level-headed than the others, understood exactly what he was about.

Tugging at the timber stacked behind him, he twisted, and pulled and then handed Devlin a short piece of sturdy lumber and two blocks.

Not wasting any time, Dev shoved two of the blocks on both sides of one of the wheels that remained upon the ground, and tucked them in snugly. This would prevent them from rolling when the wagon was pulled back into an upright position. He then grasped the larger plank under his arm and jumped up onto a stone ledge that decorated the front of the milliner's building. Tossing the lumber onto the overturned cart, he pulled himself up and climbed around to where the chit was trapped.

Large blue eyes peered up at him trustingly.

Stunned, for only a moment though, he hovered over the tiny space she'd managed to wedge herself. "Can you make room for me, sweetheart?" She was a lady, but the endearment slipped out nonetheless. Devlin had always found that women in unsettling circumstances responded well to a bit of coddling.

She gathered her pup close to her chest and nodded. "Watch the lion, though. I think his other paw can reach through if he feels so inclined."

Dev didn't fear for himself. The most he'd receive would likely be a scratch.

The girl pressed herself farther into the corner as he dropped into the space beside her. Not wasting any time, he reached up and grasped the lumber. He would find somewhere to wedge it so as to ensure the wagon would not fall on top of both of them, now.

He'd not bargained for the sweet proximity of the girl herself. So delightfully feminine.

A weakness of his.

She'd shifted her little dog to one side and reached her other arm around him, in order to make more room. "Don't put your hand too close to the cage, love." His body pressed up against hers. He still hadn't managed a thorough look at her. The space was cramped and darkened by the shadow of the cart. After hesitating a moment, he felt her hand settle upon his shoulder.

Devlin was considerably taller than she. At least by a foot. Her hair tickled his chin and as he inhaled; her perfume teased his senses. Vanilla, sweet.

Dev maneuvered himself around and propped the wood strategically. Upon doing so, a calm set into him. Until that moment, he had not realized his heart had been racing.

Having turned to address the wagon, he now found himself staring straight into the eyes of the lion.

"He's scared," the girl said from behind him.

The lion? Yes, he supposed she had the right of it. Furthermore, the beast was injured and likely aggravated by the indignities of his circumstances.

"His paw is bleeding," she added.

Devlin knew that if the lion took it upon himself to slash his other paw through the cage, it could reach him. Looking the lion in the eyes could rile it.

And so, he slowly turned back around to face the girl.

At least he wore a thick wool jacket. It would protect his back somewhat if the lion chose to become aggressive.

"Are you hurt?" He looked down at this petite miss who had remained surprisingly calm in such an upsetting situation.

She tilted her head to look up at him, and his breath caught. She was exquisite.

Creamy white skin, rosy lips, and just a hint of blush on her cheeks. Her hair hung in spiral curls, but they somehow did not look ridiculous, as he'd often considered the style on other chits.

"It's all my fault — mine and Peaches, that is. Which, in reality, means that the entirety of fault lies with me. I could not stop her barking when she watched the animals pass. And her barking upset the horses."

It was the confounded driver's fault.

The floundering idiot ought to have exerted control over his animals.

Dev would reassure this slip of a girl. "All of this? Somehow, Miss Babineaux, I do not think you can be blamed for such chaos."

She took in a deep breath and then let it out in a long sigh. In doing so, she unwittingly pressed her breasts against his waistcoat. A low rumbling sound arose behind him. Dev crowded into the little doll protectively and tucked her head into his chest. "You are doing well to keep the pup silenced now. We don't want to appear too interesting to our friend in the cage."

"Oh, I rather think he's interested," she whispered. Up

until then her voice had sounded like a song; the tenor of her whisper stirred him in a rather inconvenient way.

He touched a finger to her lips. "Any more than he already is," he clarified in a low voice. The skin beneath his finger felt soft and plump. Hell, he was growing *interested* as well.

What were the gents doing out there? Did they intend to leave the wagon tipped over all afternoon?

"Poor thing, trapped in a cage. I hope he isn't too badly hurt. Will they kill him, do you think? If he *is* injured?"

Devlin raised his brows at her question. A circus life seemed a poor substitute for the wilds the beast ought to live in. Perhaps death would be merciful.

"People used to pay to watch the lions at the menagerie eat small pets, did you know that? A very long time ago." The girl continued without receiving an answer to her first question. "Humans can be the vilest of creatures sometimes."

She tilted her head to look up at him again. "Oh, not you, sir. I simply mean in general."

But her words had struck a chord within him. He'd witnessed far too much carnage brought about by humans, to contradict her statement. "I think you have the right of it, Miss Babineaux."

And then she wrinkled her nose. A petite nose, just as her person was, and really quite adorable. "I'm afraid we've not been introduced properly."

Devlin could not help but shake his head at her turn of thought. A proper English miss, indeed! "Captain Devlin Brookes, at your service."

"Oh!" she exclaimed suddenly. "You acted as Colonel Harris' second in the duel." She knew about the duel? "It was unsporting of him, I suppose, to have, well, you know. But I rather think Lord Kensington deserved it."

Who is this chit?

"Ladies aren't supposed to be apprised of such nasty events," Devlin said, taken aback that she'd been privy to the earl's... accident. She even seemed to know the nature of the injury.

"I am well-acquainted with the countess."

Ah, well, that would explain it. Lady Kensington needed as many friends as possible. What with a eunuch for a husband now.

Contemplating Kensington's injury, Dev winced inwardly.

Miss Babineaux chose that moment to shift her weight. She was an enticing combination of sensuality and innocence. Did she realize it?

The clanking of chains dragging nearby echoed from the street on the other side of the overturned wagon. It would not be long before they had it righted, and Dev could be on his way.

He would leave the city soon. As a man of property, he would most likely become responsible, a respectable landed gentleman. It was something he'd desired, but he would miss a few aspects of the life he'd lived up until now.

On that thought, he wrapped his arms around Miss Sophia Babineaux, placing one of his hands just below the small of her back.

She furrowed her brows at him with questioning eyes.

Such a sweet bundle of womanhood. Long lashes fluttered in surprise when he slid his hand even farther and settled it upon her bum.

She tilted her head questioningly. It was all the encouragement he needed.

Ever so slowly, he lowered his mouth to hers. "Just a taste," he murmured.

At first, she compressed her lips — a feeble protest — while he used his own to coax and persuade.

But then… ah, yes.

Giving in with a sweet sigh, her mouth softened beneath his.

Dev took full advantage of her acquiescence and slid his tongue along the relaxed seam.

Honeyed lips opened for him.

"So sweet…" He growled into her mouth before delving deeper into the pink, moist flesh. He was vaguely aware of the rattling of chains as they were attached to the wagon, and then voices, a brief argument, and some sort of agreement.

Undeterred, he had time yet. He explored behind her lips and along the line of her teeth and then sucked, ever so lightly at her tongue. He would miss this. The excitement of experiencing a woman's arousal for the first time. The delight of hearing her breath quicken.

She liked it, he could tell, although he also presumed her to be shocked at his audacity. But she'd lifted her face up, closer to his. She must be on her toes.

Dev dug his fingers into the flesh of her derriere and the tremor that shook her body convinced him that, given the opportunity, she would enjoy more intimate play.

But Miss Sophia Babineaux was a lady.

He would have to be satisfied with but a kiss.

Except... He had been considering earlier... Finding some sweet thing...

"Here she goes! You ready in there, sir?"

Dev pulled away and smiled into the passion-clouded eyes of Miss Sophia Babineaux. "Carry on!" he shouted without removing his gaze.

And then she narrowed her eyes. The debutante had returned!

"You ought not to take advantage, Captain."

"Why ever not, Miss Babineaux?" he asked. "Don't I deserve a boon for coming to your rescue?" He bent down and pressed his open mouth against the side of her neck.

She shivered and, contradicting her own words, tilted her head to give him better access.

Dev knew when a woman was willing.

And, in this moment anyhow, this woman was willing.

CHAPTER 2

*S*ophia had heard of Captain Devlin Brookes.

Despite efforts to hide the nature of Lord Kensington's injury, the Nottinghams had been unable to keep secret the details of the infamous duel. It was simply too delicious for any self-respecting member of the *ton* to keep to oneself. The servants at Nottinghouse, anyhow, had been unable to do so. And everyone knew that the juiciest morsels of gossip were fueled by one's retainers.

This man, with his arms around her, Captain Devlin Brookes, had acted as second to the challenger, Colonel Harris. Sophia considered Harris something of a hero. He'd avenged his daughter's honor most efficiently.

And, well, the Earl of Kensington had deserved it! He'd betrayed one of her dearest of friends.

Although Brookes had only been the second in the duel, the nature of his association gave him stature in Sophia's esteem.

And now, he'd come along to rescue not only herself, but Peaches, too.

The captain stood so tall that she needed to tilt her head all the way back to assess his features. She ought to be shocked by his behavior, but here she stood, one hand tucked into the material of his jacket, cradling Peaches between them, and the other around his neck.

He was in need of a haircut, she pondered idly as her fingers combed through a few tendrils. She considered withdrawing but she had nowhere to go! And so...

She'd never imagined the taste of another human's mouth. Spicy, warm — and his tongue felt rough as he danced with her own.

When the lion cart began toppling toward her, she had braced herself for crushing pain, an onslaught of sorrow for her untimely demise, and then, blessed, peaceful death. Amidst all these thoughts, she'd hoped she could somehow protect Peaches with her own body.

But the impact had not come.

The cart would have landed on them, but the façades of the two buildings beside her had halted its descent at the last moment. She'd huddled, amazingly alive, only to realize she still faced danger... danger that involved swiping claws and razor-sharp teeth.

She almost might have crawled out beneath the precariously perched vehicle, for she could see daylight peeking through, but if she were to make one wrong move, yikes! She'd decided not to attempt it.

All of this had left Sophia and Peaches in close confines

with an injured lion. And although the situation was harrowing, indeed, her foremost fear was for Peaches. Most certainly, her tiny dog would provide a fine delicacy for a lion.

She'd been doing her best to prevent another fit of barking when the captain had appeared, hovering above her.

He'd materialized most heroically, a dark silhouette against the bright sky.

Such a sense of authority and power exuded from his person, that the panic of her situation dissolved unashamedly... into shivers of admiration.

And he had been so kind!

Whereas certain men might chastise her, this one expressed only concern and sympathy.

He'd not patronized her.

Nor had he berated her for this calamity; in fact, he'd scoffed at the very notion of Sophia being at fault!

How could one *not* find such a figure heroic?

He smelled divine. And he tasted... Oh, my!

She had never been so conscious of a man, of a person for that matter, in her entire life. Not even Lord Harold.

Her fiancé had certainly never held her like this — as though he would die if he could not touch her, kiss her, taste her. This captain didn't even seem to mind Peaches snuggled between the two of them.

What would Harold think if he knew? Surely, Harold would feel betrayed.

With good reason, she admonished herself as the captain gently nipped at her lower lip.

For such utter lack of resistance on her part was an unqualified betrayal of her sweet, quiet, unassuming fiancé.

She could make all the excuses in the world that the shock of nearly being crushed to death had muddled her judgment, but the reality was that she had willingly allowed another man to kiss her — a man who was not her fiancé.

And go right on kissing her.

In fact, he now seemed quite fascinated with her cheek, and the sensitive skin by her ear.

Why ever would she want to end this?

Did a person take one breath of air and then stop breathing?

Did a man lost in the desert, drink one swallow of water and then toss the canteen aside? Or perhaps more aptly, could a girl take a single lick of her ice from Gunter's only to allow the rest to melt?

Good heavens, no!

For in her twenty years of life, by no means had she ever experienced such delightful, and yet unnerving sensations.

How could she tell him to stop before he was finished?

She could not.

She did not.

Which, as an engaged woman, she found more than a little disturbing.

Why hadn't Harold aroused such feelings? Brookes, a man she didn't know from Adam, had inexplicitly lit a fire in her she'd not even known existed. What was so different about him?

Was it because she and Peaches had been in such danger? Could her scandalous behavior be excused as an understandable response to such a harrowing experience?

Or was it simply because she found herself trapped in a very private alcove with a sublimely handsome gentleman? Perhaps she could scrutinize these matters with Rhoda.

Later.

"They're going to hoist the wagon upright in a moment. Sophia? Are you well? Is Peaches unhurt? You've gone awful silent, Sophia?" Rhoda's voice penetrated Sophia's muddled thoughts.

"Keeping quiet, Rho," Sophia answered almost automatically. Really, she ought to be ashamed of herself. "Don't wish to upset the lion!"

"Oh." Rhoda sounded a trifle put-out. "I suppose…"

Rhoda faded into oblivion once again as Brookes' mouth explored the inner shell of Sophia's ear. How on earth could something so… silly… feel so brilliantly, extraordinarily fabulous?

Harold's touch never had caused these sensations. It hadn't even come close. She hummed under her breath and at the same time reflected upon the rare intimate gestures her fiancé had bestowed upon her.

He'd occasionally kissed her hand. Well, he'd kissed the air above her hand. He had never quite placed his lips upon her skin, or her glove, to actually kiss it, per se.

And on a few instances, he'd courteously offered his arm while they strolled through the park.

He… well, once he'd brushed a lock of hair away from her eyes. She'd thought he would kiss her then, but he'd turned away instead. Rarely had she found herself alone with Lord Harold.

Why, truth be told, aside from his formal proposal, they had never been alone together!

And very soon, the privacy she shared with this heroic rake would be stripped away as well. The tip of his tongue flicked inside of her ear now. And the captain was whispering something about an introduction

"May I call upon you some afternoon, Miss Babineaux? Take you for a ride in the park, perhaps?" His breath felt hot in her ear. "If you require a formal introduction, I'm certain I can arrange something."

She could barely respond, however, for all of the confusion flitting about her mind.

Harold was so very different from this impertinent captain.

Good heavens! It had taken Lord Harold nearly two Seasons to ask for a *dance*. She'd been particularly flattered when he'd told her this.

Captain Brookes lacked such patience, it would seem.

Yes, this delicious man was likely considered something of a rake. His expert touch revealed that he knew exactly how to do... all of this. No, nothing shy about him.

She probably ought to mention that she was, in fact, spoken for.

Yes, she really ought to... And she ought to thank him for his assistance...

"Although he will most likely be grateful for your aiding my rescue..." Sophia spoke into his shirtfront. Oh, how his hair felt ever so soft and springy! "...I doubt my fiancé would approve of this."

She'd barely completed her sentence when, with a great deal of creaking and groaning, sunlight landed upon them both as the carriage shuttered and was hoisted back into its upright position.

Clutching Peaches in one arm, Sophia took one step backwards and smoothed her dress where the captain's hands had been. Naughty man! Hopefully, it hadn't wrinkled too badly.

Rhoda, who rushed toward her now, would likely notice wrinkles that oughtn't to be in certain places on one's gown.

Rhoda could be counted on for this sort of thing regardless of the circumstances.

"Sophy, Oh, Sophia! You had me terrified!" Rhoda was suddenly beside her, hugging her and fussing at her dress and hair. Which said something as to the danger she'd been in, because nothing frightened Rhoda.

Ever.

"Are you hurt? And Peaches, is Peaches all right?"

The familiarity of her friend brought a shimmer of tears to Sophia's eyes. Oh, wonderful, now she would cry? She did not wish to give in to her suddenly maudlin state with all of these gentlemen and ladies looking on. Neither did she wish for the captain to see her so discomposed.

But really! What must he think of her?

Where had he gone? He'd disappeared as soon as Rhoda rushed in. If he returned, could she face him again?

"We are fine, both fine. But I wish to go home. Would

you mind terribly if we canceled our meeting with Madame Chantal today?" Madame Chantal, London's famous modiste, was stingy with her appointments and would be annoyed if they failed to attend.

Nonetheless, Sophia wished for the privacy of her bedchamber. She and Rhoda could have tea and biscuits sent up and perhaps discuss these new qualms she'd suddenly developed in regards to her betrothal.

"Of course! When we get you home, we'll send a missive telling of the accident. Why, you were nearly killed! Even Madame cannot blame you for being overset."

"But I don't want my stepfather to know about this. He and Dudley already complain that Peaches causes too much trouble, and I'd rather not give them further reason to dislike her." She'd had Peaches since she was a puppy, four years now, and had learned to try to keep her out of sight. Mr. Scofield barely tolerated Peaches and her stepbrother openly despised her.

"Of course not!" Rhoda understood.

This morning, they'd made their way on foot from the Scofield townhouse, so they had no choice but to walk back. This had seemed like nothing, earlier, but Sophia's legs felt a little wobbly now. Fear -- and other things -- had obviously weakened them.

There was nothing for it. They must walk back. Sophia tucked her reticule under her arm and gathered Peaches close.

"Why don't you let Peaches walk? You needn't carry her all the way back," Rhoda suggested.

But Sophia shook her head. "That's what started all of

this to begin with." She then told Rhoda how Peaches had upset the horses, which had upset the driver, upsetting the horses further, which had then upset the cart, which upset the lion.

"It was a most upsetting experience," Rhoda responded in agreement. She had a stern expression on her face, but Sophia understood her friend all too well. A wicked twinkle in her eyes belied amusement. Rhoda, being Rhoda, would find some humor in the situation.

"It was!" Sophia insisted. She eyed the cart with the lion. It seemed as though he were watching her and Peaches, memorizing their images so that he could one day exact his revenge. She shuddered at such a thought.

They would need to pass alongside him once again to walk in the direction of Mr. Scofield's home. She could not lose control of Peaches again.

A tingling of awareness crept over her, just then. Looking away from the lion, she realized that Captain Brookes had chosen that moment to rejoin them.

He'd most likely been discussing the removal of the carts and the re-harnessing of the horse with the caravan drivers, or other such manly matters, Sophia presumed. But he had returned, and his attention was once again fully riveted upon Sophia, Rhoda, and even, it seemed, Peaches.

He bowed and spoke in deep, formal tones. His straight spine and soldierly demeanor betrayed his military training. "Ladies, My apologies for the lack of a proper introduction."

"Captain Brookes…" Sophia spoke his name as though they were meeting in one of London's most fashionable ballrooms. "...may I present to you my dearest friend, Miss Rhododendron Mossant."

Brookes chuckled, most people had the good manners not to comment on Rhoda's less-than-common name. "Rhododendron, Miss Mossant? Beautiful name for a beautiful lady."

Was he teasing Rhoda? Or *flirting* with her?

Rhoda laughed.

In fact, if Rhoda were a cat, she'd have been lapping cream from his hand. "I consider myself the lucky one. I have two sisters, Coleus and Hollyhock. My father was French and my mother—"

"An avid horticulturist?" Brookes finished for her with a gleam in his eye.

Rhoda nodded and giggled. Was she, too, taken with the dashing captain?

Captain Brookes chuckled, garnering Sophia's attention once again. Tiny wrinkles appeared at the corners of his black eyes when he did that. His eyes were even blacker than his hair, which gleamed a near blue in the sunlight. As Sophia studied his appearance, he turned toward her.

"I haven't my conveyance, Miss Babineaux, but may I locate your coach and chaperone?" Despite his unscrupulous actions earlier, he addressed the ladies as though he were, in fact, a fine gentleman. "Or, if you haven't one, may I hire a Hackney?"

"We haven't far to walk." Sophia noted that Rhoda had blushed an annoying shade of rose.

"Then I shall provide you an escort, of course."

"We would be ever so grateful, Captain Brookes," Rhoda answered, not bothering to consult with Sophia.

A most unpleasant sensation crept into Sophia as she watched a coquettish smile dancing on Rhoda's lips.

Sophia herself was engaged, and she would have her friend be pleased, yes, but Brookes was a rake, most assuredly. And well... that kiss...

Brookes was apparently oblivious to the turmoil he'd stirred up in Sophia. He, instead, now studied Peaches and seemed to be considering the issues that had instigated this situation at the outset. "May I see your dog, Miss Babineaux? Perhaps a firm hand will extract us from this melee without further catastrophe."

Snuggled contentedly upon Sophia's shoulder, Peaches rested her chin in an unusual display of docility. The entire experience must have exhausted the poor thing.

Captain Brookes reached over and scratched behind her baby's floppy ears. "Hello, little sweetheart."

Peaches' eyes lolled back in ecstasy.

Glancing again at Sophia, he raised his brows questioningly. "May I?"

"I suppose, if she'll let you..." Sophia trailed off uneasily. Peaches hadn't taken well to many men. She barely tolerated Mr. Scofield, and her stepbrother not at all.

Apparently, the males in her life simply lacked Brookes' charm, for Peaches climbed right into his arms and tucked her head beneath his chin.

Holding Peaches safely against his chest, this large military man cuddled her baby protectively. "We won't let that lion hurt you, little one," he cooed to her dog.

These were the words that catapulted Sophia, most devastatingly — more than halfway — head-over-heels in love with Captain Brookes.

* * *

RHODA BIT into one of the warm and flaky pastries provided with the tea that had been brought up to Sophia's chamber. "Good heavens, Soph. These are divine. Did your father hire a new cook?" They *were* unusually good today. And the linens were new, as was the tea set.

But Sophia was not concerned with the tea nor the biscuits. In fact, she could barely contain herself one second longer.

She just had to tell Rhoda about the kiss.

"But not so delicious as Captain Brookes, would you not agree?" Rhoda flashed a grin as she dabbed the napkin at her lips. And then she sighed deeply. "I thought I would just die when he smiled at me. Those striking black eyes, and he is so very tall... and manly..." Blushing, she dropped her gaze to her lap. "How foolish of me! The man has turned me into a simpering ninny."

Oh, dear.

Rhoda *liked* Captain Brookes.

"If this is anything like the emotions Lord Harold has inspired in you, I now fully understand why you were so giddy when he asked for your hand."

Oh, dear!

"Er, yes, I suppose, but Rhoda, you don't even know Captain Brookes." She felt the need to interject a dose of reality into this most unreal situation.

"I know, Soph. But, oh, my, when he jumped onto the building and over the lion's cage — my heart be still! He is most powerfully built indeed."

And charming, Sophia thought with a grimace, and polite, and kind… and a magnificent kisser!

Perhaps he had this effect on all women. He'd most definitely won Rhoda over easily enough.

As Captain Brookes escorted them the short distance to Sophia's parents' townhouse, he'd politely inquired after Rhoda's hat, and then he'd teased her flirtatiously again about her long, tongue twisting name.

Rhoda had taken one of his arms while he'd carried Peaches in his other.

The entire way home.

Sophia chastised herself. She was an engaged woman for heaven's sake! She had no business whatsoever feeling any sort of… possessiveness over Captain Brookes.

Despite the fact that he'd nearly had his way with her.

Guilt washed over Sophia as she studied her dear friend.

Tall and willowy with dark chestnut hair, Rhoda was nearly completely opposite in appearance to Sophia. Her eyes were brown and serious, surrounded by the longest lashes Sophia had ever seen. And Rhoda was normally pale, but in that moment, two spots of color stood out on her cheeks.

The two girls had become friends when they'd found

themselves relegated to the wallflower seating at the balls they'd attended. It was where they'd met Emily and Cecily as well. Emily, Rhoda, and Sophia were all from families with good connections but lacked respectable dowries. Cecily had had an enormous dowry, but hailed from the lower classes.

Married a mere six weeks ago, Cecily'd been told, by the Earl of Kensington, no less, that he'd done so for the sole purpose of winning her father's money. He'd gotten his due, in the end, but that had done naught to change Cecily's unfortunate circumstances.

And now Sophia was the second of them to become engaged — quite happily so! She loved Lord Harold! He was gentle and sweet-natured. He seemed to *listen* to her. Not many men who'd been in her life had ever taken the time to hear what she had to say.

Not many women, either, for that matter.

Except for Rhoda and Emily and Cecily.

Yes, Lord Harold possessed many attractive characteristics.

And, marrying Lord Harold ensured that she would be removed from her stepbrother's proximity.

She could leave her stepfather's home.

Oh, yes, she was quite happy to be engaged.

Rhoda was fidgeting, peeling some flakes away from her pastry in an un-Rhoda like manner. "I did, er, mention to him that we would be walking by the serpentine tomorrow afternoon." At these words, she glanced up with a wicked smile on her face. "He responded as though he might see us there."

Sophia frowned. So, Brookes would simply move along to the next London miss then. "Hmph..." she said. And then realizing her friend might become suspicious as to... well, that she herself was... But she was not! "Is this an assignation?"

Rhoda fluttered her eyelashes and looked at her lap again. "I would not call it that. But, I will admit to you that I am hopeful. I—"

"Hello? Girls? You're taking tea upstairs then?" Sophia's mother peeked through the door, her silver blond curls softly framing her face. Sophia imagined, and hoped, that she would have similar looks as her mother when she herself aged. Her mother was of Sophia's same height and coloring, and today she wore a periwinkle-colored day dress.

Sophia'd not seen it before.

Finances had been tight for them until recently. The thought struck her that her stepfather must have done well with some investment or another.

"A new dress, Mama?" Sophia inquired in a cheerful tone. It was nice to see her mother looking fresh and fashionable, wearing something that put a cheerful gleam back in her eyes.

Her mother stepped in and twirled around twice. It was obviously a new dress, then, and she was evidently quite pleased with it.

"By Madame Chantal," she said. "Delivered just this morning."

Sophia and Rhoda simultaneously rose to examine the stitching and crocheted border. Another interest the four wallflowers had discovered they shared was a mutual appreciation for fashion. "Oh, this is lovely Mrs. Scofield," Rhoda sounded impressed, as she ran her fingers over the silk thread.

"I love it, Mama!" Sophia echoed, smoothing the material of the skirt.

"Did you make any purchases this morning, Sophia dear? Something pretty to wear to the theatre tomorrow night for Lord Harold?"

The girls shared a knowing glance, and then Rhoda answered. "It took longer than I'd anticipated to retrieve my bonnet. At first, the shop assistant could not locate it and then when she pulled it out, we realized one of the ribbons was loose. We waited for her to repair it, and when she was done, we were both famished!"

Sophia's mama accepted the explanation without question. "Nonetheless, Sophia dear, you should order a few new gowns next time you see Madame. As for tomorrow, we can add some lace or tulle to your rose frock. Men don't usually notice such matters, and surely we can make it look as though it is brand new."

Her stepfather must have improved their finances indeed! She would not discuss the matter with her mama in front of company. For now, she would simply be happy enough to see her mother looking so happy.

But she did wonder. Their improved status paralleled most coincidentally with her engagement.

Surely no relation existed between the two! For her marriage would mean that her dowry, small though it was, be demanded.

"I must say," Rhoda said as she watched Mrs. Scofield repair her coiffure in Sophia's vanity looking glass, "Sophia takes her looks from you, ma'am. Was your first husband fair-haired as well?"

Sophia's mother blinked and then turned away from the glass. "I don't speak of my first husband, dear. It would be unkind, unappreciative to do so, after all Mr. Scofield has done for us."

Although Sophia's mother and Mr. Scofield had been married many years now, Sophia had never seen a great deal of affection between them. They were kind to one another, however, and Mr. Scofield always treated her mother in a respectful manner.

Sophia had vague recollections of her father, her real father, holding her mother, joking and laughing. In the few memories she had of him, he was smiling. Her mother had laughed in those days as well, but Sophia also remembered finding her mother in tears more than once.

"I recall a little, Mama," Sophia said softly. "Remember I told you I thought he'd been a dream."

Her mother fussed at Sophia's hair but didn't answer.

"I remember when he brought home the kitten."

Finally, her mama's face softened, and she seemed to relent. "Foolish man!" She blinked quickly. "Barely had enough to pay the bills, and he brings home another mouth to feed."

"But you loved him, you told me."

At times, something would strike her mother's memory, and she'd tell a particular story to Sophia. Sophia was the only person in the world with whom she'd ever share

31

them, most likely. It was a world where only the two of them had seemed to exist.

"Love doesn't put a roof over one's head." Practicality won out with her mother. It always did.

Rhoda rubbed her hands together in anticipation. "Was it a love match, Mrs. Scofield, between you and Mr. Scofield?"

Again, it did not seem as though her mother would respond. Sophia knew that it wasn't, of course, but she was curious to hear her mother's answer. "Dudley, as you know, is not my son by birth. He was all of nine years old, and Sophia barely five. Mr. Scofield needed a mother for his son, and Sophia and I were nearly destitute."

Sophia remembered when her father had become ill. He'd died just after her fourth birthday.

"Ah... a marriage of convenience." Rhoda nodded sagely. "It must have been daunting, taking on another woman's child. Was Dudley troublesome for you?"

Sophia's mother shrugged. "I suppose..." She was distracted once again by her new dress. "...but a woman does what she must. And aren't we glad of it, Sophia?" Without waiting for an answer, she turned to leave as quickly as she'd come. "I merely wanted to look in on you both before I left for my visits. You are certain you don't wish to join me today?"

"Mother, they are *your* friends." Sophia wrinkled her nose, in no way willing to spend time in the company of a bunch of inquisitive matrons. "I will see you later this evening." She'd had this discussion with her mother before.

Her mother stole one more look in the mirror, nodded approvingly, and then took her leave.

Sophia frowned.

Rhoda was the only one of her friends who knew about Dudley, and she'd sworn to never tell a soul. "Please, Rhoda! You promised! I don't want Mama suspicious. She'd only worry. Please, please, be careful what you say to her."

"I know." Rhoda was instantly contrite. "I'm sorry." They'd been over this before.

Sophia straightaway felt horrible. Rhoda hadn't said anything, really. "No, I'm the one who is sorry. I don't know what's the matter with me. Perhaps it's just the events of today, what with the carriage and the lion and... such."

"Could it be something else?" Rhoda could be annoyingly astute at times. "Has something happened between you and Lord Harold? You seem a little... twitchy this afternoon."

"Nerves? I suppose the magnitude of what I've committed to is beginning to dawn upon me. Goodness' sake, I hardly know Lord Harold, really! And now I'm about to pledge myself to him forever! Look what happened to Cecily!"

Rhoda placed one arm around her shoulder and squeezed comfortingly. "Lord Harold is nothing like Lord Kensington. Up until recently, you have been singing his praises! Remember? He is kind, gentle, humble. Nothing at all like the earl! I think you are quite safe accepting him as a husband. He's not the sort of man who would ever cheat or hurt you. I'm certain of it. In fact, I believe he might actually deserve your love."

Rhoda's tone was soothing but her words not quite so. She herself had cheated this afternoon, and she'd enjoyed every second of it! How could she do something like that to Lord Harold if she loved him? Did she love him? And even if she didn't, did it even matter at this point?

CHAPTER 3

*D*ev chuckled to himself as he turned to walk toward his uncle's home. Of course, the first debutante he felt a stirring of interest for in years would be betrothed! More than a stirring of interest, a small voice nudged him, if he were to be honest with himself. No, he'd been entranced, captivated, even, for those few minutes he'd spent alone with her behind the lion's wagon.

The incident had set him back over an hour. Although her father's home was indeed, in Mayfair, it was on the outskirts, some distance from the larger, more elaborately built mansions that surrounded his uncle's home, Prescott House.

Situated in the heart of the exclusive neighborhood, the Prescott ducal townhome was set back from the street and somewhat hidden by centuries-old trees lining the walk. In addition, a wrought iron fence stood guard, providing nearly as much privacy as one would find in any country estate.

If only so much privacy could be had within, as well.

Dev's father, the duke's younger and only brother, was most likely in residence, as would be distant cousins, aunts, uncles, and other various types of relations, mostly hailing from the duchess' side of the family.

Not that they had need to do so, but with so many otherwise unused chambers, it made little sense to take lodgings elsewhere. Prescott House was something of a palace, rather than a mere mansion, large enough for any or all of them to reside inside for days without seeing one another.

That being said, whenever he was in town, since reaching his majority, Dev rented private bachelor's quarters.

He preferred a modicum of independence to the constant interference of meddling relatives. Although he had no quarrels with his aunt or uncle, he preferred, on principal, that he not be under the duke's thumb any more so than necessary. He'd seen the effects it could have upon a man. His own father, although a man of independent means, seemed to defer to the duke's wishes more often than not. Whether this was due to outright agreement or a sense of indebtedness, Dev was not certain. He preferred not discover such a propensity firsthand.

"Captain Brookes." The longstanding butler, Mr. Evans, damned near stood at attention when he opened the door to admit him. Evans, Dev had learned, had once been a military man and would forever maintain his respect for the dignity of the vocation. "Out of uniform, today, Captain?" he inquired pleasantly, but in surprise.

Dev owed no explanation to servants but nodded and winked at the man. "A disguise, Evans. Ladies are mad for the uniform, you know." And then, wanting to complete his task as quickly as possible, he said, "Is my father with his grace?"

Mr. Evans nodded affirmatively. "They are not alone, Captain. The duchess, Lord St. John, and Lord Harold joined them not thirty minutes ago."

Dev pinched his lips together. "A family meeting, eh?"

"I would not know, Captain," Evans answered predictably.

Dev grimaced and took his time as he sauntered up the stairs and down the familiar corridor.

The door was partially ajar, so he entered unannounced.

"—not necessary to hasten a wedding date." His cousin Harold's serious and somber voice carried across the large chamber. Harry spoke as though it were to be a funeral. Surely Harold wasn't referring to his own wedding?

"Who's to be wed?" he asked, not bothering to be welcomed into the conversation.

His father and their graces turned satisfied faces toward him as he strolled into the room. His father eyed him warily, noticing immediately, Dev was sure, the absence of his uniform.

"Devlin, my boy." Prescott glanced up from the papers he'd been perusing. "Harold is betrothed. You'd know this already if you'd bothered stopping by when your regiment returned."

Good Lord! Harold betrothed?

"This is true, Harry?" Devlin propped himself upon the arm of one of the long leather couches arranged precisely along the lines of an ancient heirloom rug. "Anyone I know?"

"Not unless you've been frequenting Almack's," St. John interjected, sounding as dry and as bored as usual. Lucas Brookes, the Marques St. John, was Harold's older brother and Prescott's heir. He'd been standing in the shadows, preparing to take some snuff.

Almack's. That was one venue Dev would avoid at all costs.

An image of a petite blonde with porcelain skin intruded into his thoughts. "Not yet, cousin." *She'd* probably landed her fiancé there.

"Dev, so wonderful of you to visit. Where have you been hiding?" Floating over in a cloud of perfume, his aunt placed one hand upon his arm and offered her cheek. "You've been in London over a fortnight, yet you've only just now come to reassure your family of your safe return. Naughty boy."

"My apologies, Aunt. I've been finalizing my latest assignment... and other things..." he trailed off. This was only one of the reasons he chose not to reside at Prescott House.

His father raised a brow. "Colonel Harris' duel being one of them?" Of course. The duel.

Duels were no longer legal. But when one's colonel requested a man to act as second for him...

"And other matters."

"I'd have seconded Harris if he'd asked me. Well done of

you, Dev." St. John spoke up from the shadows again. "Kensington's actions were appalling. I understand Harris has been forced to send Alice away. She's utterly ruined."

Dev would not expand on that. He'd since learned that Alice, the Colonel's wronged daughter, had not led the chaste life her father had believed. Perhaps it was best for her to be away from London. Get into less trouble that way.

Dev, though, was curious about his younger cousin's earlier words. "Harold? A bridegroom? I am all astonishment."

But Harold did not meet his eyes and laugh as Dev expected. "We haven't set a date." From Harold's tone of voice, his younger cousin was none-too-anxious for the happy event. "I'd prefer a small ceremony at Eden's Court, after the Season's end, but their graces wish to hold the nuptials here in London."

"Your fiancée has no opinion on this?" Most women, to his knowledge, were much involved in these sorts of details. And likely the chit would want all pomp and circumstance possible. She was marrying into a duke's family, after all. What debutante would not wish to share the spectacle of her good fortune with all of London?

"Her family will be amenable to our wishes." It was his uncle who answered.

Her family?

Poor chit. Or perhaps not. Perhaps she knew exactly what she was getting herself into.

Again, Dev conjured up the lovely Miss Babineaux. She embodied all that was feminine. Her groom, no doubt, eagerly looked forward to their wedding night. He would be wise to provide her with the moon and the stars.

If he didn't, he'd be a fool.

"The lady best not take issue..." His uncle spoke in a stern voice. "...for all the blunt we've put up to secure this charade." Delightful. Such pleasantness that could only be Prescott. And a charade it was to be? The puzzle pieces logically fell into place now.

"It is an arranged marriage, then?"

Harold laughed ironically. "Did you think I'd fallen madly in love?" Harold had never been a happy person, even as a lad. "Father wants to move the date up. I've resigned myself to the institution, and yet it is still not sufficient for his grace." Tension had flared between Harold and his father for years now. Dev doubted they would ever get past it.

"With everything settled, with the first installment paid, I'll have a bride for you, and I'll not wait." Harold's frown grew deeper as his father spoke. "The sooner we ease your mother's worries, the better. What does it matter to you? It's not as though it will change anything." Ignoring his son's obvious reluctance, the duke scribbled some notes on the ledger before him. "Besides, the announcements have been sent. The first of the banns are to be read Sunday."

Another example of why Dev did not dwell in Prescott House.

Harold's shoulders drooped in sullen defeat. "Does Mr. Scofield know? Does she?"

"Mr. Scofield is as eager as I to have this done. You may inform her tomorrow night at the theatre. They are to attend as our guests, of course." Prescott's disdain insulted his son more than a raving tirade would have.

"Do join us, Dev." The duchess spoke up, dispelling some of the tension. She'd grown rather adept at that, soothing over the ruffled feathers created by her husband and sons. "Welcome her into the family with us."

Dev nodded, sorry for his cousin. What a twisted world this was...

"What is it that's brought on this visit, Devlin?" His father's question broke into Dev's thoughts. "Not that we aren't pleased to be graced with your presence."

So, his would be a family discussion after all. No reason to hem and haw, then.

"I've sold out. Signed the papers on an estate in the country, and as of this morning am a landed gentleman." He would not soften the blow, so to speak. It was not his way.

He expected disappointment. He knew his uncle nurtured hopes of him achieving the status of colonel. He was less certain as to what his father's reaction would be.

The room fell silent for a moment before his aunt stepped forward and embraced him. "I am so glad!" She effused her approval.

But Dev kept his eyes upon his father. He tried not to be concerned with pleasing family, but his father's good will mattered.

Prescott reclined in his chair. "I would have provided an estate for you — something to cut your teeth on. In the country, you say? You've not much experience with land stewardship."

But Dev's father rubbed his chin thoughtfully. "You have earned it, I'm certain. You'll learn the way of the land, the ways of the people. I know that you will succeed in whatever you set your mind to."

Dev let out a breath he had not realized he'd been holding. He'd warred with a few niggling doubts. Was he taking the coward's way out? He knew this was not the case, and yet... His father's blessing reassured him of his decision.

"So, you will not be leaving England for months at a time? This is wonderful news! We won't have the constant worry for your safe return. And we will once again have your company for the holidays, and for birthdays. Oh, Prescott..." She turned toward her husband. "...this is wonderful news indeed."

St. John finally stepped out of the darkness. He was tall, slim, and Dev thought, more duke-ish than his father. "Well, if we aren't to toast Harold's wedding, then perhaps we ought to toast Dev's new status." He poured a splash of scotch in a short glass and handed it over. The others already held some sort of drink in their hands. "To Dev," they all said.

"To Dev," Harold echoed.

The drinks were tossed back heartily.

Wonderful.

* * *

WHEN MISS MOSSANT had first hinted to Dev that the ladies would be in the park this afternoon, Dev had thought it would be unwise to accept the bait.

As a rule, he never dallied with engaged women. Married women, perhaps, if they were sophisticated and knowledgeable in the ways of the world. But even so… he preferred to avoid love triangles completely. Less complicated that way.

Less dangerous that way.

However, *Miss Rhododendron Mossant* was not spoken for. The dark-haired lady seemed interesting enough and was quite pleasant to look at. Perhaps Miss Babineaux would bring her fiancé along, and Devlin could size the gentleman up. He had saved the minx's life, after all. He felt almost responsible for her!

Perhaps the ladies wouldn't even come. Or they'd been and gone already. Why, *afternoon* could mean practically anything!

With such logical intentions settled, he strolled — for no reason whatsoever — along the calm waters of the Serpentine on the appointed day at the height of the afternoon.

He'd not realized people thought to feed the water fowl. Didn't most of the *ton* come here simply to feed their own hunger for gossip? Or to show off a new hat, or bonnet, or some other faradiddle?

He laughed at himself.

And then his laughter turned to one of pleasure. She was here.

Across the grass he caught sight of a petite woman with soft blond curls trailing a leash. At the opposite end, a long reddish pup pranced along in front of her.

It took a moment for him to register that her friend

walked beside her, Miss Mossant, yes, Miss Mossant. The girls complemented each other in a most attractive way. One tall, dark, and slim, the other shorter, golden, and softly rounded.

No fiancé in sight, damn his eyes.

He watched as they reached into a cloth bag and offered pieces of bread to the more courageous ducks approaching them. It did not take long for every duck in sight to surround the two ladies.

One might think ladies of the *ton* would be intimidated by such fowlish exuberance.

Not these girls.

Their giggling and laughter floated across the park almost musically.

As he watched, Miss Sophia Babineaux, with a flourished twirling, tipped the bag upside down and turned it inside out. Any last crumbs scattered and were pounced upon eagerly.

The ducks, it seemed, had experienced this before and knew no more plunder was to be had.

As they waddled away, Dev sauntered toward the ladies.

"No chaperone, again?" he asked.

Smiling, Miss Mossant pointed toward two tittering maids seated on a bench several yards away. They were obviously caught up in their own gossip and oblivious to both Miss Mossant's and Miss Babineaux's affairs. "The best kind!"

Miss Babineaux eyed him suspiciously. He did not blame her for doing so. His actions yesterday were not exactly those of a well-intentioned gentleman.

Her canine, however, gazed at him adoringly. Taking whatever welcome he might find, he crouched down and scratched the back of Peaches' head.

"She is afraid of the ducks. She only barked at them once, and they nearly quacked her head off for it," Miss Babineaux explained.

Her voice touched something elusive inside of him. Not long ago, he'd held this little bundle in his arms, tasted her lips...

Looking up, he studied her as his hand massaged the dog's neck. "She's a good dog. How long have you had her?"

"Almost four years now." With her hair in ringlets, dressed in lace and pastels, she appeared to all the world a simple miss. And yet... her eyes were guarded. Something troubling lurked behind her smile. Something... dark?

The dog licked his wrist before Dev rose.

"You are still in town." Miss Mossant addressed him, drawing his attention away from Miss Babineaux. "How delightful for us! We can thank you again for your assistance yesterday. You are quite the hero, Captain."

"My pleasure, ladies." Dev spoke cautiously.

Miss Mossant watched him from beneath fluttering eyelashes — fluttering and *flirtatious* eyelashes. She was a beautiful woman in her own right, but the ladies seemed to be the closest of friends. This could become complicated if he did not watch himself.

He ought not to have come. He would converse briefly with the two of them and then bid them farewell.

Intentionally keeping both women in his sights, he would not appear to single either of them out.

"A circus is in town." The words left his mouth of their own volition. Good God, what was he doing?

Brilliant blue eyes flickered with interest. "Is that why the animals are in town? They're not here for the menagerie then?" He remembered now, that in spite of the danger she and her dog had been in, she'd been concerned for the lion.

"They are not. They've set up not far from Westminster Bridge, just off Church Street." Dev could escort both ladies to the spectacle.

"The lion is there?" An unmistakable light of curiosity entered her eyes.

He'd caught her attention.

Dev nodded, oddly satisfied. He'd rarely, if ever, actively pursued a lady of the *ton*. A gentleman was bound by too many rules.

He was likely to stumble into one of many traps.

All too aware of her engagement, he nevertheless could not prevent himself from watching her: the curve of her mouth, the gloss of a curl as it fell casually along her silky cheek.

She was a well-bred, genteel young woman, as was Miss Mossant. And strictly speaking, he'd not yet been properly introduced to either of them. He had no knowledge of the two women's families, nor they of his. He was going to have to remedy this.

"I've brought my conveyance today." He dared her.

Miss Babineaux seemed to consider his invitation for a moment, but then she sighed. Her expression, he noted, showed reluctance.

"I cannot take Peaches." She then looked over at her friend. "But Rhoda, you should go. I will make up some excuse and send your maid home. You oughtn't miss it for my sake."

"Really, Soph? You wouldn't mind?" It seemed, Dev thought ruefully, he was getting his due. Not that he minded escorting the other woman… but he'd hoped…

"No," Miss Babineaux reassured her friend and then glanced over at Dev and frowned.

Dev knew she was not indifferent to him, although she might wish that she were. Dev forced himself to turn toward the other lady. "Miss Mossant?"

"Rhoda, go with Captain Brookes," Miss Babineaux urged her friend once again. "I'll take Peaches home. I've a great deal of letter writing to catch up on anyhow."

Dev forced a smile. It was early in the day, and letter writing was a weak excuse indeed.

It seemed she did not intend to stray.

Again, anyhow.

"Won't you join me, Miss Mossant?" He bowed in the direction of the taller, darker lady. She was quite lovely in her own right. He ought not to feel so disappointed.

"I'd be delighted." Her warm eyes sparkled as she took his arm. Miss Babineaux scooped her dog up and turned to leave just as Miss Mossant abruptly halted their progress. "Oh, no! Except I cannot! I rescheduled my fitting with Madam Chantel for today! After breaking my appointment yesterday, I cannot possibly miss another one. Madam would be livid!"

Miss Mossant looked crestfallen and dropped his arm

reluctantly. "You go, Soph. Church Street isn't far, and I can drop Peaches off with your mother." Miss Babineaux went to protest, but her dear friend persisted as she gathered Peaches into her own arms. "I'll take care of everything. You are the one who will wed soon. You ought to have a little fun. Go, Sophia... Go!"

Not allowing for any argument, the taller girl tucked Peaches under her chin and strolled confidently away.

And just like that, Dev was alone with this engaged lady.

The lady who'd occupied his thoughts, quite persistently, for the past twenty-four hours.

CHAPTER 4

Suddenly bereft of her dog, Miss Babineaux seemed nearly as stunned as Dev.

He'd not expected time alone with her. He'd fully intended to introduce himself to a worthy fiancé today and assure himself of her well-being after yesterday's harrowing experience.

Fate had different ideas, which, if Dev were to be truthful with himself, he appreciated.

Not one to let such an opportunity pass, he winged his arm for Miss Babineaux to take before she could come up with another excuse.

But she did not.

Instead, she smiled timidly and placed her hand upon his sleeve. She appeared hesitant but not reluctant.

A warmth filled his chest, and the cloud that had been blocking the sun moments before dissipated.

"I am curious to see how the lion is faring today." She looked over at him from beneath an indigo-colored bonnet. Her skirts swished over his boots. Her scent was fresh, sweet, and uniquely female.

"Then the lion, you shall see." Dev covered her hand with his.

Her fingers were so much smaller than his own. He steered them away from the water and toward the road where he'd left his curricle with a groom. Three of them could have ridden on the rather narrow bench, but it would have been a tight squeeze.

"This is the second time we've seen you out of uniform, and yet we know you as Captain Brookes. Are you leaving military life behind?"

Clever girl. "I am. Unless necessary, I'm henceforth going to live the life of a country gentleman. Enough war for me."

She nodded.

Dev wondered if she'd felt ill-used by him. "I behaved badly, yesterday," he began. "I owe you an apology." She was a lady, a gentlewoman, after all.

"For kissing me?" Her candor startled him.

"I shouldn't have done it, but I have no regrets. Do you wish for one?"

"Another kiss?" Her glance was sharp this time, and she pulled away slightly.

"An apology." He laughed, pulling her close again.

"Oh." She resumed her stride. And then she further surprised him. "I don't know."

He knew it. She'd been affected, regardless of the existence of said fiancé.

"I don't know you," she added.

"But you will," he almost said. Something inside him insisted.

And then he considered the enthusiasm she'd exhibited in his arms the day before. "And yet, you do." Walking beside her, holding her arm, he felt the tremor that ran through her.

And she did not argue his point.

Dev had never been one to walk away from a challenge. Especially when compelled strongly by the prize.

It would require some finesse. He'd perhaps need to move a few mountains. "I had planned on leaving London in a few days' time."

Again, she glanced over and up at him. He watched her swallow. "For this new country estate you mentioned?"

"Yes. I'm to become a respectable gentleman. The embodiment of all I raged against in my youth."

"It is to be admired. The desire to live a peaceful life. You are weary of war." Her voice washed over him like a benediction of sorts. She spoke words he had not realized he needed to hear.

"You do know me, then, Miss Babineaux... Sophia." He said her name slowly; spoken out loud it sounded like a whisper.

"But you," she pointed out, "do not know me." And yet she trusted him. She was slipping away with him for a secret outing.

Alone.

He would not give her cause to regret doing so. He patted her hand once again and began listing all that he knew of her. "I know you care deeply for animals. You are not prone to the vapors, and you are a generous and loyal friend." He paused. "You are also a beautiful woman."

She tucked her head down at those words. They had arrived at his vehicle, and he turned to assist her. The cushioned bench seat was high off the ground. This gave him an opportunity to place his hands around her waist, lift her up, and linger until she was safely on board.

Dev then pulled himself up as she gathered her skirts into herself.

"Do you think anybody ever really knows another person? Sometimes I find it difficult to even know myself." She'd not relinquished their train of conversation. She'd also, he noted, ignored his compliments. Most debutantes would have fished for more.

Dev lifted the reins and guided the pair into traffic. "Perhaps in allowing the right person to know you, you can come to know yourself more fully."

A small hum escaped as she seemed to contemplate his words. "I feel that way with Rhoda sometimes, and some of my other friends." She sounded almost melancholy. "We speak of private matters when we are together, and yet, I feel they cannot ever really know me completely."

As Dev drove along the crowded road, an odd sense of intimacy wrapped around them. What a strange conversation to be having with a lady, and as they drove through town, no less. He glanced sideways at her.

So serious, and yet, for all the world, one might think she was as empty-headed as any other debutante. She wore pastels and lace, naturally. Her lips were full, and he imagined, usually inclined to smile and laugh. It was that troubled look in the back of her eyes that intrigued him.

Was it a troubled look? Anxious even? Was he imagining something that did not exist. Perhaps, and yet he'd learned to trust his instincts. They'd gotten him through more than one assignment alive. Thousands of others had not been so lucky.

"What of your fiancé?" He kept his eyes focused upon the road as he asked the question. "Does he know you?"

He felt, as much as heard, her sigh. At first, he didn't think she would answer him, but then, softly, "I've no idea..."

"Tell me about him." Did she know her fiancé at all? "How long have you been betrothed?"

Again, another sigh. "Nearly a month now." She did not sound like an enamored bride. "He is... sweet and kind. He is well connected and..." She shrugged. "...I am lucky to be marrying him. This is my second year on the marriage mart, and my stepfather had been hinting it would be my last."

An arranged marriage? Not exactly... perhaps. But a woman's choices were limited. "He is the lucky one, Sophia." Dev's voice caught for some unknown reason. He cleared his throat and then glanced at her.

She returned his gaze for barely a second before her lashes dropped and she began fidgeting with some lace on her dress. His inclination was to cover her hands with one of his own, to comfort her.

"He is a good man, and he treats me well." She spoke softly, barely loud enough for Dev to hear.

Damnit, what the hell was he thinking? He ought not to have come today. He would change the subject. "It is as much an exhibit as a circus."

Sophia looked away from him to watch the passing scenery. "I've been to the menagerie, to the tower. I'd rather have gone shopping for a new bonnet." She was a somber little creature.

This statement, he was certain, wasn't because she did not find the animals fascinating. It was not because she believed a new hat vital to her personal enjoyment.

It was because she felt deeply for animals.

"Sophia," he said, again taking liberty with her name, "would you prefer I convey you home?" He did not wish to force himself upon her if it would… complicate her life too much. He merely wanted to spend time in her company. It was odd, how he knew that she most likely usually laughed easily and smiled at everyone. She was not so easy today.

She peered over at him. Ah, yes, a troubled look lurked in the back of her eyes. "I would like to see the lion…" And then a tentative tilting up of the corners of her mouth. "…please."

Had he not been in such heavy traffic and crossing the bridge, in that moment Dev would have pressed a kiss against those lips.

This was why he'd come.

Oh, yes, he was going to have to investigate the circumstances of her betrothal.

"We're almost there." He would buy her a confection, some sort of sugar-covered pastry. She gripped his arm securely. When they'd cleared the bridge, he turned and watched for a place to pull out of traffic. Special events such as this never failed to draw crowds.

The circus tents and colorful flags created a carnival-like atmosphere. An aroma of fried foods and various animals was an unlikely combination indeed, but most definitely one aspect of the event's allure.

Helping Sophia off his curricle was even more heady than assisting her up. Again, with his hands about her waist, he slid her down along the length of his body. He didn't let go until he could feel that her feet were on the ground. "Let's see if we can locate that lion."

Sophia nodded and pulled herself out of his grasp, flustered.

Hell, if he were honest with himself, so was he.

THE CARNIVAL VARLET featured exotic exhibits and sensational death-defying acts. They were here in London on limited engagement before traveling across the empire.

Sophia had never seen anything like it. In fact, it stole her breath at first.

She noticed, however, that although the crowds consisted mostly of working-class folks and merchants, other gentlemen and ladies were present as well. She could reassure herself she was not doing something so very scandalous after all.

But what would Harold say? Or his father and mother? What would Mr. Scofield and her mother say if they knew she were here alone, with a man to whom she'd not been properly introduced?

As Captain Brookes protectively guided her through the crowds, somehow, in that moment, none of it mattered.

For even though she was acting impetuously, risking her engagement and reputation even, she'd never felt safer in her entire life. "To where have you traveled, Captain?" She was suddenly curious to know more about him. "Have you ever seen a lion in the wild?"

His teeth gleamed white as he smiled back at her. "India, Africa, of course the Peninsula and all throughout the continent. I never made it to the Americas, though. And in answer to your other question, I have not. I've met men who have, however, in fact, I attended one of their funerals."

"So, they are dangerous, then?"

He paused a moment before answering her. "They feel threatened by man. They've grown to learn that men are hunters. They've seen the effects of a weapon. Our relationship between them has developed into one of sportsmanship and fear. And so yes, they are dangerous."

"Do you enjoy travelling?" Would he regret settling down? He'd said he was going to become a country gentleman. This was somehow difficult to imagine, and yet, she could not see him uncomfortable in any situation. He seemed to be so… adaptable.

"I am intrigued by different cultures. Huge populations of people see the world in a completely different light than we, the British, the so-called civilized world do. Some worship animals. Some believe our spirits pass through to different beings after death. They eat different foods, with exotic spices and meats. Some won't eat meat at all, for they believe it to have as much of a soul as you and I."

Sophia peppered him with questions as he maneuvered her through the crowds. What would it be like to travel to such places? His descriptions and answers gradually opened an entirely new paradigm in her mind.

Occasionally, he'd point out one exhibit or another, noting something unique or amusing. She held his arm comfortably and only released it when he reached into his pocket to pay for the confectionary he'd purchased for them to share.

He handed the paper-wrapped pastry to her and paid the vendor. It was covered in powdered sugar and smelled heavenly. She'd not had tea today; the last time she'd had anything to eat was first thing this morning. She took a bite, and then a little larger one. As she did so, the other end of the pastry flipped up and rubbed against the tip of her nose. A few crumbs got away from her and fell into her décolletage.

Captain Brookes' eyes teased as he watched her, but they weren't mocking. Instead, they laughed with her, reveled in her enjoyment, it seemed, of such a simple treat.

He was having fun with her!

Sophia was so very aware of his presence, of his every move, his every breath. He reached out, holding a folded handkerchief as though he would wipe the sugar away, but then stopped himself.

"What is it?" He looked to be suddenly fascinated by something.

And then he leaned forward and touched his lips to the side of her nose. Shocked but intrigued, she froze. The texture of his tongue lingered on her skin as he licked the sugar off. Surely, she was going to turn into a puddle of liquid, right here, in the middle of the circus!

The corners of his eyes crinkled when he grinned, unashamedly. "I could not pass up such temptation as Sophia Babineaux embellished with sugar."

What did one say to that?

Heat rushed up her neck and into her face as she looked down at the pastry. Not knowing exactly how to respond, she lifted it to his lips.

Smiling devilishly, he tilted his head forward and tore off a bite with just his teeth.

Oh, Lord, help me!

She ought not to have allowed Rhoda to leave her alone in his rakishly charming company. She cleared her throat and forced her mind to come up with some coherent conversation. "Will you take me to the lions' den?"

He smiled.

And then he chuckled.

"Your wish is my command." They strolled past several vendor booths. Brookes' mind was obviously not as befuddled as hers, as he easily pursued proper conversation.

"Tell me about your family, Miss Babineaux."

For the second time in two days, she was to discuss her unusual parentage. She spoke mostly of her mother and the few memories she had of her father. She only mentioned her stepbrother and her stepfather as necessary.

"Your stepbrother," the Captain said, "he is older than you?"

Sophia nodded. "By four years." But what a difference it had made. "Oh, there he is!" Spotting the lion, Sophia tugged Captain Brookes' arm until they reached the tiny space closed off with bars. In large black, bold letters, the word DANGER was printed on a sign at the back of the cage. Below it, a drawing illustrated the lion ripping off a man's head.

"It would not be so very bad, I think," she said, "if they were to be given a larger space to wonder about, with rocks and ponds and streams. A place where they could have their needs met and take some exercise."

Captain Brookes rocked on his heels beside her. "Still a cage, though, Sophia."

"I suppose you are right," she said on a sigh. "You don't hunt, do you?"

"Not unless it's necessary. There have been times when my battalion would not have eaten had we not hunted."

He was too perfect, this man. His words appealed to her soul.

This was troubling.

This gentleman, this total stranger, seemed to understand her better than her fiancé did — better than even her closest of friends!

But Harold *did* love her. He'd said so, hadn't he? Of course, he had! And Harold would care for her and eventually, her mother as well. As she so often did when she was not having a care, her next thoughts slipped out of her mouth.

"I do like you, Captain Brookes." And she smiled at him. She did like him!

He could be a friend. A respected acquaintance.

Yes, they could be friends.

Except for the kissing... and the licking of sugar on one's nose...

An overturned log lay beside them and Captain Brookes placed one booted foot upon it. He then draped one arm across his knee and leaned toward her. "Sophia," he said, suddenly quite serious, "do you *like* this fiancé of yours?"

Oh!

How had she told him such a thing!

He was an honorable man.

"What must you think of me?" She turned her head away, but with tender fingers, he brought her chin back around so that she would look at him.

"Do you love him?"

What was she doing? "I thought I did." She couldn't lie. "He is a kind and gentle man. He is always good to me. He is not arrogant. He will not control me or be cruel to me in any way. And my family is so happy that I am finally engaged." She stared at him openly. "I haven't much of a dowry. My stepfather made some poor investments a few years back, and those funds were tied up with them... But since I've become engaged, everybody is dreadfully relieved. My mother appears ten years younger. I haven't seen her smile so much in ages."

This man, this man she'd only just met, watched her

closely. It was as though he peered into her soul. He was a good listener — too good of a listener, in fact.

"Does he love you?"

"He has said that he does, I think. I was so happy when he proposed that I cannot remember exactly what was said, but I believe he said something to that effect. He said he esteemed me greatly, yes, I think he said he loved me."

Captain Brookes tilted his head slightly. "Are you happy for it?"

Sophia gave him what she knew, most assuredly was a pained expression. "Oh, Captain, I had thought I was! I was so relieved to have matters settled! But now…" She looked down at her hands, hands which were suddenly cradled in his.

"Have I ruined it for you?"

"I don't know!" she said. "You have and yet… even before I met you, I think I was beginning to have doubts. And then when you kissed me… Your kiss…"

He dropped his foot to the ground and moved forward, protecting her display of emotions from curious passersby. "Hush, hush. I didn't mean to upset you, Sophia. But I am not unaffected by you either. If you were to become free, somehow, I would have you know that I would court you." He rubbed his hand along her back. Luckily, a large post stood between them and the vendor-lined corridor. "I would not have chosen such a public setting to have this discussion."

And then Sophia laughed a little.

For spying them from just a few feet away, with only

the bars to separate them, was the lion. "This lion is going to know all of our secrets, Captain."

"Devlin — Dev." His lips were only inches from hers.

Sophia's heart raced, and the sounds of the carnival around them faded into a vortex of emotions.

Sophia had never felt so flustered in her life. "I do not expect, nor think you ought to be compelled to say such things merely because…" Did he feel guilt for kissing her when they had been trapped together?

"Not merely because." He glanced over her shoulder at the lion and stared thoughtfully before pinning her with his gaze once again. "I want you to know, sweet Sophia, that you have choices. I am not wealthy, by any means…"

She looked up at him, pained despite her laughter mere moments before. "I am so confused, and yet I am not confused at all. I do know, however—" She took a deep breath. "—that I must return home soon. My mother is already going to be wondering…"

He watched her with an intensity that nearly caused her knees to buckle. But then, as though coming to some sort of a decision, he reached into his front pocket and removed a small pencil. Tearing a piece of paper off the pastry wrapper, he jotted down some scribbles and numbers. "These are my directions. If you have need. Promise me, if anything changes, you will send word. The top number is my place of lodging in England and the bottom my new residence in Surrey."

She would cherish his writing forever. She handed him what remained of the pastry and tucked his note into her reticule. Did she, she wondered? Have choices? The idea provoked her.

Just as quickly as the thought came to her, she froze and felt all the blood drain from her face.

For across the corridor, in front of the cage that housed a black panther, her stepbrother, Dudley, stood watching. Shaking his head in disapproval, he met her eyes mockingly. He then pushed himself away from the display and disappeared into the crowd.

Dudley could be devious. If he were anything like a brother, he would come to her, advise her in kindness, that she ought not to be seen in public with a man who was not her fiancé. Even a stepbrother would want only to protect her and keep her from finding herself in a dangerous or upsetting situation. He would offer her his escort home, and perhaps chastise her gently.

Not Dudley.

No, Dudley would lie in wait, much like the panther he'd been standing near. He would wait until she was at her most vulnerable and then pounce, so as to create as much injury as possible. His reputation preceded him.

CHAPTER 5

*I*t had not been an easy thing, Dev thought ruefully. He'd wanted to kiss her right there in front of the exhibit, where any passer-by could see. Her lips had been so close he could practically taste the sugar on her breath. And she'd been so yielding, so open.

She'd also obviously been filled with confusion.

So instead of giving into temptation again and nipping at the tender skin of her lips, he'd written down his direction for her.

The decisions as to what could, or could not be, between the two of them, was in her hands. For he would not step into such a sticky situation such as this without knowing she wanted it as much as he did. Breaking up a betrothal was not something a gentleman did.

It was unthinkable, really.

However.

However, if Sophia Babineaux were to say the word, he would do all sorts of things that gentlemen did not do.

But she must be certain.

And so, he'd handed her his address, scrawled on a sugar-covered pastry wrapper, and then escorted her back to his vehicle. She'd become as thoughtful and quiet as he.

This time, when he assisted her up, she did not lean upon him so easily. And as they drove, she sat straight and rigid beside him, only grasping his arm when they turned, or stopped abruptly.

Had he been wrong?

It was possible, he supposed. Perhaps the second thoughts she'd been experiencing about her fiancé were the typical, normal response all people have before committing themselves to a lifelong relationship.

But, deep inside, Dev did not think that was the case. He had a feeling about her, and his gut instincts were usually spot on. When he asked her address, she'd told it to him but then requested that he set her down at a nearby corner.

He understood.

This afternoon had been an adventure for her. Something of a last hurrah. As he reached their destination, he pulled the carriage to a halt and turned in his seat. Although she was impatient, it was her hand that covered his.

She swallowed hard before speaking. "Thank you... Devlin. If we... in case I cannot... I want for you to know how much I..." And then she looked away and swallowed again. Ah, she was fighting tears.

Again, he questioned his sanity. What the hell was he doing?

"Sophia…" When he spoke her name, she turned back to meet his gaze. It would be ridiculous to promise anything at this moment, and yet he wanted her to know that his intentions were not as dishonorable as his actions had been up to this point. "…if you send word to me, that you are free, or that you wish to be free, I will arrange a proper introduction. My connections are not insignificant, and I believe your parents would not find my family objectionable." Again, how did one reassure a girl who had so much to lose? "I would like to court you properly," he added and then lifted her hand to his lips.

Inhaling, he pressed his lips to the silk of her glove and held them there for longer than was appropriate. But this was perhaps goodbye.

She turned her hand so that it cradled his cheek. "Thank you," she whispered.

Thank you?

Dev withdrew and jumped down to the pavement.

Thank you?

When he assisted her down, he once again allowed her body to come into contact with his before setting her feet on the ground. He was angry, and frustrated, and not quite sure what she was thanking him for.

"I forgot my reticule." Her words returned him to his senses. "And your directions are inside."

Dev glanced up to the seat they'd just vacated. Seeing the silk purse, he retrieved it and then held it out to her.

"Thank you." Again, those two words.

After taking the reticule, she stepped away from him onto the sidewalk.

Dev gave her one last searching look and then bowed.
Without saying another word, she turned and fled.
That was likely the last he'd see of her.

* * *

When Sophia entered her stepfather's home, she did not
go directly to her own chamber. She went to her mother's
room instead. Her suddenly tumultuous emotions were
alternating between acute anxiety and fledgling hope.

Dudley had seen her with the captain! Surely, he would
not keep the information to himself.

But that wasn't all that whirled about in her mind. A
seed had been planted... Could she withdraw from her
engagement? Was such a thing possible?

Her mother was not alone. And today, of all things, her
mama had acquired a new lady's maid!

The woman was middle-aged, slim, and stern-looking.
It had been necessary last year to let go of Mother's former
maid in order to economize. Her mother had not
complained, but Sophia knew she'd felt the loss greatly.
Mr. Scofield must be doing well indeed!

"Mama?" She hesitantly peered into the room. "May I
speak with you alone for a moment?"

Her mother sat in front of her dressing table and
glanced up, only slightly concerned. "Mrs. Crump, I'd like
you to meet my daughter Miss Sophia Babineaux. Sophia,
Mr. Scofield has hired Mrs. Crump as my lady's maid! Isn't
this wonderful?"

The maid pinched her lips together before tilting her

head in acknowledgement in Sophia's direction. "Of course, Missus, but we haven't much time." She spoke in a tight voice before exiting to the dressing room.

Sophia located a chair and pulled it up to sit beside her mother.

"Mama..." She was not sure where to begin. "...I'm not... I am feeling..."

"What is it, Sophy, dear?"

Sophia heard such love in her mama's voice that it nearly brought tears to her eyes. "I, Mama, I am having second thoughts..."

"Oh, dear, are you having cold feet about Lord Harold?" At last, she had her mother's full attention.

Sophia nodded, and her mother smiled encouragingly. "All ladies feel this way! Are you afraid of the marital act? You mustn't be, my dear. It can be a wonderful aspect of marriage. And Lord Harold is not unattractive physically. He will be careful with you, I am sure. But we mustn't speak of such things yet. I will tell you all about that when the time comes."

"No, Mama, it isn't that." Was it? "What if he isn't the one? I know that you loved Papa."

Her mother frowned and turned back to the mirror. She picked up a brush and dabbed some powder onto her nose and cheeks.

"It is not so simple as that, dear. Yes, I loved your father with all of my heart. He filled my life completely. But aside from the love, aside from the joy of giving birth to you, there was not much else. We lived on my awfully small dowry, but that didn't last long. And after your father died, not only was I devastated by the loss of him, we were left penniless."

Sophia knew all of this.

"What of Mr. Scofield, then. Do you love him?"

Her mother's shoulders sagged at the question. "I feel great affection for him. He is considerably older than I, you know this. But he promised security and comfort for both of us. If not for Mr. Scofield, who knows where we would have ended up? There are aspects to marriage that last much longer than grand passion or romantic notions."

"But—"

"No buts about it, dear. There comes a time when we must make practical decisions, decisions based upon rational thought and logical facts. Is Lord Harold good to you? Does he frighten you? Has he not offered you his protection and affection? These are not small matters. Anyhow," she added. "I think that you *do* love Lord Harold, as he so obviously loves you."

"Mother, but what if I don't?"

Her mother shook her head before turning back to face her. This time her eyes were earnest and slightly pleading. "Sophia, darling, the contracts have been signed. Everything is already in place. I'm afraid you no longer have any choice in the matter."

Sophia shook her head, not quite understanding what her mother meant by this.

"Lord Harold's family is so exceedingly happy to welcome you into the family that they have placed an annuity upon Mr. Scofield, Dudley, and myself! They have set funds aside for you and your future children. Have you not noticed that we are keeping the candles burning longer? That the food has improved significantly? Not to mention the new clothing for myself, your trousseau, and Mrs. Crump! Darling, your Lord Harold has quite been the answer to our prayers."

Sophia was stunned. She ought to have known though. The pastries, the visits to Madam Chantal, and yes, the candles had been left burning longer. Some misguided optimism inside of her had attributed it to Mr. Scofield's ingenuity. When it fact it was all due to her betrothal.

She ought to have known, but she'd been too caught up in her own world.

"Is this not something I ought to have been informed of earlier?" She loved her mother. She wanted her mother to have her heart's desire. But knowing of such payments, she suddenly felt… sordid.

Was it a simple matter of Lord Harold's benevolence?

"How large are the annuities, Mother?" she asked gently when her initial question went unanswered.

Her mother looked up with wide eyes. "I wouldn't know the details, dear. You know how Mr. Scofield is regarding financial matters. And you ought not to worry about them either. I simply told you so that you would be reassured of Lord Harold's love, that he holds you in such high regard as to ensure your family's security."

What? This made no sense at all. Of course, she'd expected her husband to provide for herself upon her marriage, and perhaps eventually, her mother. But this… was most unusual, was it not?

When Cecily married, it had been *her* money which had gone to the groom's estate.

Her mother waved one hand in the air. "It is of no matter, darling. Now, oughtn't you to be getting changed?"

But Sophia continued to sit facing her mama, feeling confused. "I wish Rhoda were joining us tonight." Rhoda had a way of making sense of these things.

At the change of subject, her mama brightened. "Why don't you send a messenger to invite her. I had planned on bringing Aunt Gertrude, but she is under the weather. Her grace won't object, I'm sure, if we substitute one guest for another. The numbers will still be the same."

Yes, yes, this was an excellent idea. Sophia sprang to her feet and went to find one of their manservants. She mustn't delay, as Rhoda would need time to dress. Oh, she hoped Rhoda could attend. Sophia had so many questions, and her friend was so much worldlier than she.

She wished it could be all four of them, Emily and Cecily as well, but since Cecily had married, nothing was the same.

And now Sophia was to marry as well.

When had her life become so complicated?

* * *

"If she is not here in five minutes, we will leave without her, Sophia." Mr. Scofield stood at the mantel, glass in hand, not at all pleased to be delayed.

"Really, Soph…" Dudley clucked his tongue. "…your friend ought to show some consideration. Shouldn't surprise me, though, I'd always thought Miss Mossant an irreverent sort."

Rhoda had failed to arrive at the exact designated time. What ought to have been a normal family gathering had become somewhat uncomfortable.

"She did not receive her invitation until late." Sophia lifted her chin. "She is filling in for your sister, Mr. Scofield, as a favor. She will be here any minute, I am certain."

Her stepfather pinched his lips and pulled back the curtain. Dudley threw a satisfied smirk her way. He'd still not said a word about seeing her at the circus. Had he known who Captain Brookes was? Most likely.

Dudley was a friend to Lord Kensington and was adamant that the duel had been unsporting. He would know who Captain Brookes was, most certainly, even if he'd not personally met the man.

"There she is now." Sophia's mother stood, reaching for her reticule.

"Hurry along." Mr. Scofield held the door. "I do hope the duke isn't insulted by our tardiness."

"Walter, my dear," her mother soothed. "Isn't a lady allowed to be late? I'm sure Lord Harold will be all the more pleased when Sophia arrives."

Mr. Scofield, somewhat mollified, glanced at Dudley who was chuckling to himself. "Of course, my dear, of course."

As Rhoda rushed in, they gathered hats and wraps and what-nots and were quickly ushered outside to a carriage with the Duke of Prescott's insignia on the door. It had arrived nearly half an hour ago. Her father and Dudley sat in the front-facing seat and the ladies slid onto the opposite bench.

Mr. Scofield inspected and touched the plush upholstery in approval. "Beautiful, beautiful. The duke has excellent taste." It was the most satisfied he'd sounded since Sophia joined them in the drawing room.

"He does at that," Rhoda quipped, never one to be intimidated by arrogance or self-importance.

The rest of the short journey passed in silence. Sophia knew Rhoda wanted to ask about the afternoon spent in Brookes' company, just as Sophia was anxious to discuss all that she'd discovered today. Rhoda would most definitely have opinions on all of it.

And Sophia valued most of them.

But, of course, the girls could discuss none of it in her family's presence!

So, they settled for cryptic glances, and half smiles, until the coach came to a halt at the front of the theatre.

Her fiancé and his brother awaited them outside, both somber and unsmiling.

Sophia, drawing upon manners instilled in her since birth, presented Rhoda to the Marques St. John while Lord Harold stood by, impatience on his face. "My lord, may I present to you my dear friend, Miss Rhododendron Mossant. Rhoda, the Marques St. John, Lord Harold's older brother."

Looking slightly less bored than he had a moment before, St. John stepped forward and bent over Rhoda's hand. His gaze, Sophia noticed with some concern, lingered perhaps longer than it ought to upon Rhoda's décolletage.

But the play was due to begin any moment.

Without further delay, Lord Harold led them into the theatre.

"I'd hoped to speak with you before the play, Miss Beauchamp. In the future, please, I'd appreciate it if you can avoid such tardiness." His voice was tight and disapproving. Casting him a questioning glance, Sophia was surprised when he refused to meet her eyes.

She took his arm tentatively as he ushered them through the emptying corridor.

"I'm sorry, my lord," Sophia breathed. Oh, why could he not be in a better mood this evening? She'd so hoped to find reassurance in his company, tonight of all nights.

Mr. Scofield escorted her mother while the marques offered his arm to Rhoda. Dudley followed alone. Sounds of the crowd could be heard as Lord Harold rushed them along.

Just as they stepped into the duke's box, the lights began to dim.

Not before, however, Sophia took in the curious and disapproving faces awaiting them.

Except for one, which looked as surprised as she felt.

Sitting in the corner, next to the duke and the duke's younger brother, was none other than the man who'd licked her nose earlier that afternoon.

Captain Devlin Brookes.

* * *

IT COULD NOT BE HER! Surely! The lights dimmed, and he had to stare at the woman closely to see if his mind was playing tricks.

She'd invaded his thoughts on and off all afternoon. Ever since he'd watched her walk away from him.

"I do like you," she had told him. He did not believe she'd meant to speak such thoughts aloud. It had been more as though they'd escaped her mouth unwittingly.

She had blushed.

And then, perhaps, regretted her words.

She'd become distracted and nervous, insisting upon returning home.

An engaged lady, for Christ's sake. He was not the sort of man to interfere with another man's betrothed.

And so, he'd ignored his instinct again, to pull her into his arms and kiss her senseless. Gentlemen did not ravage young ladies on the street for all to see. Unless, that was, he was amenable to getting caught in the parson's trap himself.

Which he could have been, had he been willing to compromise her.

Ha, parson's trap indeed!

But that was not his way. He would have a lady make her own choices.

Furthermore, as she'd attempted to point out to him earlier in the day, they did not really know one another at all.

He did not know her family, nor where she was from. And she knew nothing of him.

And yet, despite all of that, their souls had connected.

Which ought to have sounded ridiculous but somehow did not.

When she appeared in the box, clutching Harold's arm, Dev had wondered at his own sanity for just a moment.

The lights went down before any introductions could be made.

By God, it *was* her though.

Sophia Babineaux was Harold's betrothed.

This knowledge, as it raced through Dev's mind, raised all sorts of questions. It also, perhaps, provided a host of answers.

Of course, if the duke had already made payments to her family, she could not back out of the engagement.

A sweet deal, indeed. Miss Babineaux had landed a husband who would make no physical demands upon her whatsoever, but provide financial security — hell, abundance — for the rest of her life. For both her family and herself.

She sat with a ramrod straight spine, not touching the back of her seat, her eyes pinned to the action on the stage.

She'd seen him, oh yes. Those angelic eyes had widened in shock for the briefest of moments.

She would not look back.

Of course, she could not.

Dev stared at her profile as the stage lights whispered across her features.

His cousin, Harold, sat beside her, quite unimpressed by everything. He was not happy, Devlin knew, with his father's decision to hasten the wedding date. Harold's shoulders pressed into the corner of his chair, away from

Sophia. Plenty of empty space separated the engaged couple.

Sophia was in an arranged marriage.

She'd insisted her fiancé loved her, that he was a kind and gentle man. It would not do to appear so mercenary. She was a sweet young thing, after all. She would not ruin such an impression by admitting she was marrying a man for his money.

Devlin was disgusted. With her, with himself, with his uncle. It was difficult to be disgusted with Harold. It was not his fault, really. Harold would not have chosen this for himself if it had been his decision to make.

Sophia had not known Devlin was a member of the Prescott family, a distant heir, even, to the duke himself.

No, the look on her face had portrayed dismay and surprise.

Miss Mossant attended as well. Seated beside Sophia, she'd gotten a look at him, too. Perhaps she'd sent him a shy smile. He could not remember.

He'd had eyes only for Sophia.

But now he turned toward her friend. Had Miss Mossant known?

The taller woman wore her chestnut hair high upon her head with curling tendrils dropping to her shoulders. And although a little slimmer than his normal tastes, she was a desirable woman in her own right.

Lucas sat beside her, nearly as uninterested as Harold.

Such a delightful party.

Across the aisle, in the front row, Dev presumed the older couple to be her parents. Yes, the blonde was most definitively Sophia's mother. She had the same petite beauty. The man on the aisle next to them must be the brother.

Sophia'd not said much about the brother, but upon some inspection, Dev realized he had some knowledge of the man — an itinerate gambler and a wastrel. The fellow mingled in circles who spent lavishly, and as far as Dev knew, most likely held several of his vowels.

Another reason for Sophia to sell herself to his uncle.

Goddamn it.

It was not what he would have believed of her.

He could only wait for the first act to be over. He'd already seen this performance, a week prior, and it was mediocre at best. He'd attended only to appease his aunt and father. And he'd been mildly curious as to what sort of lady had sold herself to Harold.

He would leave at the intermission.

Until then, he had difficulty keeping his eyes off her.

Did she feel him watching her? Could she feel his anger?

A few minutes into the production, Sophia turned toward Harold. She placed her hand on Harold's arm and whispered into his ear.

Her manner appeared contrite, cajoling even. Harold took her hand in his and raised it to his mouth mechanically. He then quite deliberately replaced it back in her own lap and relinquished it.

Sophia's countenance deflated.

Did she know Harold's secret? Had she been expecting Harold to respond lovingly?

She'd told Devlin her fiancé had said he loved her. Hadn't she? Was Sophia merely a chess piece in a game she didn't know was being played? The look on her face gave him pause.

And then another question taunted him.

Could anything be done about it?

CHAPTER 6

*S*ophia both dreaded and looked forward to the moment the lights would be brought up to signify the first of two intermissions. Why was Captain Brookes here? Had he intentionally sought her out? Of course, he would not! Would he? And what of her fiancé? Why was Lord Harold so irritated with her? Surely, she and her family's tardiness was not such an affront as all that.

She was jarred from her thoughts by the applause of the crowd followed by beginning murmurs of relief from the audience members at sitting for so long. The glow from the gaslights grew until she could see all the faces about her.

Harold made a pained look, stood, and turned formally. "Miss Babineaux, may I present to you my cousin, Captain Devlin Brookes. Dev, my fiancée, Miss Sophia Babineaux."

What should she do? Should she pretend they had never met? Instead of wondering why he was here, she ought to have been figuring out what she was going to do about it!

Dudley watched her with narrowed eyes.

Sophia glanced at Rhoda, who shrugged and laughed. "Not necessary, Lord Harold. We've already had the pleasure of meeting Captain Brookes. He rather came to my rescue, you see, in a skirmish on the street a few days ago. But we did not know he was a relation of yours. What a delightful surprise."

Oh, thank you, Rhoda, you quick-thinking girl!

Dudley's eyebrows rose. "So that would explain, Sophia, why you were in his company this afternoon at the circus. I did make an attempt to capture your attention, but the two of you moved along too quickly, before I could reach you." He then sent a satisfied-looking gloat in Sophia's direction. "I did not, however, see Miss Mossant."

All eyes turned toward Sophia upon Dudley's words.

But Rhoda again came to her rescue. "You ought to have tried harder, Mr. Scofield. And you would have been most welcome to join us. An outing is always more pleasant when the numbers are even. Would you not agree?"

He raised one brow. "My apologies. In the future, I will heed your advice, of course."

But Lord Harold was not interested in who was with whom at the circus. He returned his attention to his cousin. "How unexpected, Dev. I am pleased to hear of your acquaintance. No one was injured, I hope? In the skirmish?"

Rhoda was doing such a fine job explaining all of this that Sophia merely looked to her friend to answer. "Heaven's no, and all thanks to Captain Brookes. He is quite the hero." Rhoda then went on to describe the events most dramatically, omitting the role played by Peaches and telling it as though it were she, rather than Sophia, who had been trapped.

From the corner of her eyes, Sophia watched Captain Brookes.

He would not contradict Rhoda. He must understand that she had not deceived his cousin willingly.

She hoped so anyhow.

Oh, this changed everything! Her heart, which already had felt heavy this evening, now plummeted to somewhere around the vicinity of her feet.

Captain Brookes would not meet her eyes. He simply followed the conversation with an unreadable expression.

"And today..." Rhoda wrapped up her story most convincingly. "...he offered to take us to view the lion in a more civilized setting. As we'd already fed the ducks, how could we deny ourselves?"

"How indeed?" Dudley chimed in. Of course, he had likely guessed that much of the story was fiction. But to call Sophia out, again, in a most public setting would have no beneficial outcome whatsoever.

For now, it seemed, Dudley's attempt at creating trouble for her had been foiled.

All attention turned away from Sophia when a few of the duke's acquaintances presented themselves at the door to the private box. She fixed a smile upon her face and turned slightly so as to appear interested in the various introductions and greetings. Her mama was in heaven, and Mr. Scofield most satisfied with his newfound importance.

She ignored Dudley, who still watched her.

Rhoda turned and whispered near Sophia's ear. "That was somewhat alarming. Did you realize Dudley had witnessed you with Brookes? I wish it had been me who'd gone. And would you believe? Madam Chantel, ironically enough, canceled my appointment. You can only imagine how frustrating that was." She spoke softly even though a great deal of noise droned around them.

Sophia wished to discuss all of this with Rhoda but was also aware of her fiancé beside her, and even more so, of Captain Brookes' presence a mere few feet behind her.

Lord Harold placed his hand upon Sophia's arm. "I would discuss a matter of importance with you, Miss Babineaux." He sounded a little more his normal self, soft-spoken, quiet, humble.

Rhoda waved her hand toward Sophia and, turning toward the aisle, stood up. "My legs are positively exhausted from all this sitting." Glancing pointedly at the few gentlemen not engaged in conversation, she hinted, "I would like for nothing more than to take a turn about the theatre before the production resumes."

Both Captain Brookes and the marques rose. "Would you allow me to escort you?" The marques bowed in her direction. Looking a little disappointed, Rhoda fluttered her lashes and executed a pretty curtsey.

"I'd be honored."

Which left Sophia and Lord Harold alone in the front

row and Captain Brookes lounging in his seat behind them.

Lord Harold reached for her hand. "Miss Babineaux," he said, such earnestness in his eyes, the same he'd had when he proposed, "...I cannot wait much longer to make you my wife. I would have that we set a wedding date, three weeks from Sunday, here in London, at St. Georges."

This was the last thing she'd expected him to say! Good Lord, for a moment she had thought he was going to ask her to call the entire thing off.

"So then, you are not angry with me for arriving late this evening? You've not spoken to me in such tones before."

He had the good grace to look sheepish at her words. "My dear, I was merely worried that you were not coming. Will you accept my apology for such boorish behavior?"

Sophia furrowed her brows. "Well, of course, I will, but as to the other..."

"Father has sent the announcements to the papers. Chalk it up to an anxious bridegroom if you must, but I really must insist."

He was to insist upon this now? He'd not insisted upon anything until this point. A sickening suspicion began growing inside of her. "I am not ready, my lord," she said. "I've barely begun to build my trousseau, and I had hoped to finish the Season with my family first."

Mr. Scofield had apparently been eavesdropping. "Nothing that cannot be remedied, Sophia." And then to Lord Harold, "Of course, my lord, his grace mentioned this earlier. Sophia has no objection to moving up the date. Do you, my dear?"

Her suspicions held more merit than she would have wished. Mr. Scofield, the man who held the key to her mother's happiness, stared at her sternly, as though threatening her to contradict him.

Payments have been made...

She then caught sight of her mother, smiling, laughing at something the duchess had said. She looked younger and more carefree than she had in months. Sophia swallowed around the huge lump that had appeared in her throat.

She shook her head, unwilling to admit to herself that this was, indeed happening. But why?

She wanted to marry Lord Harold. Did she not?

Was she making a mountain out of a molehill?

"Do you, Sophia?" Mr. Scofield's voice sounded closer now, more menacing.

The intensity of the moment must have caught her mother's attention, for she too, now watched for Sophia's response.

Sophia turned back to Lord Harold, her gaze traveling past Captain Brookes' narrowed stare as she did so.

"Of course not," she said. "Whatever you wish, my lord."

* * *

THE REMAINDER of the evening passed in a daze. It was almost as though Sophia herself was not there.

A shell of her person went through the motions, applauded at the end of scenes, and then wished her fiancé and his family goodnight before climbing back into the opulent carriage.

After dropping Rhoda off, Sophia sat across from her mother and Mr. Scofield as they rolled along the now quiet streets toward their modest townhome.

"Await me in my study, Sophia." Her stepfather's voice jolted her as the carriage came to a stop. When mother glanced at him questioningly, he patted her gently on the hand. "Not necessary for you to join us, Mrs. Scofield. I'd simply iron out a few details with the bride-to-be."

Her mother nodded, unwilling to question her husband.

Sophia took a deep breath as a sensation of spiders creeping across her skin made her shiver. She nodded in agreement and climbed out of the conveyance. Pulling her shawl around herself comfortingly, she braced herself for what she was certain would turn out to be more unpleasantness.

But perhaps it would not, a quiet and rational part of herself argued with her more tumultuous thoughts. Perhaps Mr. Scofield would be fatherly, protective and reassuring. Perhaps he would tell her that she did not, indeed, have to move the wedding date forward if she were not comfortable doing so. Perhaps, he would tell her she did not even have to go through with the engagement if she were having doubts.

Don't worry unnecessarily, Sophia, this part urged her.

The other part, the queasy spidery one, responded bitterly. *Don't be a fool.*

Sophia admonished them both, entered Mr. Scofield's

study, and found a chair near his desk. The candles were lit, but he'd yet to have arrived himself.

When he did appear, he was not alone.

Dudley followed him into the room.

Both were unsmiling as Mr. Scofield closed the door behind them.

At this point, she suspected that the spidery voice had had the right of it. She planted her slippered feet firmly upon the carpeted floor and sat up straight as she awaited whatever reckoning was to come.

"Sophia…" her stepfather began, sitting himself behind the large desk.

Dudley did not sit. Instead he leaned against the closed door with both arms crossed.

"…you are no longer a child, and I will not treat you as such. Neither are you like other ladies your age, free to fritter about Society for years on end. You have responsibilities. You have duties."

"Yes, sir," she said. *Out with it, please! I wish to know what I am dealing with!*

"This, er, engagement of yours… I wish to remind you that you are under my protection until you are wed, and upon your marriage, you will be subject to the will of your husband. And as your husband is a member of such an esteemed family as the duke's, you shall be subject to their will as well."

Sophia merely nodded. Although this was not the way she'd imagined a marriage to be, she knew he spoke the truth, as far as the law was concerned, anyhow.

"The responsibilities you have as a daughter and as a

sister..." He glanced toward Dudley. "...may be relinquished, for the most part, upon your marriage. But until then, you will do as I tell you, knowing I always have your mother's and Dudley's interests high on my list of priorities. And yours, of course."

"Of course," she mimicked. She had to bite her tongue to keep from saying more.

At this point, Mr. Scofield's face hardened. "Your marriage, as it is, legally has already occurred. Amongst the papers you were asked to sign last week, concerning your dowry and whatnot, you signed a marriage license and said license has been witnessed. Your bridegroom has signed it already as well. Payments have been made, and all necessary contracts have been filed by the solicitors."

She was not sure she understood what he was saying. And then, when she did grasp his meaning, she found it difficult to believe. "But why? Why would such trickery on your part have been necessary? For I do feel as though this is a form of trickery."

Her stepfather narrowed his eyes at her. She'd never before argued with him. But this was important! This was *her life!*

"It is simply the way matters are accomplished when dealing with such an aristocratic family as your fiancé's. It was not trickery, my dear. It was business. Ladies are incapable of understanding these finer details. I would never have told you had I not sensed a... hesitancy upon your part this evening regarding the changes to the wedding date. I will prevent you from causing scandal or legal troubles for this family. I doubt your mother's poor heart could handle such humiliation and dishonor."

"But is the marriage not disputable until a ceremony has been performed, and… well, consummated?" She flushed as she said the words. She wished Dudley were not present. She would rather have had this conversation in private.

She would rather have avoided such a conversation all together.

"It could be disputed with an exam, I suppose," Dudley interjected from his side of the room.

But a knowing look lurked in his expression, and his eyes were hooded and mocking.

"That won't be necessary, my dear. As I've said, my concern is for your mother. Has she not glowed with health and happiness as of late?" His voice dripped with condescension. "And it is of no matter, is it? It has been my own opinion that you are happy to marry Lord Harold. I would only bring all of this out into the open with you, as I have said, since you seemed hesitant about the date.

Sophia barely comprehended all that had occurred over the last few hours. She sat, seething, as her stepfather spoke to her now.

"Surely, you won't make any trouble. All I ask is that you continue frolicking about town with your friend, shopping and preparing for your wedding. Nothing distasteful in any of that, now, is there?"

And then she found her voice, low and steady and edged with a steel all its own. "How much?"

His brows rose. "Pardon?"

"How much have they paid you?"

He did not say anything, merely moved a few papers about on his desk for a moment or two. And then, glancing up at her, he confirmed her worse fears. "Enough," he said. "Enough to eliminate this family's debts, Dudley's included, and for your mother and me to live comfortably for the rest of our lives. Would you put your mother's future in peril, Sophia?"

Bile rose in her throat, but then subsided into her heart.

She stood. And then another question dawned on her. Turning back, she demanded, "But why? Why would the Prescotts pay so much? Why would they pay at all?"

At this, it was Dudley who answered, "Because, dear sister, Lord Harold is so very enamored of you. He's leaving no chance for another man to snatch you away. You ought to be flattered."

Flattered?

She'd done naught but consented to an *engagement*.

She'd trusted all of them while signing those papers. Was that not what a betrothal was for? A time of contemplation? A time to develop trust? A time for the couple to assure themselves of the decision they'd made?

It was awfully high-handed of them — of Lord Harold. She'd not thought he would be such a husband as to act so arrogantly in regard to their life together. She hoped he would not do so again.

For it seemed, she realized as she made her way up to her chamber, she was already, a married woman.

CHAPTER 7

"*H*e would cut me off completely, Dev." Harold spoke into his half-empty pint glass. The performance at Drury Land ended hours ago, and the two cousins had drifted from one club to another until finally settling into the tavern of the lesser-known, and not at all prestigious, King's Pot and Porridge.

Despite Dev's decision earlier that day, the evening's events had compelled him to learn more about this so-called betrothal between his cousin and Miss Sophia Babineaux. Normally, he would not immerse himself in such family affairs, but, well, he had an interest here.

What he ought to do was pack his belongings and make the trip down to Dartmouth Place, forget he'd ever met Sophia Babineaux, and begin carving this so-called new life out for himself. With the commission sold off and the property purchased, nothing was left to keep him in London.

He could ignore the twinge of regret he felt at losing something he'd thought he'd found.

He could resign himself to seeing her, occasionally, on those rare family get-togethers he would feel compelled to attend.

There were other women.

There were always other women.

Harold had been reticent about his engagement for most of the evening. Instead, he spent his energy complaining of the high handedness of his father.

Dev did his best to keep from shaking his cousin.

"That's why I've never allowed myself the luxury of living at Prescott House, Harry," Dev responded. "I won't have another man making such decisions concerning my life."

But this did nothing to relieve Harold's situation.

Of which Devlin wanted to know more.

He wanted to know more about her, about Sophia.

"She believes you are in love with her, Harold?"

Harold took a long swallow before answering and then laughed with no amusement whatsoever. "Isn't that a hoot? She's a fine girl. And a looker too, if I say so myself. Not much in the brains department, but that's to be expected. She was thrilled when I began courting her — believed everything I told her."

"What did you tell her, Harry?"

Harold stared straight ahead, not really looking at anything. "I told her I'd been besotted since the moment I saw her. That I'd been too intimidated by her beauty to approach her. I held her hand a few times, pretended she meant the world to me. Grand performance, if I say so myself."

Dev felt sick.

So, Sophia had been fooled. He'd doubted her.

"She believes you love her," he confirmed.

"Yes, yes, I rather think so." Harold took another long drink.

"I presume her parents know the situation." Devlin conjured the image of the elder Mr. Scofield. He'd looked rather like the cat who'd swallowed the canary.

"Her father, and the brother, I think. Not the mother though... But that's not the worst of it."

Good God, how could this get any worse?

"The marriage is a done deal, as far as the legalities. A license was stowed in with all the paperwork both of us signed last week. We've both already signed the wedding papers, as have witnesses. It is done. She has no more choices, and neither do I."

Dev wanted to knock the mug out of his cousin's hands in that moment. He tempered his actions but not his words. "Do you realize what a cruel thing you've done, Harold? Do you realize you've ruined a young and innocent girl's life through your own selfishness?"

Harold nearly choked on a sob at the admonishment. Good, Dev thought. A morsel of guilt, a morsel of conscience was most definitely in order.

But it sounded as though everything had been finalized. And, knowing his uncle as he did, no loopholes would be left open. Even if Mr. Scofield wished to put an end to it, he would be subject to all manner of legal action — even though the contract had not been executed legally. The duke would find a way around that little detail.

Sophia's family would be required to return any funds they'd accepted, with penalties and interest, most likely. Funds of which, Dev was quite certain, the family would not have.

His uncle would be livid. The scandal, the talk, the rumors would force Harold to flee England.

Goddamn, but Sophia was caught between a rock and a hard place.

And, guilt pricked at him, he'd only made the situation more untenable for her. By wooing her, by telling her they could have more...

Except that, she would have discovered the truth eventually. She'd been bound for heartache from the moment she accepted Harold's proposal, hadn't she? Dev felt sick at heart.

She deserved none of this.

He'd watched her withdraw into herself after intermission. And for one of the first times in his life, he'd felt utterly helpless. He was a man of action. A man who could jump in and fix any situation. Could he call out her father? Could he call out Harold, his uncle? Would Sophia even want him to?

He had no idea. None of this made sense to an honorable man. But it was the way of the *ton,* the way his uncle would address Harold's *inclinations.* It involved choices far beyond himself, choices only Sophia could make. Or Harold. Except the choices were limited now for both of them, and the repercussions quite unthinkable.

When she'd acquiesced so easily to Harold's demand that the wedding date be moved up, Dev had wanted to shake her.

And yet he'd understood.

He would wish to have this conversation with Sophia, but as that was currently not an option, he turned to Harold, took a deep breath, and began looking for some solutions. "What do you want to do, Harry?"

* * *

AFTER CECILY'S debacle of a marriage, Sophia thought she'd never see anything worse.

On the couple's wedding night, seconds after divesting Cecily of her virtue, Lord Kensington had stood over her as he dressed and told her that he did not love her — just like that.

He'd only married her for her father's money.

And that was what confused Sophia about her own engagement.

If — and it was becoming an especially big *if* — Lord Harold did, in fact, love her, why had he felt the need to be so highhanded, and yet generous, with such unconventional marriage contracts?

And why all the secrecy? And the trickery?

She would march over to Prescott House this very moment and demand answers if it would not be so exceptionally outrageous. But she could not. A lady simply did not show up at the doorstep of a gentleman, even if he was her fiancé.

She tossed and turned all night. Just one week ago, she'd been so happy about her engagement! Now everything had changed! Was it because Captain Brookes had kissed her? She'd done nothing to put him off! Likely she deserved this!

Or was she fretting over nothing?

Would any of this have made any difference if she'd never met Lord Harold's cousin?

Oh, fiddlesticks! She wished Cecily were here, and Emily and Rhoda.

At least she could see Rhoda tomorrow, and Lord Harold, if at all possible. She must attempt to have an honest discussion with him.

She'd likely not see Captain Brookes again for quite some time. If ever. Even though he was Lord Harold's cousin.

When the sun finally crept over the horizon, Sophia donned a well-used bonnet and one of her older day dresses. She ignored the closet full of newer gowns. They represented the sordid nature of her engagement. She felt sickened at the thought of wearing them.

They'd not been purchased with her stepfather's money, but with her fiancé's family's money.

And she could not help but think of it as the money that had bought and paid for herself.

Tiptoeing down the corridor carrying Peaches, she hoped to escape the house with nobody being the wiser. But Mr. Carstairs, her father's ancient retainer, bowed upon catching sight of her and offered to summon a maid.

Sophia waved his concerns away. "I'm to meet with

Miss Mossant, and she will have her maid with her," she told him. "I will wait outside."

Not giving him time to press the point, she pushed the door open and stepped outside onto the front stoop. Carstairs would most likely report her actions to her stepfather, but in that moment, on this particular day, she didn't care.

Of course, she did not wait; rather, she and Peaches strode purposefully along the sidewalk and quickly covered the short distance between hers and Rhoda's home.

If it had been any normal day, she would have relished in the feel of sunshine on her shoulders, her head, her face. Not a single cloud marred the blue sky, and although it was early yet, the air was already warm and fragrant.

But it was not any other day, and the day wasted its beauty on her.

Arriving at the townhouse Rhoda's family leased out for the Season, Sophia determinedly raised the knocker and then waited several moments before the door opened.

The manservant, although disapproving of her dog, knew Sophia well. He reluctantly gestured her toward Miss Mossant's chamber.

Finally, she and Rhoda could scrutinize this situation together!

Bursting in, Sophia found Rhoda sitting at her dressing table, fully dressed and ready to face the day. Catching sight of Sophia in the looking glass, she swiveled around and held out her arms. "I will hold Peaches while you tell me everything!"

"I... hardly know where to start!" She handed her pup over, who eagerly licked Rhoda's chin. "But oh, Rhoda, you were wonderful last night! My mind went completely blank when Lord Harold presented me to Captain Brookes."

"I'd figured as much. But it was more than that. You were not yourself for the rest of the evening. You didn't laugh at any of the funny parts of the play, and then you just kept smiling with an odd look in your eyes."

"Lord Harold — Mr. Scofield — and the duke..." Sophia hardly knew where to begin. "Payments have been made to my family to ensure the betrothal." But it was not really a betrothal any longer. It was already a marriage!

Rhoda narrowed her eyes. "Why would they do such a thing?"

Sophia made a face of disbelief. "I'm told it is due to Lord Harold's great affection for me, but..."

Rhoda pinched her lips. "Exactly. As delightful of a gentleman as your fiancé is, I cannot imagine him ever overwhelmed with great affection for anyone. No insult there, Soph."

"None taken."

"But the question remains, why? Was it a large sum?"

"Staggering, Rhoda." It felt so good to discuss this with a person who would not question her grasp of reality.

"Were funds so very lacking?"

In for a penny, in for a pound. "If it were not for these payments, my stepfather would be nearly destitute. And you've seen my mother as of late. She is not so wan-look-ing. She is glowing again, smiling."

"Dudley had gambling debts as well, I'd imagine."

Sophia tilted her head to one side. "You suspected? Why was I so unaware?"

"I don't know how you do it, but you tend to only see the good around you. Unfortunately, you are also the last one to see the bad."

"And you are one of the first."

"Yes," Rhoda said, "usually. But Sophia, I understand how all of this is disturbing, yet if you love Lord Harold, where is the problem? You've been over the moon since your engagement."

Just then a tapping sounded at the door. When Rhoda bid the maid enter, a footman followed her, carrying a large bouquet of a colorful variety of blossoms. A hopeful smile spread across Rhoda's face. "Is it possible, do you suppose, that these might be from our Captain Brookes?"

Uneasy, Sophia licked lips which had suddenly gone dry. He'd sent flowers to Rhoda?

"Perhaps they are from Lord St. John. He did, after all, pay you compliments last night."

But Rhoda had opened the envelope and was reading the contents. A second, smaller missive had been folded inside the elegant parchment. "It is from Brookes." But her expression had turned to one of disappointment. "Perhaps I'm beginning to understand your dilemma." She handed over the second envelope. "He's asked that I kindly deliver this to you."

Sophia reached out and took the sealed missive. Unwilling to hide anything from her friend a moment longer, she blurted out the truth. "He kissed me, Rhoda.

But I was not ever going to see him again. I did not know that... I did not wish to..."

"Open it," Rhoda said, obviously not wishing to hear Sophia's explanation. But then she burst out with, "What is the matter with me? Why do I have such poor judgment where gentlemen are concerned? I truly thought he'd wanted to get to know me better! And it was you all along!"

Although it nearly burned a hole in her hands, Sophia could not open the missive while her friend felt so dejected. "It was confusing. Even for me. He kissed me, and I — well, I — I didn't stop him! And then I didn't know how to tell you..."

Both girls sat in baffled silence for all of a minute before Rhoda gestured to the missive once again. "Unless you wish to open it in private."

"No, no, that isn't it at all." She would tell Rhoda everything today. She would not keep anything from her friend. "Lord Harold and I are already legally wed." She went on to explain the deceit surrounding her engagement, her stepfather's meeting with her, and even Dudley's cryptic comment.

At the end of Sophia's long explanation, Rhoda frowned. "It certainly does seem a little devious." She tapped her fingers against her lips with a perplexed look in her eyes. And then she glanced into Sophia's lap. "Soph, I don't know about you, but I personally cannot wait a moment longer. For heaven's sake, open the missive! I'm dying to know what he's all about."

No further encouragement was necessary. Sophia broke the seal and opened the fine parchment.

She read aloud to Rhoda. As she said her own name, she realized that she spoke it softly, caressingly, as he had done on a few occasions.

SOPHIA,

I will not reveal all in this missive, considering the possibility that it never reaches your hands. When you next feed the fowl, as your habit leads you to do, I will await nearby. We have much to discuss. If you do not attend, then I will accept your decision to leave matters as they are. I would simply ask that you trust me.

SHE LOOKED UP. "He signed it *D.*"

He was giving her an entire week to consider her answer. For she was aware that he knew their habit was to feed the fowls on Wednesday.

Today was Thursday.

Placing both hands upon her cheeks, she looked up at Rhoda with a blank stare.

"What are you going to do?" Rhoda asked. "No, that's a foolish question. You'll meet him, of course."

"I will?"

"You will."

"Yes, of course. What have I to lose?"

CHAPTER 8

The next six days were possibly the longest of Sophia's life. Rhoda and she tried to keep occupied, but shopping had lost its allure.

She no longer felt comfortable charging frivolous items to Mr. Scofield's accounts. Although she'd canceled all of her appointments with Madam Chantel, she could do nothing to keep her mother from the steady stream of spending she'd commenced since the engagement. Every time her mother appeared in a new dress, or bonnet, or pelisse, Sophia felt the ropes tighten around her.

On a positive note, Dudley had made himself scarce. She presumed he was out gambling again. Which ought to upset her further, but she appreciated his absence, nonetheless.

And Mr. Scofield was spending a great deal of time at White's, from what she understood. Her entire family, it seemed, was perfectly amenable to this entire situation.

She would not discuss anything with Lord Harold until after she met up with Captain Brookes. For the life of her, however, she could not imagine any plan that could extract her from this intolerable situation.

But she would meet him. How could she not?

Sophia felt forsaken by her family. Even her mother, whom she knew loved her dearly, avoided being alone with her.

But Sophia was not alone. She took solace in the fact that she had Rhoda.

And she had Peaches.

And, of course, Captain Brookes.

His very existence gave her comfort.

Because, as he had asked of her in his missive, she *did* trust him.

Soon to marry into the Prescott family, she was compelled by duty to attend a few soirees — a recital, two unremarkable balls, and one garden party. She'd done her best to don a cheerful demeanor and appear as normal as possible. Rhoda remained by her side as much as she could.

But Rhoda had, most surprisingly, found an interesting distraction. Or perhaps the distraction found her.

Lord St. John, on more than one occasion, had sought her out most specifically. He'd danced with her twice at both of the balls and then sat beside her at the recital. Rhoda said he was pleasant and charming. He did not make any demands or promises.

Of course, Rhoda was suspicious of him, believing he'd participated in the details of Sophia's engagement. But...

It wasn't every day that a handsome marques singled one out.

He may simply have paid her compliments since she was his brother's fiancée's bosom friend. Then again, perhaps he was a little besotted.

The weather had turned dreary, and any light from the windows the following Monday was dismal and filtered. When the storm finally organized itself, the deluge prevented Sophia from venturing out at all. Peaches hated the rain, and Sophia would not leave her alone.

With the marques' help, Rhoda had, in fact, quickly gotten over the loss of Brookes' affections.

Wrapped in warm shawls, the two women passed the afternoon in Sophia's chamber. Once tea was delivered, Sophia locked the door, as always, and tucked her feet beneath herself on a comfortable chair.

"What if it rains on Wednesday?"

"We take umbrellas," Rhoda said, adding sugar to her cup.

"Of course. But the bread will get wet." Sophia worried her bottom lip and then turned away from the window to take a better look at her friend. Something was... different. "He's kissed you, hasn't he?"

The blush creeping up Rhoda's neck was a sure sign Sophia had the right of it. "Oh, good Lord, Rhoda, do not be sorry! He is not an enemy! We don't really know he had anything to do with my engagement!" She grinned, remembering the kiss behind the lion's cart. "Did you... tingle all over?"

Rhoda sat her tea on the tray and covered her face with

her hands. Pulling them down to cover just her cheeks, she peeked out at Sophia. "It was... incredible."

"Oh dear," Sophia said. And then an odd notion struck her. "We could become sisters!"

"I dare not even think it. I am so far below him — he cannot possibly be considering me — oh, but Sophia, I never knew!"

"It does complicate matters." The girls stared at each other, apparently thinking the same thing.

Their recent interactions with gentlemen of the *ton*, had not ended well at all.

"How does one know?" Rhoda moaned. "Cecily was, well, so certain of Lord Kensington's affection. And you were over the moon to be engaged to Lord Harold."

And now, all Sophia could think of was Captain Brookes.

But it had been nearly a week since they'd spoken. Had her emotions for her fiancé been so fickle? With Lord Harold, she'd known a tenderness, and an enormous... gratitude? *Surely not.* Whatever she chose to call it, it was nothing like the euphoric attraction she felt for Captain Brookes.

"I don't know, she answered. "Is it only an illusion? Is love nothing but an illusion?"

"It can't be," Rhoda asserted.

"My mother loved my father, but she also resented him for leaving her penniless." Sophia had considered this before. "Are there different kinds of love? If I were madly in love and somehow able to marry a man who swept me off my feet, would I love him through the difficult times —

hardships and trials? If we had no money to live, could I love him regardless? And if so, for how long?"

Rhoda shook her head, at an obvious loss. "If I were to fall in love and marry the man of my dreams and then later discover that he has been involved in treachery, could I love him still?"

Both girls fell silent at their musings.

Sophia tucked her knees under her chin and sighed. "I hope it doesn't rain on Wednesday."

* * *

It did, in fact, rain on Wednesday.

No, it *poured* on Wednesday.

Rhoda and Sophia were to walk from Sophia's house after sharing a light nuncheon with her mother.

"You girls must forgo your outing today, surely! We will read, or better yet, finalize some wedding plans." Her mother made the announcement matter-of-factly. Why would any sane person wish to walk outside, by the river, on such a dismal day?

"The ducks and the swans are expecting us, Mother," Sophia said firmly. "I will not disappoint them."

Her mother dropped her napkin and scoffed. "That's foolish, Sophia. You'll catch your death. I won't have a daughter of mine falling ill just days before her wedding."

"Fifteen days, Mama. That's over a fortnight." Sophia's stomach was in knots. She could barely swallow her food. What if Captain Brookes didn't come? What if he presumed she would not attend due to the weather? What if he simply forgot? "I won't fall ill. I never fall ill. In fact, I'm more likely to fall ill if I have to spend another day inside — stuck in this blasted house!" She searched for some way to convince her mother as panic threatened. "Nerves about the wedding. I need to be outside. It calms them — the outside that is, the outside… weather. It calms my nerves." And then she stood up. She could not wait a moment longer.

Rhoda placed her half-eaten sandwich onto her own plate and looked to Sophia's mother, who reluctantly nodded.

"Very well, I don't want nerves making you ill either. But carry an umbrella and wear your winter mantel. And be quick about it. Once the rain soaks through, you'll feel the cold for certain."

"I know." And then, after giving her mama a quick kiss on the cheek, Sophia pulled Rhoda away so that they could be on their way quickly.

So quickly, she almost forgot the bread.

She'd barely stepped outside before a gust of wind blew icy moisture into her collar. "Blasted feathering English weather," she cursed beneath her breath. The umbrellas might as well have been non-existent, for all they were worth. The silver lining to this blustery weather was that it did not take Sophia and Rhoda much effort to convince their chaperones to wait for them in a teahouse. Of course, the chaperones knew the girls were up to something, but for sweet biscuits and a warm fire, they were quite willing to relinquish their responsibilities.

Peaches wasn't allowed inside the teahouse, however, and would have to come with them to the park.

Burrowed into Sophia's cloak, the pup began shivering before they were out the door. Sophia would not leave Peaches behind. Even though she hadn't seen Dudley lately, she would take no chances.

She snuggled Peaches close and marched determinedly toward the park. Rhoda carried the bag of bread and led the way.

When they arrived at the river's edge, Sophia's heart plummeted.

Not another soul in sight. Not by the water's edge, not near the pavilion, and not on any of the paths.

He hadn't come.

But before she could utter her dismay, Rhoda tapped her on the shoulder and pointed.

A black, non-descript carriage was parked in the distance with a man standing beside it, rather nonchalantly, really.

As though the rain were not wet, as though the droplets were not cold.

It was Captain Brookes.

It had to be him.

At a vigorous wave from Rhoda, he pushed himself away from the vehicle and ambled toward them. Sophia handed Peaches to her friend and nodded. "You wait in the comfort of his carriage. I'll speak to him in the pavilion." Rhoda had no cause to argue with such a plan and made a quick dash toward the coach.

Sophia stood in the downpour as he approached her.

She no longer felt the rain even though it had, by now, soaked through her shoes and hat. She barely noticed when a drop slid onto her hair and down her cheek.

She'd wondered how she would feel in this moment.

She'd wondered if she would feel indifferent, or resentful even.

And now she knew.

Every part of her body came alive at the sight of him.

He wore all black. His hat, his coat, his boots, even his gloves. The hair that was not tucked under his hat was slick with water. Shiny.

Practically blue.

And, despite the dire reason for their meeting, his eyes danced with amusement. The grin that lit his face revealed white, even teeth.

He was laughing!

She could only chuckle, herself, when he grasped her free hand and led her toward the covered building nearby. "Can you believe this wicked weather, Sophia Babineaux?" His voice held laughter as they dashed across the grass. "Nothing like a little rain to keep things interesting."

She relished in the warmth of his hand as they neared their destination and could not help but glance over at him. "You're here!" Until that moment, she'd not known how fearful she'd been that he would fail her.

She had trusted him… but just as she'd trusted her stepbrother… her stepfather… her mother… and Lord Harold… well, she'd grown wary of disappointment.

He stopped, for just a moment, and peered under her umbrella. "Where else would I be?"

It had not been an illusion. This feeling of closeness, of knowing another person's soul.

She blinked away a few raindrops. The relief she experienced nearly caused her knees to buckle as they walked the rest of the way. "Oh, I don't know, beside a cozy fire, perhaps, or wrapped in a warm blanket with your dog and a good book."

"Ha," he said. "Not me. I'm a military man, remember? The ground is my bed. A pretty lady is my fire..."

And then they were under the shelter. Several shrubs grew all around it, lending them more than a little privacy. What with no one else in the park, it was as though they were completely alone.

They did not have a great deal of time, though.

"My engagement is not at all what I thought," Sophia began, apologetically.

"I know," he said.

"How much do you know?" she asked.

"Pretty much all of it." He took her umbrella from her and set it aside. It seemed the most natural thing in the world when he then embraced her reassuringly.

Sophia felt warm.

Safe.

"And I've spoken with Harold. He's none too pleased, either."

That was something she'd suspected, but not yet comprehended to be true. "So, it was a performance on his part. And this... payment... It has nothing to do with a grand passion for me."

Still holding her close, he nodded solemnly. And then

he tucked her head under his chin. "It's all a pretense. You are a decoy. If I'd any idea what was happening, If I'd had any notion at all…

"Your uncle is a powerful man."

"He's no power over me, Sophia."

She nuzzled deeper, inhaling his scent. "So, Lord Harold, he is in love with someone else, with somebody your uncle deems unsuitable?"

Dev stilled. "Yes, yes, I believe that's the crux of it all. And yet he did nothing to halt his father's plans."

"Why me? I am a nobody. Surely, countless marriageable ladies would have readily agreed to such an arrangement."

"Likely," he said. And then, answering her question more fully, he added, "Mr. Scofield and my uncle have long been acquainted. They wished for all intents and purposes that yours and Harold's betrothal appear to be a love match. You have an air of… innocence about you."

"Such nonsense!" She felt all the wonder of being in his arms, but also all the hopelessness of it. "Nothing can be done now. I've thought on it for hours and hours. My mother—"

And then he was just as serious. "There is a way. My cousin, you'll be glad to know, has more of a spine to him than I'd thought. He admitted to me that he does not wish to continue living as his father's pawn. He refuses to make a move, however, until Prescott releases his funds, presently in trust. And that transaction will not occur until after your wedding ceremony." Sophia pulled away to consider his words doubtfully. "We've discussed the circumstances at length, and... come up with a plan. If it works, your parents will be safe from legal action. But most importantly, both Harold and you will be free. It's going to take some time, however. Details need to be ironed out."

Stunned by his words, she could almost believe him. "You are not joking? You are not teasing me?"

He shook his head. "I am not."

"Can you tell me more?"

Dev looked as though he would, but then he grimaced. "There are secrets that are not mine to reveal." He touched her cheek lightly. And although he wore gloves, she could feel the tenderness within him. She would believe all could be set right, for now.

"And then what?" she was compelled to ask.

Dev touched the corner of her mouth with his thumb. "Then, I think you and I can begin to get to know each other."

"Dev..." She pressed her cheek into his hand. "...are you real?" She laughed. "Is any of this real?" If only... If only she could believe it.

She could easily guess the details of their scheme, and she could not disillusion him.

Yet.

She knew that all of it was only a dream.

But she could not tell him. It was too mortifying.

She would have to tell Lord Harold, eventually. Harold. Her husband.

Before he did anything drastic.

"Sophia," Dev breathed. One of his hands had moved to

the back of her neck, his other caressing the small of her back.

She tilted her head back and parted her lips. *Kiss me.*

She did not need to say the words. He would hear. He would know.

And he did. He knew exactly what she needed — exactly what she wanted. But how? Why?

So perfect, soft and searching and then confident and giving. His taste evoked safety, comfort, and desire all at once.

She was one of the lucky ones. Millions of women in this world would never, not in their entire lives, experience the magic of a kiss from Captain Devlin Brookes.

She would take as much as he would give her today. For eventually, he would know the truth. He would discover she was a fraud.

Good Lord, she was as much a fraud as her fiancé.

She and Lord Harold were likely perfect for each other. But she would not think about that now.

She would savor her captain, surrender to his touch, allow him to believe that she too, was his dream.

Dev pulled away and buried his face in her neck. His height required that he bend his knees to do so, even though she stood on her toes to accommodate him.

"God, Sophia," he breathed again, "we need to be patient. We need to wait."

No one had ever considered her wishes so thoroughly. Not that she had suffered overtly, or been neglected, but no one had cared much to know what she wanted, or what she needed. An overwhelming sense of love filled her.

It was too soon, far too soon, she knew, but the words escaped anyhow.

"I love you." She felt him stiffen. She needed to explain! "Not in a silly, whimsical feminine way, but because you would save me. And not because of how you make me feel, but for the goodness within you. Your heart, it speaks to me. You give me a foolish hope. And for that, I thank you."

By now he had raised his head and was watching her closely.

She touched his face and memorized his features.

Tiny creases around his eyes indicated that he'd laughed whenever given the chance. She studied his nose... strong, aquiline, his cheekbones, and the dark whiskers already threatening to reappear. She would one day remember his dear sweet lips and his concerned brows.

He grasped her by the shoulders, sensing her melancholy. "Have faith in me, Sophia. Everything *will* work out, and yet you are looking at me as though I'm headed for the grave. Believe me. Believe in me? Won't you?"

She nodded for him.

One last kiss. A promise from him, a wish from her, and then they returned to the black carriage. The rain had stopped and the sun barely peeked through the thick heavy clouds. Rhoda climbed out and handed Peaches over to her. Brookes offered to give them a lift home, but Sophia was adamant. This was goodbye.

He reached out, scratched Peaches behind the neck, and winked at her. "Don't be downcast."

"I know," she said.

And with that, he jumped into the carriage and was whisked away.

Rhoda turned to her. "Well, what did he say? It sounds as though he has a plan."

Sophia sighed and then gave Rhoda a halfhearted smile. "It's hopeless."

CHAPTER 9

*S*ophia, under normal circumstances, would have been over the moon at the prospect of planning her wedding. She was a girl who'd always appreciated fashion, flowers, and the details involved in such a grand spectacle.

Not that Mr. and Mrs. Scofield had ever had the funds to throw any lavish events themselves, but she'd attended enough to know the difference in a well-planned party and one thrown together by a novice.

But this wedding was not something she anticipated, and she did not experience the excitement of a normal bride. So instead of reveling in the questions she was asked regarding color, flowers, flavors, and whatnot, Sophia, rather endured the meetings she and her mother attended at Prescott House with the duchess and a various collection of Lord Harold's aunts.

A pre-wedding ball would be held the night before the ceremony at St. George's, and then a celebratory breakfast would follow. She and the groom would spend their first night as a married couple at Prescott House, for there really was no reason to stay anywhere else, and nowhere else would be finer, that was for certain. And then the day after, to signify a premature end to the Season for most of the family, they would all travel in an assortment of distinctively ducal vehicles to one of Prescotts' large country estates adjacent to the sea. After a few weeks, Sophia and Lord Harold would travel to a nearby estate which had been gifted to them by the duke.

Sophia was becoming numb to all of it. It had been decided that Rhoda and her mother and sisters could join them following the wedding. Sophia'd not asked for much, after all. Such a simple request by the bride could be honored.

Sophia rather thought of herself as a mannequin to be dressed, an actress reciting her lines. It did not matter, she surmised, who she was, merely that she existed.

That was why, on one of these visits to Prescott House, the duchess caught her unawares when she requested a moment alone.

Her grace, always regal and poised, exuded confidence and calm. Since their first meeting, Sophia had been some-what in awe of the woman.

As the two walked together through one of the endless corridors that wound through the mansion, Sophia realized that her future mother-in-law's presence was not due to any great beauty. Upon closer inspection, the duchess was, in fact, rather normal-looking.

She had the same brown hair and eyes which had

attracted Sophia to Lord Harold. Her grandeur was not derived from beauty, rather from her bearing and her dignity.

When they came to an iron gate blocking the corridor, the duchess took a key from a hook on the wall and then unlocked it. As the structure rested upon wheels, it slid off to the side easily, into what must be a deep narrow compartment.

"I thought you'd appreciate a glance at some of your future husband's ancestors." She spoke graciously as she hung the key back on the wall. She then took Sophia by the arm again and led her into the portrait-lined galley.

"I want you to know, Sophia, my dear, that you are welcome in this family. It can be overwhelming. I understand." The duchess led Sophia along at a leisurely pace. Sophia was intrigued. This stroll was not about Lord Harold's ancestors. "I remember when I was a new bride, how daunting it all was. And although Harold is not the heir, and God-willing, never will be, he is my son. His happiness matters greatly to me."

Sophia didn't know what to say to this. She'd barely had two words alone with her fiancé since that dreadful night at the theatre. The feelings she'd had for him were now, not just clouded, but stormy. In contemplating the reality of her betrothal, she only could rely upon her previous acquaintance with Lord Harold and Captain Brookes' opinion of his cousin. But what could she say to the duchess?

"As it does to me," Sophia said cautiously.

The duchess nodded approvingly. "And, my dear." Her

grace patted Sophia's hand reassuringly. "I have learned from my own experience that if I wish for my children to find comfort and contentment with their spouses, then the best I can do is ensure their spouses are as content, themselves, as possible. That they always feel safe and that their concerns matter within this family.

"I have watched you, and I feel as though I have come to know a little of who you are, Sophia. I think you are often underestimated, for your compassion, for your courage, and for your ability to love deeply. These last few weeks you have been subdued, however, and I think, overwhelmed."

The portraits on the wall had taken them through centuries of dukes and duchesses and a few landscapes. When they rounded the corner, Sophia could not help but smile.

"I thought to myself, what would make Sophia feel at home? What could I do to help her feel as though she belongs with us?" The large, prestigious portraits on this wall were of dogs. Enormous long-haired dogs, Thin, spindly, short-haired dogs, a pug, a poodle… and…

…Peaches.

It really was Peaches!

Sophia laughed for the first time in days. The duchess released her arm and stepped aside. "Oh, your grace," Sophia said, moving closer to the painting and shaking her head. No one had ever done anything like this for her! "When…? How…?"

"When the maids would take Peaches out for those little constitutionals during our meetings, our family artist awaited her. I commissioned the painting the first time I saw you with your pet."

"I don't know what to say," Sophia said. She wanted to touch the painting. The hair, the eyes, the tilt of her head — the likeness was uncanny. "Thank you, your grace."

"You are protective of her. I want you to know that she will always be safe here. I quite understand." Her grace gestured to another portrait of a poodle. "Figaro lived to be eighteen years old. He was perhaps a little spoiled. But not a day passed that he did not love me. And I realize we humans cannot always say that about one another." She laughed at herself then, a little self-consciously.

"Your suites will always have the conveniences you will need for Peaches to make herself at home, wherever you and Harold stay."

Sophia reluctantly backed away from the painting and turned toward the duchess. "Your gift warms my heart," she said.

The duchess nodded at Sophia's compliment. Her grace had said that she, too, had been overwhelmed when marrying into the dukedom. Had her marriage been an arranged one, Sophia wondered?

After staring at the painting for a few more moments, the woman gestured toward where they had come.

"Your mother must be wondering where we've wandered off to. Shall we return and finalize the details of this wedding of yours?"

What could Sophia do? She smiled. "Of course, your grace."

The duchess turned back and led them out of the

gallery, sliding the gate closed behind them. Sophia was not marrying into a family of monsters! Lord Harold, except for those few moments he'd shown her his irritation, had been nothing but kind and gentle toward her.

But he had indicated an affection for her, even though he was supposedly in love with another woman.

If this was, in fact, the truth.

Could the captain have been mistaken?

Self-doubt encroached again.

Was she imagining the unfairness?

The corruption?

The manipulation?

Even the duke himself had never so much has uttered a single threat toward her.

And what part did Devlin play in all of this, really?

Oh, God, for the millionth time she reminded herself that she'd blurted out that she loved him!

Everything had felt so romantic, so tragic, as they'd stood in the pavilion, his arms tightly wrapped around her. Was that the love her mother had warned her about? The kind that caused her to see an upcoming wedding as a prison sentence? The kind of love that caused her to stand in a frigid rainstorm, telling a man she'd known less than a fortnight that she loved him? If it had been possible, in that moment, she knew she'd have given herself to him.

He affected physical, emotional — egad — even spiritual feelings that altered her perspective of the world. Was that a good thing, or was it a very, very bad thing?

Even Rhoda could find no fault in Sophia's future in-laws. They presented a united front to the world, they lived together quite peaceably — if one discounted Devlin, of course, — and they were free from scandal.

In addition to all of this, it appeared that St. John was respectfully courting Rhoda. Rhoda was of a well-connected family, just as Sophia was, but nobility did not exist in her ancestry. In fact, both girls had lived most of their lives near the shadow of hovering poverty.

Did not these facts reveal compassion and a liberal-minded attitude within the Brookes' family?

Had the payments to her parents been, perhaps, merely an exaggerated gesture of charity on their part?

Again, sitting amongst Harold's womenfolk, Sophia tried to concentrate on tying the ribbons at the base of the paper cutouts of wedding bells. The paper was of the finest parchment, the ribbon of the finest silk.

She looped and tied and stacked, listening to the casual conversation floating around her, until her mother stood, indicating it was time for them to leave. Rhoda had not attended this meeting. Lord St. John had offered to escort her and her sisters to the tower this afternoon. Rhoda had expressed interest in a temporary exhibit, and he'd quickly offered his escort.

His offer showed a gentleman of kind spirit, did it not? And such a gentleman would not be of an evil family.

Sophia glanced around before they made their good-byes and was forced to admit something she'd been resisting. Her fiancé and his family were not, in fact, ogres and demagogues.

So, what did that make her?

And what did that make Captain Brookes?

Her mind was tired from trying to figure it all out.

With the wedding less than a week away, one would think she'd be more panicked than she was.

She had seen Captain Brookes at various social occasions. And even though, around his family, he'd treated her with a proper respect and distance, she had found a comfort knowing he was near. She'd felt... peace in seeing him, even knowing their love — if that was what it was — was bound for disappointment.

When they last spoke at the park, he' been supportive of both her and of his cousin, Harold. She was trying to think of Lord Harold by his first name. He'd not asked her to, but knowing that he was already her husband...

And that thought set her off again; she bristled at the high-handedness of it. Why had they done that? Why had they stolen her choices?

The questions never came with any answers.

She only wished she could quiet them somehow.

THE EVENING of the pre-wedding ball, Sophia couldn't help but have a sense of expectancy. For surely, *surely,* if anything could be done to stop the ceremony, it would be accomplished tonight. For even though she'd already signed the license, Sophia could not help but hope for Captain Brookes to somehow produce a miraculous discovery, discrediting it all.

And in her wildest imaginations, Sophia had dreamed up numerous scenarios whereupon she stumbled upon thousands of pounds and could refund the monies paid by Harold's family. Not that she truly expected any of this but...

A girl could hope, couldn't she?

If she was to be saved from this marriage, it would happen tonight.

With such ridiculous expectations in mind, she stood in the reception line beside her fiancé and greeted each guest pleasantly, as though for all the world she were a blushing bride. Lord Harold did the same.

Nearly every young lady who greeted her was most likely envious. Harold was the son of a duke. He was good-looking, kind, and wealthy. She'd achieved great success on the marriage mart. She must be over the moon!

And she might have been... but appearances could be greatly misleading.

Sophia had, as of yet, failed to find a single moment alone to speak privately with her fiancé. Had he designed it that way intentionally? Was it his way of avoiding her accusations?

With questions whirling around her brain, she would not pass up an opportunity, no matter how brief, to speak privately with him tonight.

Such a chance arose as she and Harold greeted an endless train of guests in the receiving line before the ball. The duke and the duchess -- on one side of them -- were earnestly listening to an elderly man, and her parents -- on the other side -- could not escape the one-sided conversation of Mr. Scofield's sister. Sophia and Harold had only each other with whom to converse.

She determined to make the most of it.

Leaning in, she wasted no time. "Your cousin says you are in love with another. Tell me, please. I know nothing can be done, but be honest with me. Is this true?"

He'd not been looking at her when she first hissed these words, but as he realized what she was saying, he turned to her, initially making an attempt at shock and denial.

"Do not play me for a fool, my lord. I hold no malice but I would have you be honest with me. Please."

And then he let out a long breath.

And nodded. "Dev spoke with you?" His tone held more sincerity in that moment than she'd heard from him... well, ever.

"He has." Glancing toward her mama, and realizing she'd not a great deal more time, she had to ask the next question. "I can never find a chance to speak privately with you. But I wanted, well, I need to be certain, to know..." Oh, how did one say such a thing? "We aren't going to consummate this marriage, are we?" She wished she could have been allowed some privacy with him before now. Lord Harold's eyes flew open wide, but no sooner had the question escaped her, when they were interrupted again.

"Lord Harold, Sophia dear." Aunt Gertrude and an elderly man who often acted as her companion stepped forward. "What an exciting night for both of you!" Her aunt, whom she'd only just seen at nuncheon, gushed as though it had been months. She exclaimed over how handsome a fiancé Lord Harold was and how honored Sophia must be to marry into such a fine family.

Sophia wished to stomp her foot in frustration. She'd

wanted an answer from Harold, by God. And if it proved to be the wrong one, she would have an argument. She was tired of the lack of transparency she'd experienced these past few weeks, and, well, a girl needed to know this sort of thing.

Because she most certainly did not want to do, well, *that*... with Harold.

She would not.

Not as matters stood.

And he needed to know that.

Of course, he would not expect to, would he? Especially in light of Brookes' plan — whatever that was.

Nonetheless, if Lord Harold had any expectations in that quarter, she'd felt it best to set him straight tonight!

On the heels of her Aunt Gertrude came Harold's Great-Aunt Florence, and then his second cousin on his mother's side, Mr. White, and then his mother's dearest friend, Lady Catherine — Caroline — Camilla — something or other...

Before she knew it, the reception line was dwindling, and the guests of honor, primarily, she, her parents, Dudley — damn him — and Harold were announced.

No further chance at privacy arose.

Even the single waltz they were allowed was performed with the entire ballroom of guests looking on. Thank heavens, she knew the steps well. As, of course, did Lord Harold.

It was as though every guest, note of music, and rule of etiquette was designed to keep Sophia from discussing anything of import with her fiancé.

Surely, he would not intentionally avoid such an important matter, would he?

As the evening progressed, Sophia resigned herself to the fact that she would simply have to make herself clear to her fiancé when the time came.

Furthermore, she had another matter on her mind. Well, another man, that was. At the beginning of the evening, her mother had handed her a dance card, prefilled of course!

God forbid the bride be a wallflower.

Was all of this planning performed out of some misguided sense of altruism, or was it blatant manipulation? She'd become quite cynical in that the details of her life were now organized by some all-knowing, unseen force from above.

She'd been thrilled to see, however, that somehow, Captain Devlin Brookes had managed to reserve a waltz with her.

It was to be the last set of the evening.

BROOKES, being a gentleman in a gentleman's world, had, in fact, found several occasions to speak privately with Harold. And they'd not wasted time discussing the weather.

In addition to their original plan, they'd discussed a myriad of other possibilities, no matter how farfetched. By this time, their options were narrowed down to two scenarios.

Harold's self-confidence was their largest stumbling block. He'd never been known for his courage, nor for his strength of will.

Dev did not blame his cousin. As an adolescent, Harold's father had criticized him relentlessly. And not with simple rebukes, rather with persistent attacks to Harold's dignity.

Harold had had little reason to doubt the duke.

On some days, Harold was bold, outspoken, and ready to act. Unfortunately, on those other days, he questioned himself, the core of who he was and what he deserved in life.

Devlin's support persisted.

He knew Sophia had doubted him, despite her words.

Good heavens! She'd told him she loved him!

At first, he'd been shocked. He'd not considered love, romantic love or otherwise, a great deal in his life. It was something that existed, between himself and his father, his other family members, and at times, between a captain and his men.

It was never spoken. It was just there. It existed.

It existed when Devlin visited his father, when they shared a drink. It existed when he'd protected another soldier, putting himself at risk. It existed when he and his men sat around a fire on a harsh, cold night with little protection. When they'd lifted each other up, knowing that melancholy was a dangerous thing.

And so, when Sophia had told him she loved him, at first, he'd felt… irritated by it, suffocated.

HELL IN A HAND BASKET

No, that was not the right word. He'd felt frightened that she would insert such a word into their situation.

But then she'd expanded on it. She'd gone on to explain that it was not in a *silly, whimsical feminine way, but because he would save her*. And not because of how he made her feel, *but for the goodness within him*. "Your heart, it speaks to me." She'd said. "You give me a foolish hope."

And suddenly, it had not been enough.

It was insane. He barely knew her, and yet...

Something shifted inside of him.

He wanted her love in every way possible, including that silly, whimsical, and feminine way.

But he must wait. He'd not spoken the sentiment to her, not verbally, anyhow. And, then later, almost like a lovesick schoolboy, he wondered if she had been offended at this.

He'd been forced to watch Harold squire her about for over three weeks now. Of course, he was not jealous! How could one ever be jealous of Harold?

But as time passed, she'd softened toward his family. He'd seen it in her eyes.

Had her feelings for him been a temporary infatuation? He'd swooped into her life, literally, and saved her from a lion. At which thought he scoffed at himself. Anybody could have done it. Most likely, she'd been in no danger at all.

He'd kissed her with passion and yearning. God knew, she'd not shared anything like it with Harold.

And then, when she'd discovered some duplicity within her family, and on his family's part, he'd supported her opinion that it had been manipulative, devious even. He'd promised to rescue her.

She'd told him once that they did not really know one another. Had she merely been swept away by the unique moments they'd experienced together? Those brief interludes had been filled with romance, passion, and an abundance of sentimentality.

On a few occasions, when he'd caught her watching him from a distance, he'd done his best to send her some sort of reassuring signal, a nod, a wink — hell, he'd even sent her a smoldering glance or two.

He was to dance the waltz with her tonight.

She looked, to all the world, like a beautiful young lady, caught up in a fairy-tale, marrying into a prosperous, dynastic family. But Dev saw her differently. And the troubled look behind her gaze persisted.

Dressed in something flimsy and floaty, she was separate. The underskirt of her gown was an icy blue with a lacey, gauzy confection floating over it. It was cut just low enough as to give a hint at her feminine curves, but not so low as to be common or gauche. And those curls, those delightful golden curls, somehow were less bouncy, the style, subdued.

He also noted that she wore one of her grace's necklaces, a sapphire pendant on a white gold chain.

She was never alone.

And so, when at last their dance was next, Dev strode toward her with resolve.

In that moment, he was eager to breech the distance

that had grown between them. He wanted another chance to address the troubled look in her eyes.

Eyes cast downward, she dropped into a curtsey when he stood before her. He bowed and then plucked her away from the various protective family members and chaperones she'd had in her midst all evening. And once they reached the middle of the room, he pulled her into his arms.

This waltz had originally been claimed by another, but Devlin would settle for no less. He'd erased the name and written in his own.

He needed to touch her. To hold her.

As did she, he thought.

He hoped?

"Where's Peaches tonight?" he whispered above her ear.

And then the music began. She raised her eyes, and he led them into the dance. As they moved, her perfume teased his senses.

"Silly man," she admonished.

"Tell me what you're thinking," he spoke softly as he steered them through the crowded floor. She was too quiet, too withdrawn.

"I don't know," she finally said. "I hardly know what to think anymore! I'm not really afraid of your cousin, or your uncle, or even..." She shook her head, trailing off. "I'm rather afraid of myself, of my own thoughts... Am I paranoid?" She glanced up, confusion raw in her gaze.

"And me?" He could see the crack in the trust she'd professed to have for him just a few weeks before.

"Are you even real? I mean, of course I know that. Of

course you are real. You are live flesh and blood, here before me. But am I making more of this than I ought? Oh, how fickle and foolish I must seem! But these feelings... Are they real? Are they like vapor? Will they disappear when the sun comes out?"

He twirled her expertly and then pulled her close again. She was not fickle or foolish. Her very concerns proved this to him. He'd known she was experiencing such qualms.

He steered them around another couple before answering.

"I've never been compelled to obstruct or hinder anything my uncle has ever attempted to do. I've disagreed with him. I've doubted him. But I've never before interfered in either of my cousin's lives..." He twirled her again. "...but—"

"But?" she prompted.

"—I've never wanted a woman as badly as I want you." Was it fair of him to tell her this?

"But am I real?" He would address all of her concerns. "I am here. I have a strategy, and I intend for it to go as planned. Are these feelings real?

"Real enough to keep me awake, several nights in a row. Real enough to cause me to think of nothing but you, even when other women are readily available. Real enough to be painful at times. Are your feelings like vapor?

"If the sun comes out, what will become of them? Will they dissolve into nothing but a fine mist on millions of blades of grass? And what if the sun disappears? Will they turn to ice?"

At his words, she chuckled.

"Are you mocking my attempt at poetry, Sophia?" A few wisps of her hair tickled him when he bent down to speak near her ear.

She glanced at him out of the side of her eyes. "I'm mocking myself..." She spoke so softly that he almost missed her words. But she had smiled. "...for doubting something more real than anything I've ever known."

He twirled her again, pleased that she'd smiled for him. A real smile, too, not that halfhearted one with the distant look in her eyes.

He pulled her close, perhaps closer than he ought. "Ah, Sophia," he whispered. "Trust me?"

SHE SHOULD TELL HIM. No matter they were on a crowded dance floor.

It was not that she did not trust him, but she knew.

His plan was doomed to fail.

How would he feel about her then? Knowing she was tarnished? He'd said his feelings for her kept him up at night. But how much of that was based on the image he'd created in his mind? For she was not so innocent as everyone thought. And when he discovered...

"'Sometimes we are less unhappy in being deceived by those we love, than in being undeceived by them,' my captain."

It was his turn to laugh. "Are you quoting Lord Byron to me?" But his eyes creased as he smiled. This was how she would remember him. Long after he'd left her life in search of something attainable. "And very cryptically. I'm not sure I delight in your answer."

"I trust you." She held his gaze unwavering. "And I adore your poetry." This drew his laughter again. She would lock this moment away, in the safest part of her heart. She would pull it out and cherish it as she grew into an old, forgotten woman.

For that was how she was beginning to picture herself as Lord Harold's bride.

CHAPTER 10

*I*n the early hours of the morning, just as Sophia climbed into bed, she was startled by a light tapping at the door. "It's Mama, Sophia. Let me in, dear."

After hopping up, she unlatched the lock and opened the door wide for her mother to enter. Apparently, her mama intended to discuss the marriage bed with her after all.

Except that there would be no marriage bed for this bride. Sophia was quite certain of that. Thank heavens, the days were gone when the lady's maid presented a stained sheet to the family, or God forbid, when the family looked on while it was performed.

She was merely obliged to undergo this short, informal discussion that her mama wished to have with her tonight. "It's late, Mama. Is this really necessary?"

Her mother had donned her dressing gown and slippers and wore a mop cap over her silvery blond curls. "Oh, dear me, yes, darling. Good, the hearth is still warm. Let's sit over here and chat." Her mama led her closer to the dying embers and curled up on the small settee there. Sophia joined her, their toes touching. She would humor her mama in this.

"Your husband, your future husband," Mama clarified, "Lord Harold."

"Yes," Sophia said.

"Tomorrow evening, he is going to come to you."

Sophia nodded. Yes, she understood this.

"You will have the services of your new maid, Penny. You must allow her to assist you in bathing, braiding your hair, and dabbing perfume in a few delicate places. Such as behind your ears and on your wrists. You will want to be an oasis to your husband, darling. A fragrant, soft oasis."

Well, perhaps, it seemed, she might learn something from her mama after all.

"Instruct Penny to braid your hair loosely, only after brushing it one hundred times. Tell her to tie the end with a loose bow. We do not want for your husband to struggle with it, when the time comes. We want him to feel manly and powerful. He will pull the bow off easily, and your hair will flow freely in his hands."

Her mama smiled conspiratorially and added, "Men love hair, darling, especially long, flowing, shiny hair such as yours."

Sophia raised her brows. Her mother had thought this through quite thoroughly.

"Relieve yourself before he arrives."

"Relieve my— Oh! Yes, well, yes, of course." Sophia was slightly shocked. How much detail was her mother going to go into? This might come to be more embarrassing than she'd originally presumed.

"And well, the perfume. Always remember the perfume." Waving her hand through the air, her mother then dismissed this aspect of the conversation. "You might wish to climb into the bed before he arrives. It saves for some embarrassment on your part. Anyhow, your role is to simply lie back and look beautiful. Smile as though you have a mysterious secret. Close your eyes, as though his touch gives you ecstasy. And contrary to what many women say, I believe you ought to move with him. Do not lie still like a plank of wood. Do not keep your eyes pressed firmly shut as though you are tasting something bitter... even if it is bitter, for darling, it will be, most likely, quite painful in the beginning. Although I cannot imagine Lord Harold to be so large as to— No matter. You are a maiden, and your body is not used to such... well, such a visitor as it shall welcome tomorrow evening."

Oh, this was mortifying, hearing her mother speak of such things! Perhaps, more existed to her mother than she'd imagined. And as for Mr. Scofield... At which thought, Sophia brought her musings to a screeching halt.

She would not allow herself to speculate on such things! Good heavens!

"Move with him, Mother?" Sophia had not thought of any of this. When she'd been near Captain Brookes, she'd had inclinations. She'd felt an overwhelming impulse to open herself to him in a most indefinable way, but she'd not considered actually doing so. She'd rather denied such things existed ever since... well, ever since.

Her mother nodded sagely. "Yes, yes, rather like rowing a boat, dear. There is a rhythm to it all. You will know. Your body will know."

Sophia sat up straight. "What if I get it wrong?"

Her mama laughed. Patting her hand, she smiled at her daughter warmly. "That, my dear, is the beauty of marriage. You shall have years and years to practice. And unlike the pianoforte or learning a new dance, it is an assignment you both shall enjoy."

Sophia looked at her mother again and felt she'd learned more about her in the past ten minutes than she'd known these past twenty years.

Her mama kissed her cheek and then rose to her feet. "Now, off to bed with you, my darling. You've a big day ahead of you!"

If Sophia had been a real bride...

If Lord Harold had been a real groom...

If they had been in love with each other, rather than other people...

If, if, if... So many ifs. Doubts and thoughts flew about her mind in a frantic but taunting manner.

For if all of the above were true, or even slightly true, her wedding would have been a dream.

The sky was a beautiful blue, and the sun provided the perfect amount of warmth. Birds sang as she climbed out of the barouche upon reaching the church. Her mama

glowed, Mr. Scofield smiled at her proudly, and Dudley—
Well, dearest Dudley was nowhere to be seen!

Sophia's dress could not have been one iota more fashionable, nor even the tiniest bit more suited to her figure and
coloring. Periwinkle blues trimmed with yellow and gold
emphasized all of her best attributes. The flowers everywhere
were newly in blossom. How had the Prescotts arranged for
such an occurrence as that? They were powerful indeed.

When Sophia entered the church, the scent of candles
and beeswax brought decades of childhood memories to
mind.

The air was magical. Something divine was to occur in
this grand, impressive, revered building today. Two people
were to become one.

Even Rhoda, who was to stand up beside her, glowed.
She hugged Sophia, and both of them looked at each other
with a strange sort of shock on their faces. How could
anyone not have hope on such a beautiful day?

"Sophia..." Rhoda shook her head, obviously puzzled.
"...you are the most beautiful bride I have ever seen in my
entire life."

Sophia's mother stood behind her, fussing at Sophia's
gown but answering in agreement. "Just what I have been
thinking all morning, Miss Mossant — Rhoda, my dear."
Even Rhoda would bask in her mother's happiness today, it
would seem.

Before any more words could be spoken, the organ
struck a loud, majestic note, and a hush fell over the building. Penny had arrived earlier, as had Mrs. Crump. They

handed bouquets to both her and Rhoda. Dudley, ah, there he was, stepped out from behind a column, and Mrs. Crump sent both him and her mother down the aisle to the pew at the front of the church. Fully in command of the spectacle, she then pulled Rhoda to stand at the end of the center aisle. Gripping Rhoda's arm for a moment or two, Mrs. Crump seemed to be counting inside of her head, and then gently shoved her into the sanctuary.

Sophia and Mr. Scofield were next.

She'd not looked forward to walking with her stepfather. She'd felt betrayed. She'd felt as though she'd trusted him to be a father to her and that he'd instead used her for profit.

Except, for almost the entirety of her life, he *had* been something of a father to her. He also, apparently, cared deeply for her mother. How could one feel animosity knowing both of these things to be true? She tucked one of her hands through his arm and clutched at the bouquet in her other.

She would almost believe she was like any other bride. But all the tradition, all the flowers in the world could not change the nature of this wedding.

Her stepfather's solid grasp held her back as she would have dashed down the aisle at a much quicker pace. Did she merely want to get this over with? If she rushed through all of it, she could then pretend it never happened. Mr. Scofield spoke quietly into her ear. "Be patient, Sophia. Your groom is not going anywhere. I told you this was what you wanted, my dear. You'll do better to trust the men in your life." And then he chuckled.

That was the moment when she looked to the end of the aisle, to her groom she was walking toward.

Lord Harold, dressed in a fine suit with lace at his wrists and a gloriously embroidered waistcoat, looked, it seemed, almost as though he were in pain.

Beside him stood his brother, Lord St. John. Sophia glanced over the right side of the church.

Captain Brookes sat three rows back. He was formally dressed, mostly in black, relieved only by a freshly pressed white cravat. His dark eyes tugged at her.

"This is not what I want!" She wanted to scream at the congregation. *"It is what all of you want!"* And they were getting it!

She held Devlin's gaze with her own, and he must have noticed the panic in hers. For he lifted his chin and steeled his eyes. *"Be strong,"* he seemed to be telling her. *"You can do this."*

Sophia pushed back the tears that had sprung out of nowhere and nodded, such a small movement only he would see. And then, unless she was to crane her neck backwards in order to stare at the man she really wished to marry, she turned her head up to the altar where Harold stood.

And then she was there.

Beside him.

Her groom.

Mr. Scofield turned her slightly, so that she faced Lord Harold and the bishop.

When the organ stopped playing, the only sounds in the building were the rustling of dresses and creaking wooden pews. This was a place of solemnity, of purity and tradition.

"Who giveth this woman to be married to this man?" The priest addressed Mr. Scofield in a booming but solemn voice.

Oh, no, my good sir, Sophia thought acidly. *Who selleth her?*

"Her mother and I do," her stepfather answered with great conviction. He then bent forward and awkwardly kissed her on the cheek.

In a formal manner, Mr. Scofield lifted her hand to the bishop, and the bishop placed it in Lord Harold's.

She wondered, at that moment, if it was always thus so with her husband, his touching her only when absolutely necessary.

The bishop recited a few prayers for all to be in agreement with and then turned his attention to the bride and groom.

"Repeat after me, my lord." The bishop bowed toward Lord Harold, who nodded and turned to face her. He echoed the bishop's words dutifully. "I, Harold James Farnsworth Michael Brookes, take thee, Sophia Ann Babineaux, to be my wedded wife, to have and to hold from this day forward, for better, for worse, for richer, for poorer, in sickness and in health, to love and to cherish..." He choked up a little, and Sophia wondered at the woman he did love. "...to cherish, till death us do part, according to God's holy ordinance, and thereto, I plight thee my troth."

The minister than directed Sophia to take Harold's hand and repeat the same. She stumbled a little at his name. She'd not known he had so many, although she ought to have assumed so as he was from such a dynastic family. She spoke the words flatly, woodenly, much as, she thought with an insane impulse to giggle, the way her mother had described some women lay on their wedding night.

Which suddenly made the words hilariously funny.

The image of a wooden woman lying beneath Lord Harold's reluctant attentions took hold of her, the surreal nature of this moment notwithstanding.

A giggle escaped her.

The bishop looked at her in surprise, and then after a moment's consideration, in admonishment.

Lord Harold glanced at her as well, but his reaction was quite the opposite of the holy man's.

His lips twitched, and an unusual twinkle gleamed from behind his gaze.

The absurdity of this moment was not unnoticed by him.

When he compressed his own lips tightly together, it took all the focus Sophia could muster to keep her demeanor in check. She forced herself to stare solemnly at their hands together, repressing any further giggles.

Except...

The harder she dwelled on the inappropriateness of her hilarity, the greater the urge became.

Harold's hand clasped hers lightly, as though he were giving her one last chance to break free and run away. She pictured this scenario in her mind as well.

How she would love to take that mad dash.

This moment was not of solemnity and love.

It was a farce.

More pressure built inside her.

Oh, God, please don't let me laugh, please don't let me laugh... She chanted the words in her mind over and over again.

The priest turned again toward Harold.

Lord St. John had handed a ring to his brother, and Harold nearly dropped it. Sophia noticed his shoulders begin to shake unmistakably until St. John elbowed him.

Appearing overly solemn and serious, he slid the ring upon her third finger, fumbling as he did so. His discomfort with her was obvious. Why had she not noticed this when he proposed?

Again, reciting after the priest, Harold began to speak, his voice shaking. Peeking up, he surprisingly met her gaze. The shimmer in his eyes confirmed that he was struggling as much as she.

None of this was remotely funny.

It was tragic, in fact.

And yet, here they stood.

Sophia had to cover her mouth and push down another most inappropriate giggle.

"With this ring, I thee wed, with my body—"

He whimpered a bit, but Sophia knew it had been going to come out as a chortle of laughter.

"—I thee worship, and with all, with all, with all of my wohor — whor — orldly goods, I thee endow..." Red-faced, Lord Harold finished reciting the vows more confidently.

"...in the name of the Father, and of the Son, and of the Holy Ghost. Amen."

He appeared greatly relieved to have gotten all of that out.

Scowling, the bishop turned and ordered them both to kneel before the altar.

"Let us pray," he ordered them austerely. And he went on and on and on.

Sophia could feel Lord Harold shaking beside her. And she turned a few of her own giggles into what she hoped sounded like sobs of sentimentality.

The bishop placed both of his hands upon theirs together. "Those whom God hath joined together, let no man put asunder."

He gave one last stern look and then turned to the congregation. "Forasmuch as Lord Harold James Farnsworth—" more hilarity from Sophia. "—Michael Brookes and Miss Sophia Ann Babineaux have consented together in holy wedlock and have witnessed the same before God and this company, and thereto have given and pledged their troth either to the other, and have declared..." On and on and on he droned. "In the Name of the Father, and of the Son and of the Holy Ghost. Amen."

"Amen," Sophia said firmly. She could not do this much longer. Either she was going to burst into uncontrollable laughter, or she would burst into tears.

Focus, she chanted. *Focus on the floor. On the frayed edge of the carpet.* Thank heavens. Her heart was slowing. Lord Harold must do the same, however, or most assuredly, one of them was going to lose control completely.

"Amen." She heard him say beside her.

The rest of the ceremony was spent in rather dry, familiar prayer.

They both managed to endure it without embarrassing themselves further. It was the closest she'd ever felt to him. Even closer than when he'd proposed marriage.

He did not attempt to kiss her in the end, but he did take her hand and smile.

They could be friends, perhaps.

When Lord Harold assisted her down the steps of the altar, Sophia glanced at Captain Brookes. Unashamedly, he brushed tears of unleashed laughter from his own eyes. He was shaking his head at them both.

Sophia covered her mouth. Beneath it, she allowed some of the mirth she'd suppressed during the ceremony to escape. As the music rose, she, Harold, and Brookes could contain themselves no longer. All of them laughed out loud.

As did Rhoda,

And even, surprisingly enough, did St. John.

CHAPTER 11

*N*obody mentioned the bride and groom's loss of composure at the altar, as friends and family of both sat down for the elaborate breakfast that followed. Sophia wondered if people merely had not noticed or if they were being polite. The breakfast was to be the final celebration to commemorate the launching of hers and Lord Harold's connubial bliss.

Sophia ate little, but smiled and nodded throughout it all. Everyone was friendly. Everyone was happy for her. Some told her she was positively glowing.

She did her best but... it was with a great sense of relief that she bid the guests farewell and was finally allowed to disappear upstairs into a chamber connected to Lord Harold's. Presumably to... Oh, the thought was too embarrassing to consider!

She refused to give such mortification any heed. She would simply be grateful for the time alone.

Upon entering her elaborately furnished chamber,

Sophia was greeted right away by Peaches, who stood on her little hind legs and begged to be held. Feeling like a mama who'd ignored her child for too long, Sophia gathered her pet up and snuggled her like a baby.

The sound of footsteps and a nearby door closing reminded Sophia that her husband was near, disturbingly near, in fact.

Best to get this over with now. A peaceful nap would elude her, for certain, if she did not. And more than anything right now, she simply wanted to sleep.

She pushed through a door to the adjoining sitting room and knocked on Lord Harold's.

The man who opened it was not her husband, but must, she thought with a frown, be his valet. He was handsome indeed, and young, nearly as stylishly dressed as Harold had been that day.

He bowed. "My lady," he said. And then opened the door wide.

"Is Lord... I'd like to have a word with my — Lord Harold," she told him. But she felt as though she had entered a very masculine, very private, domain. The gentleman's gentleman disappeared through a door across the room without saying another word.

After a moment or two, Lord Harold returned alone. He did not seem pleased to see her. But he was polite, as he'd proven to be throughout their engagement.

"I..." She'd thought they ought to at least make an attempt at friendship. "May we sit?"

He pinched his lips, as though he would rather have this meeting over quickly, but nodded and indicated she take a seat on the sofa. He sat across from her in a winged-back chair.

"What can I do for you?" he asked. "I had thought... that you understood."

"Well, Harold," she said, irritated, herself now, by his reticence at discussing anything with her, even now. "That is precisely why I would have a word with you. And why I would expect that you and I can at the least be clear regarding a few... matters..." And then she could not help but tack on one more word. "...honestly."

His eyes did not meet hers.

Sophia persisted. "I asked you for some reassurance on a concern of mine last night, and I would have it now..."

His brows rose. "Oh, God, no! I mean. Of course, not. I've no plans whatsoever..."

Pleased, and yet somewhat shocked at his vehemence, Sophia could not help but feel a significant amount of feminine outrage. But then, as she looked at the floor and noticed he wore only stockings on his feet, she remembered. "Is she, is she terribly devastated by your marriage?" She could not claim it as theirs.

"She?" He wrinkled his brow, then a light dawned in his eyes. "Oh, yes, yes. Um... well... I suppose I have been able to offer... *her* some reassurances."

Sophia nodded. *That is something,* she supposed. "And so, I have no reason to worry that you will wish to...?"

"Oh, no, absolutely not." He was most convincing. Apparently, for now anyhow, she had nothing to fret over.

Sophia sat primly and nodded, wondering if he would make any gestures of friendship whatsoever to her; if he was not going to, then she would make one. "I was terrified one of us would lose our composure completely — at the altar," she clarified.

But he seemed distracted. His eyes glanced toward the door from which he'd just emerged.

Surely, his lover was not in his bedchamber? Of course not. His valet was in residence. Furthermore, despite their agreement, that would be the height of disrespect, and yes, she would appreciate he not make a joke of her, as Lord Kensington had done to Cecily.

"You will not flaunt your infidelity?" she asked.

This caught his attention. "Of course not. Oh, Miss Babineaux, of course I would never."

Sophia sighed and looked at him much as one of her governesses had when she'd forgotten something simple. "You must call me Sophia now."

"I suppose that would be appropriate," he agreed.

Sophia waited. "And…" she prompted him.

"Well, yes, of course, please call me Harold."

They'd settled that at least.

"You are ready for travel tomorrow?" she asked, again, seeking some sort of rapport with him.

"I am. Yes, yes, I am." And then he stood, indicating the end of this rather lovely conversation. "Is there anything else you need of me today?"

"No, it's just…" She wanted to tell him her secret, but he was more than a little distant at the moment. She would wait. They had all the time in the world. "No, no… I— Nothing that cannot wait." And she rose as well so he could escort her to the door.

Back in her chamber, Peaches jumped up and greeted her once again. "Would that he had even one tenth of the enthusiasm you have for me," she said to the pup. *Well, not really...*

Penny crept quietly into the bedchamber and assisted Sophia out of her wedding clothes. After a long, hot perfumed bath, having her hair brushed and braided, and then more dabs of perfume, as per her mother's instructions, Sophia was happy to send the maid away for the day.

Penny stepped out of the room, and Sophia locked all the doors.

Not that it was necessary here, but old habits died hard.

She reached for Peaches and climbed onto the large canopied bed. The mattress was soft, and she had no other place in the world to be. Sleep came quickly, even though the sun was yet high in the sky.

It was done.

When Sophia awoke, the room was in complete darkness. She fumbled around for a flint and managed to light a nearby candle. Holding it up to the large clock, she could barely make out that it was nearly midnight. She'd slept for ten hours!

She'd missed tea and supper, and...

Yes, yes, now she was quite hungry.

A bump from next door told her that Harold was awake too. Perhaps he'd had some supper brought up. Sophia did not wish to use the bell pull and awaken a maid. They'd already been called upon to do so much extra work that day for the wedding breakfast.

Stepping into her slippers and pulling on her dressing

gown, Sophia tiptoed into the adjoining corridor between their two rooms. She would not knock, just in case the noise she'd heard had not come from his chamber. But she would take a quick peek and see if he were relaxing in his sitting room. Perhaps he would be more receptive to what she had to tell him, now, after resting up from the wedding, himself.

She did not carry a candle with her so it was easy to see the light shining through a minuscule crack near the door hinges. Ever so quietly, she turned the knob and gently pushed it open. Just a tad, and if he were sleeping—

He was not.

Sleeping, that was.

Nor was he alone.

By the light of several well-placed candelabras, Sophia had difficulty making sense, at first, of the sight before her.

The valet — yes, that was the handsome valet — bent over Harold, who was face down over the arm of the sofa where she'd sat earlier.

Neither of them were clothed.

Their bodies, together, formed a kaleidoscope of masculinity and passion. Harold's hands were above his head, seemingly captured by one of the valet's and pinned in place. The valet was slimmer but more muscular than Harold. If not for the tenderness she could see as his other hand stroked Harold's thigh, she would wonder if he were not attacking him.

Harold moaned as the other man…

What was he doing from behind? Oh, good Lord!

Oh, good Lord.

The scene ought to be repulsive, her logical mind reminded her, but instead, it was oddly...sensual.

And suddenly provided the answer to so many of her questions.

She pulled the door closed. She did not wish to intrude! She would perhaps be more horrified than either of them if her presence were to be discovered. The door closed with only the lightest of clicks before Sophia let out the breath she'd not realized she'd been holding.

No wonder.

No wonder!

Oh, what a stupid, stupid fool she'd been. Had her stepfather known? Of course, he'd known! And the duke! And St. John! And even the duchess, most probably. Yes, that was perhaps why she'd gone out of her way to be kind to her.

Sophia was to be the mask for her husband's... unusual preferences.

Had Brookes known? Of course, he'd known!

Sophia returned to her own chamber and began pacing. What did this mean? Did this change anything?

No, not really, not at all.

Except that now she could be quite, *quite* certain she would not be expected to lie with her husband.

Could he even? She wondered? What if she wanted a child? This image of her turning into the prunish spinster as his wife was becoming more and more of a reality as she considered the ramifications of what she'd just seen.

She'd known they were to be trapped together, and

perhaps she'd thought that if so, perhaps after a few years, or several even, they might decide to have a child.

But could such a man?

Her restlessness woke Peaches, who now danced circles around her and intermittently scratched at the door.

Sophia was no longer thinking of food, but she could not stay inside of her chamber either. She would take Peaches outside. Even though she and her dog were in a strange place, with a host of virtual strangers, she felt no worry for her safety.

With a candlestick in one hand, she slipped out of her bedchamber with Peaches following her enthusiastically.

Which way were the kitchens?

Turning to her left, Sophia aimlessly meandered along the corridor.

When she came across a stairwell, she moved the candlestick to her other hand, picked Peaches up, and carefully maneuvered them both downward. The steps were steep, and the small dog had not mastered staircases. She most likely never would. Her legs were far too short.

At what she presumed to be the ground floor, Sophia placed Peaches on the floor and entered a different corridor. This one was oddly familiar, but she was not entirely certain why.

Ah, yes, she'd walked with the duchess through here. Peaches burrowed behind a curtain and revealed a glass-paned door leading outside into what appeared to be a small courtyard.

Perfect. It was perfect.

Not wanting to be locked out, Sophia propped the door

open with a nearby rock, and Peaches dashed past Sophia into the moonlight.

Obviously, her little dog had been here before. Peaches sniffed around in a large circle and found a place to squat. Well, that was one less thing to worry about, anyhow.

"Good girl, Peaches," Sophia whispered and then shivered a little. Although the day had been warm, a chill hung in the air. When Peaches returned, Sophia removed the rock and allowed the door to close. Only now that she was inside again, she had no idea how she was going to find the kitchens. Navigating one's way about Prescott House was difficult enough during the daytime. She ought to return to her room and call a maid.

Perhaps the maid could bring her some ratafia.

Anything to stop the image of her husband and his lover together, replaying itself over and over in her now lurid imagination.

She did not hate Harold for what he had been doing. She did not hate him for being... of such a disposition.

But she was furious!

Furious with him, with Devlin — with all of them for keeping it from her!

Little detail she ought to know, perhaps?

For it did change things. Didn't it?

It effectively extinguished any long-term possibility of her ever having any semblance of a normal marriage. Or, she thought most likely, children.

For she was more certain than ever that Brookes and Harold had been considering an annulment as the means with which to end this marriage... but that was out of the

question. Ever since Dudley had mentioned the require-
ments for such...

Would she never be a mother? Could she embrace a life
of infidelity for herself?

But for her want of children, and but for the emotions
she had experienced with Captain Brookes, she most likely
would never have any need...

Giving up on her quest for food, Sophia called to
Peaches, who'd begun sniffing around curiously. "Let's go
back to bed!"

The animal ignored her completely.

She'd caught the scent of something interesting, it
seemed.

"Peaches!" Sophia whisper-shouted. "Peaches!"

The little dog looked up again and then took off at
a run.

In the wrong direction, of course!

Sophia followed her to that large rolling gate and
groaned inwardly. Peaches had slipped through the bars
near the floor.

Blast! The tiny fiend must have hidden a toy sometime
earlier behind one of the statues. Gnawing at a mangled
doll, her tail wagging happily, Peaches showed no sign of
returning to Sophia anytime soon. "Come back here,
Peaches!" Sophia whispered loudly. This was the last thing
she needed tonight. She loved her pet, but, oh, sometimes!
"You beetle-headed little monster, come out of there!"

At Sophia's tone, Peaches paused, appeared to consider
her mistress for but a moment, and then went right back to
gnawing at the toy.

Not wanting to unlock the gate and push the noisy apparatus into the wall, Sophia got down on her hands and knees to attempt to reach through. If she could get a hold of the toy, then Peaches would follow it back to this side.

Sophia could almost touch it.

She slipped her head between the bars, and her arm could now reach a few inches further. Almost...

Yes! She had it.

But as she went to slip back out, the metal bars halted her.

Sophia adjusted her position and, reaching up to tuck her ears down, attempted again to slide her head through the bars.

How had she slipped through so easily, moving forward?

She cocked her head to one side and pulled again.

And then to the other. She tried standing, and then sitting lower, until her lack of success began to chaff nearly as much as the sides of her face.

Sophia had heard swear words spoken by Dudley and his friends. She'd never used any of them, however, until the frustrations of this particular situation overtook her.

Releasing a long stream of profanity, she maneuvered into a position that would be somewhat comfortable. How was she to get out of this debacle? On her knees, she placed her elbows on the bar so that she could rest her chin on her hands.

That was slightly better.

She was trapped in a ridiculous situation.

The irony of it did not escape her.

CHAPTER 12

Normally, Devlin would not have stayed at Prescott House, but since the purchase of Dartmouth Place, he'd let go of the lodgings he normally kept in London. He now sat in his uncle's library and wondered if he should be sent to Bedlam.

For he was beginning to make plans for when he moved out to the country. Plans that might involve bringing a wife along with him.

For Harold, he was certain, had committed to their chosen course of action.

Devlin would travel with the family to Priory Point and provide his assistance in the matter.

Sophia would also have need of him. The fallout could prove tricky, indeed.

It could be a beginning for the two of them, if all went as planned. It would be necessary that they wait, of course, but they would take this one step at a time.

If it was what she wanted.

He was reasonably certain it was her desire to be with him. She'd told him she loved him, for Christ's sake. But so much needed to be resolved.

And much of it hung upon the courage of a cousin who had lacked confidence for all of his adult life, a man who doubted his own right to happiness because of deep-seated guilt and shame.

Dev threw back one final mouthful of scotch and contemplated the possibility of taking Sophia with him to Surrey. An interesting thought on today, of all days — her wedding day to another man.

He chuckled to himself as he recalled the spectacle the bride and groom had nearly made of the formal ceremony. Devlin had had eyes for only her, and he'd realized what was happening the first moment she'd stifled her laughter. She must have been near hysteria. The farce of it too much.

Thank God, they hadn't lost control.

They did not need any further complications. Dev would have Harold execute their plan so that he, Dev, could propose, get a special license, and then take such vows himself with Sophia.

And mean every damn one of them.

The clock on the mantel showed it to be nearly one o'clock in the morning. With a long day of travel planned for the morrow, he probably ought to try to get some rest tonight, something he'd resisted for some reason. Or something he thought might simply elude him.

What with knowing that Sophia, on her wedding night, slept in the same house…

Alone…

He stood and stretched before extinguished the few candles he'd left burning. Just as he turned to head upstairs, the pitter-patter of four tiny feet caught his attention.

Peaches stood on the floor before him, tail wagging. She spun in an impatient circle and let out one quick bark. She then spun in two more circles.

It was obvious the dog wanted her to follow him.

Had she gotten locked out of Sophia's room, somehow? He strode quickly behind the red, exasperated little body, as she ran forward and then back, returning to make sure he was following, several times. They were not headed toward the wing where he knew Sophia's chamber to be.

Growing more curious by the moment, Dev dutifully followed the impatient little canine.

And then, as he rounded a corner near the gallery, he could not help but smile at the unexpected sight before him.

This must be the reason he'd not gone to bed earlier. For, shoved into the air, in a childlike sort of pose, was Sophia's nightgown-clad bottom, wriggling temptingly before him.

At first, he could not discern what she was doing, but then he realized her blond head was bent awkwardly forward, poking through the bars of the gate leading to the gallery.

And she was cursing like a bloody soldier.

His assistance was, indeed, most necessary.

"Sophia, Sophia," he said as he got closer to the little bundle of frustration, "what on earth are you doing?"

"Oh, just sitting here, staring at the floor." Makin a vain

attempt to pull herself out, she winced at her efforts. "What does it look like I'm doing?"

"Er, well..." Was this a trick question?

"Oh, Dev..." She moaned as she said his name, unable to turn her head toward him. She suddenly looked quite defeated. "...oh, Dev, I'm so glad it's you." And then, as though she'd remembered something beyond belief, she shrieked. "You should have told me! Why did you not tell me the truth? About Harold?"

She was on her knees and could not look up at him, so he crouched down beside her.

Ah, so Harold had told her. He was surprised, actually. It was a secret his cousin had guarded all his life. "It was not my secret to tell, love."

"What a fool I've been. To think I had imagined him in love with me! I had no idea! I'm not really even certain as to the mechanics of it, but he does rather seem to enjoy it."

"He told you this?"

"Oh, no," She tried to shake her head but flinched as the bars prevented her from doing so. "I was going to see if he wanted to look for something to eat with me, since I heard him moving about, and I peeked in and I, well, I... saw them... together..."

Dev did not know what to say to this. "I'm sorry. I wanted to tell you, but I hoped perhaps it wouldn't be necessary. If everything works out as planned—"

And then a small sob escaped her. "It's not going to work out. Your plan is not going to work. I can never be granted an annulment." She seemed suddenly quite frantic, for which situation, he wasn't certain.

An annulment had been one of their scenarios, but not the one they'd decided upon. Harold had been mortified at the thought that people might guess as to why. But what was she saying?

"Why not, love?"

"The examination. The impossible examination." And then gritting her teeth, she choked on another sob. "Can you free me from this blasted barnacle?"

He cursed himself for not liberating her right away. Redness had appeared where the bars had irritated the skin along the sides of her face, and it looked as though she'd cut one of her ears. "Of course." He looked around and could not see anything sturdy enough to pry the heavy iron bars open. Slipping off his waistcoat, he folded it and helped place it beneath her knees.

Her pitiful little knees were red from the cold marble floor. And her feet were frozen.

"I'm going to find something sturdy enough to pry this apart, and some oil for the sides of your face." Standing, he turned back toward her. "Don't go anywhere," he said to her sweetly feminine bottom.

He chuckled as he heard her growl but then rushed away to find what he would need. She must have been there a while. Once he pried her out, they could discuss whatever it was that she was so upset about.

An examination? And she'd mentioned an annulment. She must be thinking an exam would be required to ensure she was still a maiden, which was quite simply not the case. Hadn't been for centuries, to his knowledge. Annulments, in fact, were far more complicated than that. Sophia was the one who could demand an annulment, if Harold refused to consummate, but that was not a part of the plan either.

He located a fire poker and some lavender oil and rushed back to where he'd left her. As he approached, he could hear her talking to Peaches. "Telling me not to go anywhere. Does the addle pate not see I would do just that if only I could? Aw, you're a sweet baby."

"Sophia?" he said, crouching once more. She could not turn her head to look at him, and he decided that would be the first thing he would address. "I'm going to open the gate, so that I can get around to the other side. Can you move sideways on your knees so I can move it, just a few feet?"

"I can. Just get me out of here before morning. I'd rather the duchess and duke not discover me here on their way to breakfast."

It was the least of his concerns. But if it bothered her... "We'll get you out, love."

He rose again, unlocked the gate, and then, slowly inched it open just enough to slip through to the other side.

When he got to the other side, he sat down on the floor, legs crossed in front of him, and pulled the oil out of his shirt pocket.

"Look up, Sophia," he said. She did so, and he saw tearstained cheeks rubbed nearly raw on the sides. "You're rather pitiful, aren't you?" He warmed some of the lavender oil on his palms before raising his hands to the sides of her face. Leaning forward, he kissed her softly on the lips.

"This ought to calm any swelling but also help you slide through. Don't move, that's a good girl. Relax." He watched her eyes close and noticed a few more tears escape through her lashes.

"Devlin, I know you were going to help me. I know that you and Harold thought you could get us out of this, but I'm not... I'm not..."

"Shh..." He would set her racing mind to rest. "The idea of testing for your maidenhood is a medieval one. The law does not do that. The church does not do that. There is not one damn soul on earth who I would allow to do that to you. Not now, not ever." Was that what this was about? Was she simply afraid of such a thing? Or was she afraid because she had already lain with a man?

That thought brought him up short. Did it matter? He supposed, on some base level, every man liked to think he was the only one. But had she been in love with somebody else? Was she still?

"Is there somebody else?" he asked, even as he rubbed the oil on her cheeks, her neck, her ears.

She shook her head slightly, moving what little she could, from side to side. "There is not," she said seriously. "But, I am not... untouched."

He moved his hands down her neck to her shoulders, which were rigid and tense. "Did you love someone before? You don't have to tell me, if you do not wish to do so..." A part of him wanted to know, and another part did not. He was tired of all the miscommunications though, and the secrets. She seemed to have been worrying over this for some time. Best to get it out now.

"It was a long time ago," she said.

"How long?" he asked. Hell and damnation, she was barely twenty. Some cad most likely had taken advantage of her naiveté when she first had come out. Young innocents, not chaperoned properly, were easily susceptible to a well-practiced, unscrupulous rake.

She seemed to be mentally counting back. "Nearly seven years."

What the hell? "You were a child!" He rose abruptly from the floor. A burst of violence shot through him. Grabbing the fireplace poker, he looked for a strategic place where he could secure it between the bars. He needed to free her now.

Touching her hair, almost without thinking, he soothed her as he wedged the bar into place. "I'm going to pry these apart so that you can slip back out. Tell me when you are ready."

Had she been raped? Goddamn it! She must have been. Who? Had the bastard been punished?

"All right," she said, "I'm ready."

"Who was it, Sophia?" he said as he put all his weight into leveraging the rods apart. "Now, Sophia, try now." He watched carefully as she wiggled a little. "Don't flinch. Relax your face. The muscles will stop you from sliding through."

She did as he'd said, and before he had to release the bars, her head slid backwards and out. "I don't want to talk about it."

She rubbed the sides of her face and then stretched her neck from one side to the other.

"You were a child." He extracted the poker from the gate. He'd barely moved the rods at all, but it had been enough.

"I'm safe now. I got good at that. And now it's over." She winced as she attempted to stand up. Rushing around the gate, Devlin assisted her the rest of the way to her feet.

"How long have you been down here?"

She shrugged and then winced again. "I came down a little after midnight. Did Peaches find you?" It had been someone she'd known. Someone she'd trusted.

"Scofield?"

She glanced at him quickly and saw the question in his eyes. "You mean my stepfather? No, no. Leave it be, Devlin. Please?"

But icicles of disgust and outrage curdled in his veins.

The son then. He knew it. He knew it to be the truth. But he would not press her tonight.

She had gathered up the candle and Peaches and was turning as though to return to her chamber.

He slipped on his waistcoat, snuffed out his own candle, and set it on a table nearby. Then, without giving her any warning, swooped her and Peaches into his arms.

One slender arm reached up to grasp him around the neck. The other one held fast to her dog. "I can walk, you know," she said before tucking her head into his neck, "but I like this better."

Devlin chuckled as he carried her through the familiar

corridor. "Of course you can," he said. "But I like this better, too."

He turned into the stairwell and adjusted her weight slightly. She was a tiny little thing, but these back stairs were steep.

"Did you know your aunt commissioned a portrait of Peaches?" Sophia said out of nowhere. "Despite everything, your family has been awfully kind to me. Her grace, I think, truly wants me to feel at home."

Dev was not surprised. His father would not have stayed at Prescott House if good will was lacking. It was never a matter of his family not loving one another. Loving one another too much, perhaps. They would protect one another, regardless of who might get hurt. Such an unquestioning loyalty was not always for the best, he knew. They did not always consider the well-being of outsiders when it came to their actions. Nor did they always consider matters such as right and wrong, due process, and lawfulness.

"Her grace is a good person. Their hearts are in the right place," he conceded, "if not their heads." He did not wish to criticize his family to her, but he also knew that she was somewhat confused by it all. "If you'd known the true circumstances, would you have accepted Harold's proposal?"

She thought for a moment or two. Devlin reached the floor where Sophia's chamber was located and turned sideways to exit the stairwell with her. She tucked her feet down so they could pass through more easily.

"Honestly, before I knew you, I cannot say that I would

not. But... I did meet you, and, well, that's changed everything."

He grinned over at her and then placed a quick kiss upon her lips. No one would see them. The halls were lit by one tiny candle, and it was close to two in the morning.

When he got to her chamber, he raised his brows questioningly. "Your maid?"

"Has left me for the evening. She believes I am sharing a romantic night with my husband."

Hmm... this could be advantageous for the two of them. He opened the door and carried her through to her bed.

"Are you still confused?"

She hesitated only a moment before answering. "No, I rather think I see the truth of it."

He did not want her suffering belated attacks of guilt. "And that is?"

"Your family and my parents have manipulated circumstances so as to each achieve their own ends — without my consent or knowledge. Your family has done so to provide protection for Harold, and mine for financial security."

"And so, it is quite understandable that you might feel justified in rebelling against such deviousness." He would have her be certain of these facts.

"I suppose." She scooted across the bed and placed Peaches on a blanket at the foot.

"Are you sleepy?" he asked her. "Or still hungry?"

"I am still hungry," she said, "but I've no wish to awaken a maid." She would have continued, but he raised one finger to her lips.

"Then do not awaken one," he said. "I have personal knowledge of where the cook keeps rations for just such an occasion." Devlin held up a hand, indicating for her to stay put. "I shall return shortly, my lady."

* * *

SOPHIA TUCKED her feet beneath her, rather than lock the door behind him as her first instinct demanded. She was safe here. She seemed to be safe whenever Devlin was near.

Perhaps they could talk. She was finally getting some answers.

It wasn't long before he returned with a tray of various fruits, breads, and cheeses. He'd also discovered an opened bottle of wine. As he entered the room, he shrugged. "If your maid believes your husband is sharing your chamber with you, we might as well provide her with evidence to that effect."

"That looks delicious." Opening a small blanket, she set out what was like a picnic on her bed. "You are going to join me, are you not?"

His answer was to remove his shoes and climb up next to where Peaches sat. "You are always telling me that we do not know each other. This is our opportunity to remedy that. Now, what sort of activities did you and Harold participate in before you became engaged?"

Sophia reached for the knife and cut off a slice of melon. "Well..." she said as she held it out to him.

He reached forward and took it from her with his teeth.

"...um..." It took her a moment to regain her train of

thought. "...we danced at various balls. We, well, he took me for a ride in the park." This was more difficult than she would have thought. What had they done together? "We, er, discussed the weather at great length." A self-mocking smile lifted the corner of her mouth. "And his affection for me... Yes, we discussed that on numerous occasions."

Devlin held up his hand and began checking off points. "You and I have danced," another finger, "I've taken you for a ride in my curricle, and I believe, I've given you some indication as to my affection for you." But then he frowned. "I know what our problem is. You and I have not discussed the weather."

"Oh, but we have," she joked. "In the park, the rain, we discussed the weather then."

He swallowed his bite and looked over at her. "So, there, you see, we are acquainted well enough."

"My dearest friend, Cecily, Lady Kensington now..." Sophia paused.

Dev waited. He was a good listener.

"...Cecily married the earl after what seemed to have been a loving courtship. He was the opposite of your cousin. But after she married, she learned he'd been even more of a liar and deceiver than Harold. The entire relationship, for him, had merely been a charade to get his hands on her dowry. I guess that I thought, with Lord Harold being so quiet and undemanding, that he was more likely to be sincere."

Dev reached out and pressed a strawberry to her lips.

Sofia opened her mouth and took a bite of the sweet juicy fruit. The rather simple action suddenly felt far more than intimate than simply taking a bite of food. She knew he watched her. And he had a hungry look in his eyes.

The juice squirted onto her lips and down her chin. Dev's hand still held the fruit, and his thumb reached out to slide some of the juice along her lips. Her breath caught momentarily.

"So, how do we ever know anybody, Sophia?" He asked the question sincerely, as though it was something he'd pondered himself on occasion.

"We've had this discussion before," she said. "Remember? By perhaps knowing ourselves better?"

"And by having good friends, finding people who prove that they can be trusted," he reminded her.

"You have done so much for me already. You have saved me from a lion, braved an icy thunderstorm, helped me to escape from the gate tonight, and now you are here. And yet, I am most certain that there are dozens of women who would cause you far less complications. I must ask this, Dev. I'm tired of misapprehensions. Why?" She needed to know.

He stared at his lap and then back up at her. "There isn't an explanation, to be perfectly honest." He gathered the bread and the plates and moved them all from the bed. "I would hold you while we have this discussion," he explained as she watched him.

And then he climbed back onto the bed, wrapped his arms around her, and lay them down together, her back against his chest. "Since I met you, I have felt something. I thought it would pass, but then I had to see you again. And when I did, it was still there, only stronger. Each time since then, that feeling has spun a web around me, connecting me to you somehow. It would feel unnatural, wrong even, to walk away from this… from you."

Sophia twisted around to consider his expression.

He looked so serious, so sincere.

She lifted her lips to his.

He kissed her back tenderly, gently.

But what of the future?

"What is your plan? Dev? How do you and Harold intend to void this marriage if an annulment is not possible?"

This — to be held in Devlin Brookes' arms, to discover the truth about everything – was what she needed. She would be kept in the dark no longer.

"As children," he began, settling into this mood, "Harold, Lucas, and I spent hours playing together. We were together nearly as much as if we were all brothers."

"Your father raised you on his own?" She'd remembered hearing that Dev's mother had died in childbirth.

"Yes, with assistance from my aunt and uncle." He looked at her sideways. "Anyway, Priory Point, where all of us are traveling tomorrow, is on the sea. It is built on high cliffs with the moors rolling out behind it. And, as boys, the moors were much less interesting to us than the cliffs."

Of course, they were!

"And so," he continued, "against my father's and uncle's direct orders, we climbed every cliff possible and explored each nook and cranny. We were quite satisfied with ourselves, I'll have you know, when we discovered an intricate system of tunnels and caves."

"I imagine her grace worried endlessly."

"Most likely." He chuckled. "Some of the caves had been used by smugglers at some point. I think my uncle may have even received a few shipments through some of them in order to keep his cellars filled. But there was this one cave, almost completely vertical. I don't think my uncle or my father ever knew of its existence.

"It was not visible from the beaches below. When I climbed down through it, though, I discovered a pool with a hidden tunnel that exited into a lagoon below the cliffs. The lagoon was treacherous — rough when the tide came in but swimmable when the tide was low. We never let on to anyone else about it. We knew we would be banned from the cliffs altogether if anyone were to discover our antics."

"What sort of antics are you referring to?" As a woman, thinking of small boys exploring such a dangerous site, she was horrified.

"At high tide, we dove into the lagoon and would then swim through the tunnel to the cave, which we climbed up and out of."

"You, Harold, and Lord St. John?"

"Yes, and another boy, but he moved away long ago."

"And what, pray tell, does this have to do with unmarrying Harold and myself?" She was almost afraid to ask.

She felt Devlin take a deep breath. "Harold is going to fake his death."

CHAPTER 13

She sensed an unusual tentativeness in him, for he'd suddenly gone quite still. "I told him there are other ways, but he wants to leave England for a place where nobody knows who he is. He wants to find a place where he can live with Stewart, without having to worry about censure and scandal."

"Stewart is his…"

"Stewart is his… valet."

"Does such a place exist?" Sophia asked. This was all quite surprising. And harrowing!

"Perhaps. Harold thinks there may be an island in the West Indies. He would have to become something of an explorer for a while, perhaps for a few years. But he told me he's always dreamed of setting his own course for his life. Without his father directing it, or his brother, or the *ton*. It would be a decision made by him and his… valet. It has not been a hasty decision on either of their parts."

Sophia lay quietly as she considered such a plan. "It is dangerous," she finally said.

"It is, and yet, it simplifies matters considerably. And it is a stunt we've done before."

"As boys."

"Yes. He will practice it." She was of no doubt that Dev would as well. He would not let his younger cousin attempt it first, after going years without knowing exactly how time, and water, had affected the tunnel. "The timing, the execution. Everything will need to be done in a precise manner. And we'll need witnesses. People willing to testify that he perished in the sea."

"You are sad for your cousin to leave?"

"It is as much what he wants as it is what you would want. What his partner wants. And what I want. But yes, I am sad. It is so very... final."

"And you are frightened for him."

"I am. I have been active, what with drills and exercises these past years, but Harold has led a sedentary life. The swimming maneuver, it is not a given for him."

Not only did Harold wish to be free of her, he *needed* to be free of her, and his family, and all of England! So much so that he would risk his life. "Dev?" she said finally. "Thank you for telling me all of this, for not glossing over the dangers of it. I want you to know — I want Harold to know — that if he finds he is unable to do it, we will find another way. He mustn't feel pressure to go through with this mad scheme if he has second thoughts."

She felt him nuzzling the top of her head.

"And that, my dear," he said, "is why I am enamored of you."

She chuckled. This was nice. Cuddling.

"Now, will you tell me something?"

"Anything." She felt most open in that moment.

"You will approve if I dispatch of your stepbrother?"

He knew. Somehow, from what she had said, he'd guessed.

He had just told her everything. He had trusted her. He'd been open and honest with her. How could she be anything but with him?

"I am safe from him now," she said.

He squeezed her protectively, but she felt a new tension emanating from him. "Thank God for that. That is why you were anxious to marry, was it not?"

"It was."

Sophia remembered some of her first encounters with Dudley. He would pinch her, or poke her, trip her, step on her toes — anything that he could do without the adults catching on. And when she told her mother or Mr. Scofield, he would deny it, indicate that she was being overly fussy. She was a girl, after all.

"I think he resented taking on a sister. I was a baby, and he was a growing boy. He did not like that my mother had entered his life and stolen some of his father's affection. Dudley could not treat my mother poorly, but he found me easy prey."

"Was this ongoing? Did it happen more than once?"

He nuzzled her ear from behind. She shook her head, just enough so that he could feel her answer and then closed her eyes and remembered. "After he got into my room that one time, I locked my door whenever he was home from school. He tried, but I was diligent. And since he was away most of the time, I had breaks from... from the threat of him."

She'd been such an idiot to ever trust Dudley!

"When he returned from school that one year, he'd changed. His voice had deepened, he had hair growing on his face, and he was taller. His friends were all taller too. Although they told me I was an annoying child, I knew things were different. And I, well, I did not find objections with much of it. They were handsome older boys. They teased me. Some of them flirted with me."

She did not wish to keep talking about this but continued anyway. "In all honesty, I do not know for certain what happened. I struggled with him, tried to shove him away, but he struck me. When I awoke, there was evidence... but, I don't actually remember any of it. I should not have let him enter my chamber. Since then, I always lock my door. It never happened again."

She felt Dev swallow hard once and then again before he spoke. "You never told your mother?" he asked.

She covered her face with her hands. She'd been such a coward. She'd not told anybody until she'd met Rhoda. "I just wasn't... I didn't..." Oh, this was mortifying. "I told Rhoda last spring."

Strong arms tightened around her. And then, "She is protective of you."

"And Peaches," Sophia added. "I do not trust him with Peaches. I caught him kicking her once. He snarled and told me that nothing would make him happier than to see her hanging from a tree."

"So, he would hurt a pet," Dev pointed out. "He hurt you. Might he hurt someone else?"

This man whose arms held her so tenderly wanted to dispatch of Dudley. What did that mean? Dev was a military man, a captain. He would wish to mete out some justice. Not just for deeds Dudley had done in the past, but to prevent him from injuring another. Which, as she considered it, was a reasonable possibility. Dudley was not above using violence and force, and if the lady trusted him...

"And so, you would wish to... dispatch of him. Could he not simply be punished? I would not wish his death on your hands, nor on mine."

Dev was quiet for a moment. It was obvious he wanted to say more, ask more questions, but he was being sensitive to her feelings. "If that is what you wish, I will honor it. If you wish nothing to be done, I will honor that as well. But bullies such as he need a deterrence. They need to suffer repercussions." Although he lay calmly, anger shook his voice.

"Then so be it," she said. Dudley would not be allowed to hurt another.

Sophia did not want to think about Dudley. She tucked her face into his Dev's chest. She hated the subject of her stepbrother! She would erase him from her every memory if possible.

"So, this Stewart fellow... He is Harold's valet then? And they... love one another? Do the duke and duchess know?"

Her gown had ridden up slightly, and the wool of his pants brushed against her bare legs. She felt the strength of his calves and thighs through the fabric.

"He is. It allows them to be together in the way that they would wish. And, yes, I believe his parents know... or have guessed anyhow."

Sophia continued, slightly in awe. "They were unclothed. The valet, Stewart, he is a handsome man. When I met him earlier, I thought he had a sort of presence unusual in a servant. I'd never considered this sort of love. Is it the same, do you think, as men and women feel?"

Dev's hand slid along her shoulder, down her arm, to her hips... "It is difficult for me to imagine, Sophia, but it is real enough. Harold has fought it in himself for a long time. He would not have chosen such a life if it were not ingrained within him. Much like the color of his eyes, or the shape of his face."

Sophia tilted her head back as Dev's lips trailed down her jaw to the base of her throat.

"I don't think I will ever understand it completely. My imaginings run more along the lines of sweet-smelling blondes. I have imagined none other but you since that first afternoon."

"Oh," Sophia said. She forgot what she'd been talking about for all of at least a minute.

The growth of his beard grazed her skin while the heated moisture of his mouth stoked a fire within her. Sophia felt helpless to such sensations as he kissed and then tasted the skin at her nape. A hunger to pull his head lower, toward her breasts, fought with another to urge his mouth higher, so that she could kiss him properly.

"Dev, please, please, kiss me?"

"I would kiss every inch of you, Sophia," he whispered, and his lips trailed lower. His hands at her back, loosening her gown. "I would touch every inch of you, taste every inch of you." Understanding dawned as to her mother's insistence that she dab perfume in all manner of places about her body. Dev had untied her gown and was edging it off her shoulders.

Sophia squirmed, and, perhaps sensing her hesitancy, Dev took possession of her mouth again. Ah, but she could kiss him for hours. "Every inch?" she barely managed to get the words out as his tongue danced with hers.

He quite stole her breath away.

Sophia gasped when cool air hit her skin. But with him kissing her thusly, his tongue exploring her teeth, his mouth nipping at her lips, she no longer felt any modesty. One warm hand covered her breast, and all she could think was that she wanted him to pull her into him, into his hands, into his mouth.

"Every God-given inch of you, Sophia," he whispered in the midst of this perfect assault.

But it was not an assault. He lay siege at her insistence, at her longing, at her willing.

Up until that point, she'd tucked her hands innocently against his abdomen and chest. But his words exploded a need within her, a similar curiosity to explore and know all of Devlin Brookes. She tugged at the bottom of his shirt to no avail. When it refused to slide out of his breeches, she pulled at it harder. What in tarnation? The shirt refused to budge.

Without any warning, Dev sat up and in one fluid motion pulled the damn thing out of his breeches and over his head.

Moonlight cast rippling shadows over well-toned muscles. Unlike Harold's and Stewart's, Dev's skin was golden and smooth with a smattering of black hair disappearing into his breaches. His eyes burned back at her as she trailed curious fingers down his sternum, not quite stopping at his navel. Impatient and demanding, he brushed her hand away and covered her with his body once again.

"Sophia," he growled. His mouth latched onto one of her breasts, while a warm hand molded the other.

This feeling, this hunger, was what he'd awakened that day behind the lion's cage. It was aroused by him and him alone and had changed the entire course of her life.

She would have him pull harder with his mouth; she would have him squeeze and pinch tighter with his hands. And he did, as though her thinking commanded it. But just enough. Just the perfect amount.

Her hands gripped his shoulders. She wrapped a leg around his waist. She would be closer.

No longer two, but one.

Another growl against her breast caused a moan to roll through her. Was that her? It must have been.

"Sophia." He stilled his mouth, but not his hands. "I would have that I'd said those vows to you today. I would want you to have no regrets or doubts when you give yourself to me." He kissed the cleft between her breasts. "And this is going to kill me."

"Oh, Dev." She suddenly knew what he was about.

He was going to stop. He was going to respect her, of all things!

He lay thusly, one hand cradling her breast, the other gripping her bottom, for all of a minute before pushing himself away.

He was far more handsome than Harold's valet.

He was hers. He would live in her heart forever. Whether she and Harold untangled their marriage or not, Devlin Brookes would always be her one true love.

With his hair mussed and his lips swollen from desire, he made her ache. This most likely was what if felt like to die.

She did not want him to stop!

She would be a temptress. She stretched her hands lazily above her head, found the end of her braid, and slid the ribbon off. As though she did so without thought, she absentmindedly unwound the braid easily and played with the long, soft strands.

"And *you* are going to kill *me*, Devlin Brookes." Her voice came out lower than normal. That was want. That tone in her voice was her own desire.

As Dev did his damnedest to tamp down his need, Sophia lay before him like a fantasy, the belle of the ball, sent from heaven to tempt him. She was so goddamned perfect in every way.

The devil's own debutante.

The other half of him.

Why had he stopped?

He'd had the best of intentions only moments before. But suddenly, with her long blond curls luxuriously spread about her doll-like face and petal-soft skin, his arousal nearly consumed him. She arched her back slightly, drawing his eyes to two perfect breasts. One nipple was moist, where his mouth had been; the other begged to be loved as well.

He'd never claimed to be a saint.

"You are certain?" He was surprised when his words came out a whisper. Her voice had tugged at parts of his body where a mere voice had no right to affect.

"It is my wedding night, after all." Again, desire wrapped around him even tighter.

Her words ought to have reminded him — reminded him that she'd married his cousin earlier that morning.

But she hadn't really.

Except for Dev, the age-old words had held great meaning, and the vows had touched him.

And so, he knelt beside her. Taking one of her hands in his, he spoke solemnly.

"I, Devlin Roderick Michael Brookes, take thee, Sophia Ann Babineaux, to be my wedded wife, to have and to hold from this day forward…" Somehow, he knew them by heart. He'd heard them dozens of times before. "…for better, for worse, for richer, for poorer, in sickness and in health, to love and to cherish till death us do part, according to God's holy ordinance, and thereto, I plight thee my troth. With all of my heart..." He'd changed the words, for he hadn't a ring. "...I thee wed. With my body, I thee worship, and with all of my worldly goods, I thee endow." He looked down at their hands solemnly.

He meant every word.

She gazed back, her eyes wide and her lips slightly parted.

"You needn't say them to me, Sophia." An awkward wave of embarrassment washed over him. But she'd seen too much of the fickleness of man. "Not until you can do all of these things openly, legally. But I wanted you to know..."

She sat up and threw her arms around him, her gown falling away to drape itself around her thighs. She pressed enthusiastic kisses along his face and neck. His hands fell to her naked waist.

This moment brought to mind the feelings he'd often experienced the night before a battle.

Sometimes a moment was a gift. It was a precious event placed in one's life, and one must take it gratefully. One never knew what the outcome of tomorrow would be, nor the next day, or the next hour.

Sophia was his gift. This moment was a gift to both of them. They would not pass it by.

He dipped his head and claimed her mouth again.

CHAPTER 14

*H*e loved her. He did not need to say the words. In his actions, in his deeds, he'd showed her time and time again.

He'd shown her he loved her when he'd sat in the church today and somehow given her the courage to get through that ridiculous ceremony.

He'd shown her when he'd presented himself in the park on such a cold and rainy day.

He'd shown her by the care with which he treated her dog, let alone her own person.

He was not like Lord Kensington, or Harold, or any of the others.

On her knees before him, she pressed her body into his, loving the feel of his naked chest against her own. Soft hairs caressed her breasts. His abdomen trembled when she ran her hand downward.

"Sophia..." He whispered her name. He always made it

sound like a whisper, even when he spoke it aloud. "Sophia."

His hands reached for the top of his breeches, and he fumbled to unfasten them. She would help him with such a task but had no idea how. She pulled back slightly so that he could be quicker. At her impatience, laughter glimmered in his gaze. His muscles rippled beneath his skin as he worked the buttons.

And then, having unfastened them, he pushed her back onto the mattress. He rolled her onto her back, trapping her with his body. The hunger in his gaze thrilled her. He wanted her.

Sophia's hands reached into the back of his breeches while he dispensed with her gown.

All the while, their mouths devoured each other.

"I should slow down," he said, his hand between her legs, "but you're so wet, so ready."

She didn't want for him to slow his pace. She'd waited a lifetime for this. Feeling emboldened by her desire, she used both her feet and her hands to free him of his breeches.

His full arousal was now quite exposed and quite apparent.

So natural, so beautiful. Sophia wrapped her legs around his thighs.

"I *am* ready. I'm ready for you." She whispered the words, urging him.

What was he waiting for? She suddenly felt frantically empty. Moving her hips, she slid along his length until the tip was near her opening.

"Oh, God, Sophia, you're killing me, after all," he murmured against her skin.

She shifted and moved along his silky hardness but knew there must be more. There was a liquid down there! She should be embarrassed, but she only felt need.

And then he assumed command befitting of his rank.

He lifted up for a moment and hovered at her entrance. Gazing down, his eyes were hooded with desire. She watched him, trustingly, until she could not stand it one second longer.

And then he took her.

He felt hard, hot, slick… and right. He was thick, but her flesh eased open around him. She welcomed him even as he stretched her, meeting each thrust of his with one of her own. She would have him take ownership of her entire body.

And then his thrusts grew stronger.

She reached up and grasped the rails of the bedframe. She would meet him. She would take him.

As though her life depended on it.

The muscles he used to hold himself off her began to shake. Sophia did not want him to hold himself away from her. She pushed at his elbow, causing him to collapse.

"Hellcat," he muttered into her neck. But he continued driving into her, slower and longer now.

"Don't hold back, Dev," she said. "Don't protect me. Don't hide anything from me."

He pumped into her, deep and purposefully, with a violence, almost. Resting atop her, his weight pushed her into the mattress. But he did not pause for long. Instead, he lunged into her again with equal ferocity.

Sophia arched her back, welcoming his passion, all of his touch. The two of them had grown slick from their exertions. She tasted the salt on his skin and nipped at his shoulder with her teeth.

His pace quickened again, and she followed his rhythm.

This was not to be slow and gentle.

This was not to be a tentative love.

It was meant to bring all of their feelings, their emotions, to the surface… just in case.

She was so close, so close…

And then Dev's entire body turned rigid; he adjusted his angle and surged into her twice more.

She clutched at his buttocks, her fingers and hands squeezing and pulling at him.

The world was white, and then black, and then she shuddered. She felt a heat at her core, and she would have tightened her legs about him if she'd had any strength whatsoever.

Dev collapsed. He was motionless but for a twitch and a pulsing inside of her.

"You will always be mine, Sophia," he said into her neck. "Always."

"Mmm…" was all she could manage.

He chuckled and must have used the last of his strength to pull the covers up around them.

And so, on the night of her marriage, she finally slept, safe and comfortable in the arms of the man she loved.

Dev crept out of her chamber just before sunrise, no one the wiser, she hoped

THE PROBLEM with having a lady's maid, despite being attended in luxury, was that one tended to sacrifice a great deal of privacy.

And Sophia would have appreciated some that morning, instead of awakening, completely naked, to find Penny placing a tray of some hot, steaming drink beside her bed. The maid then casually picked up her nightgown, smoothed out some wrinkles, and laid it along the foot of the bed.

The tray left over from her and Devlin's picnic the night before was nowhere to be seen.

Her maid must think that she and Harold...

Sophia grasped her gown quickly, all the while clutching the blanket in front of her, and then slipped it over her head with as much grace as she could muster.

The maid merely glanced over her shoulder with a secret smile. "I didn't think he had it in him!" she said. But upon realizing exactly what had just escaped her lips, and to whom the words had escaped to, she suddenly turned white as a sheet and covered her mouth with one hand.

Sophia realized that Harold's... husbandly abilities... had been in doubt, with a servant, this servant, anyhow, and most probably with numerous other servants about the house.

This was exactly why the duke and duchess had been

adamant about his marriage. For Harold and his… valet to do what she'd witnessed last night was not only scandalous, but dangerous. What was it considered? She'd read about it on one occasion. Oh, yes, an unnatural crime.

Society was far less lenient in their judgment of such matters than she and Devlin apparently were.

By having Devlin stay the night with her, creating the appearance of a night of lovemaking, well, they'd done something of a favor for the duke and duchess.

And, she supposed, for Harold… and Stewart.

Giggles threatened to erupt, but she could not do that to the horrified maid.

So, she settled on a secret smile before reaching for the hot drink. She had plenty of secret thoughts to smile about: Dev telling her of his childhood, Dev unclothed, Dev on top of her, Dev inside of her…

"I didn't know if you preferred chocolate or tea in the morning, so I brought both." The maid was quite obviously grateful to not have been chastised for her ill-timed comment.

"Chocolate, this morning," she said. "But tea usually." Most certainly her thoughts had caused her to blush.

"Very well, Lady Harold, my lady," Penny said.

Sophia bristled at her new title. She was not Harold's *anything!*

Penny continued her cheery speech. "Her grace has instructed me to ready you to leave this morning. I've most of your trunks packed for the footmen to take down already, an overnight valise, and clothing laid out for your journey. I'll have a bath readied for when you are done with your chocolate?" Her last statement was something of a question.

This new relationship between lady and lady's maid was an intimate one. Sophia did wish to bathe, however. And then as a few muscles protested when she stood, she wondered if Dev had left any marks on her. The thought, although embarrassing, was also oddly thrilling. Their lovemaking had not consisted of feathery kisses and a quick joining in the dark.

Harold might gain quite the reputation.

After the hot water had been brought up, Penny led Sophia into the dressing room and assisted her with her gown. Sophia caught sight of herself in the mirror. Yes, a few bruises smudged her hips, and a red streak stood out against the pale skin of her breast.

Feeling like a wanton, she sank into the hot water.

She would hold fast to the sensations and imprints left by Dev's lovemaking. They reminded her that it had been real. It had not been a dream, nor a figment of her imagination.

As Penny poured water over her shoulders and into her hair, Sophia relived some of last night's moments in her mind. She wanted her memories to remain vivid, just in case...

This morning she did not feel so hopeless as she had before.

Of course, any number of things could go wrong with their crazy plan. Harold might well come to his senses and decide that freedom was not worth risking his life. Or he might reconsider abandoning the privileged lifestyle to which he'd grown accustomed.

With a wife now, it would be safer for him to continue his relationship with Stewart in secret, indefinitely.

As could she with Devlin.

But...

It was not the same.

No, living in secret, living a lie, was not living at all. She and Dev had stolen a night of passion together, but he had been forced to leave before sunup.

She would have that they awaken each morning together. That they walk in the sunlight together... have children...

Upon which thought she bolted upright.

She'd forgotten all about that!

This could become complicated, indeed. No, a life filled with secrecy was not something she wished for.

Her maid handed her a washcloth and some soap.

"Oh, dear, my lady." The maid turned away quickly.

Sophia glanced down to where the maid had been looking.

A remarkably obvious bruise in the shape of a hand stood out boldly upon her upper thigh.

* * *

DEV WAS SURPRISED when he finally went down for breakfast the next morning to discover that the duchess' entourage had yet to depart for Priory Point. They were all to be delayed, it seemed, by three days, as per the duchess' orders.

Her grace had decided the newly married couple must be given a few days of solitude and privacy together. Word was, Dev soon learned, that Harold's little bride just might have *cured* him.

This, he was informed of, by one of the duchess' younger sisters. She'd heard it from her grace, who'd heard it from her lady's maid, who'd heard it from Sophia's lady's maid, who had gleefully announced that the newlywed couple had enjoyed a night of passionate lovemaking in the bride's chamber.

This conclusion had been based upon evidence of various bodily fluids on the sheets, an unclothed bride in the morning, as well as various markings on the bride's body. None of this was spoken of in so many words, which made it all the more astounding that he was able to gather so much from the middle-aged spinster.

Good heavens!

Again, reason to live in one's own private lodgings.

Lord and Lady Harold, he was informed, had embarked upon their journey a few hours ago.

And upon hearing this news, an emptiness he could not immediately identify, filled him.

She was no longer just a few steps away. She was not even a short drive across town. Sophia was miles away from London by now and this, yes, this fact was the source of his sudden dispiritedness.

His aunt had ordered everyone to wait three full days

before embarking upon their own journeys to Priory Point for the elaborately planned house party.

Dev found himself at loose ends.

For all of two minutes.

One very important matter required his attention. When Sophia told him what had happened to her as a young girl, that Dudley Scofield had forced himself upon her, it had required all of Dev's self-control not to seek him out that very night.

He'd wanted to search out the bastard and place a pistol between his eyes. No, that would be too easy. Justice might best be served by inflicting an injury like that of Lord Kensington's. Dev had scene red.

But Sophia had been curled up beside him.

She'd not wanted him to abandon her in favor of a violent errand. She'd wanted... him.

In a most primitive and passionate manner.

Which he could not allow himself to dwell upon this morning.

Today, he would address Mr. Dudley Scofield.

It was not difficult to obtain information on the craven lowlife, as Scofield enjoyed a lavish lifestyle and enjoyed considerable, although unfavorable notoriety. After recently paying off most of his vowels, the younger *gentleman*, Dev had been informed, had gone on something of a gambling spree. And just this morning he'd embarked upon a race down to Brighton. The gents involved had mentioned a possible journey over to the continent.

Dev didn't have enough time to be led on a merry chase right now. Harold was going to need him at Priory Point if he was still of mind to follow through with their plan. So instead, Dev would head over to Surrey, inspect his new property, and then journey alone to Priory Point. Scofield would pay for his misdeeds when he returned to England. Dev would make certain of it.

Meanwhile, Dev would not sit around like a lovesick fool missing Sophia.

Which was exactly what he felt like.

She had been… a revelation.

Behind her delightfully innocent looks lay the passion of an Italian opera singer.

He'd thought, as far as women were concerned anyhow, that not much could surprise him.

He'd known that he loved her, yes. He'd known that she was sweet and filled with goodness and courage — of course she was — but last night she had invoked sensations and emotions in him that had shaken him to the core.

He'd discovered scratches on his backside that morning.

Every time he thought of them, he could not help but smile.

Little, sweet Sophia Babineaux, indeed!

His groins tightened at the merest hint of reliving parts of last night in his memory.

He'd save that for a more convenient time. It was going to be close to a week before he could see her again.

And when he did, he felt an unspoken agreement existed between the two of them. They would wait to be together in an intimate fashion again, until all was settled with her marriage.

He'd already possibly complicated all of this, he'd realized, by releasing his seed inside of her. For if she were to become with child, as Harold's wife, the repercussions for paternity were damn near unthinkable.

He'd have any child of his recognized as such.

And so, it would be in their best interest to abstain.

But good Lord, Sophia Babineaux was almost impossibly irresistible.

For him, anyhow. Thank God, her husband didn't feel likewise.

CHAPTER 15

*S*ophia had not considered that she would be riding the entirety of the way to Priory Point, which was just a little past Dover, in a carriage alone with her new husband.

With her mother, perhaps, with Rhoda or Penny. In her dreams, with Devlin, but not — Lord help them both — with Harold.

Her mother-in-law, it seemed, thought the two of them would appreciate this.

Lord Harold did not question why his mother had made such an assumption.

Stewart and Penny had been sent on ahead of them along with their luggage coach and would be awaiting them when they reached their scheduled stop for the night. The duchess had packed a picnic lunch with wine and delicacies and instructed the driver to locate a romantic setting where the newlywed couple could stop and take their luncheon in a leisurely fashion.

To deny her wishes was not an option.

Harold had alighted behind her with a sheepish look and explained these details to her as the driver maneuvered them through the crowded London streets. She wondered if he felt as forlorn without his... Stewart, as she did without Devlin. Except Stewart was just a few miles ahead of them, whereas she was leaving Devlin behind.

Neither of them spoke much after that, content, apparently, to mull over their disappointment in silence. Harold had settled himself against a pillow along the window on his side of the coach, and she'd done the same on her side. Both of them sat front-facing. Harold, of course, had told her early on in their *relationship* that he became sick if he rode backwards in a carriage.

They'd been on the road for a few hours when Sophia felt compelled to speak.

"I imagine you miss him." She would not pretend that she did not know. To do so, for her anyhow, would be rather like ignoring an elephant riding along in the carriage with them.

Harold glanced over at her suspiciously, his pale blue eyes narrowing, a lock of his light brown hair falling across his eyes.

His looks were considerably different from Dev's. Was he going to respond to her? Was he even going to acknowledge her statement? But then he sighed.

"So, you know," he said.

"It is only fair that I should know such a pertinent fact regarding my husband, would you not agree?" He would have to speak with her now. He could not get up and leave the carriage, or dismiss her, as he'd done before.

"Wonderful," he said. "Now you can be disgusted of me along with everybody else. I hope you realize there is a confidentiality clause in the contract. If anything comes out publicly, your parents are liable for paying back the annuities in full, plus interest." He spoke bitterly, as though she would become an enemy to him.

"I'll admit I was… surprised. But I am not disgusted with you, Harold. And of course, why would I tell anyone your secret? Would I not be considered a fool for marrying such a man? Besides…" She looked away from him. "…one cannot always decide who they will fall in love with." She remembered her mother's regret at falling in love with her father, a poor man. She considered the love that Cecily had said she had for Lord Kensington.

Harold absentmindedly plucked at a piece of thread that had come loose on his waistcoat. "How is it that you are not disgusted?"

She shrugged.

"Dev told you, I suppose," he added, conceding the conversation's subject matter.

She was not going to dissemble. "I discovered myself. Last night, I came looking for you late, hoping we could raid the kitchen together."

At her words, Harold moaned and covered his face with both hands. Bending forward, he practically buried his face in his lap. "Oh, God, Sophia. I would never in a thousand years have had you discover that way. I may call you Sophia, may I not?"

"Of course, I believe I've already called you Harold on more than one occasion." She reached over and touched him. "I'm not made of glass, you know." And then rubbing his back soothingly, she continued, "He is very handsome, though, isn't he? How long have the two of you known one another?"

He sat up and shook his head. He then smiled self-consciously. "We met at Oxford. He's far more intelligent than I. He could become a professor, if he wished. But then we could not be together." Harold glanced down at his cravat. "I tied this, by the way. He's a horrible valet."

Sophia laughed. An excellent irony, indeed!

"I don't suppose your father would have approved of you becoming Stewart's valet."

Harold winced at her words. His father was obviously something of a sore spot for him. "My mother seems to think you cured me last night. What did you do, Sophia, to give your maid such an impression?"

He was being open and honest with her. They seemed to be bound together in a web of secrets. "I am in love with your cousin," she said simply. Let him infer whatever he wished from this statement.

"Dev?" He nodded slowly, to himself. "I wondered at Dev's sudden interest in my affairs. He's known, I think, along with most of my family, but we've not spoken until recently. And so much has occurred since he went off to war."

And then he lifted one brow. "So, the maid was not making up stories, then?"

Sophia felt herself blush. It was her turn to cover her

face with her hands. What a discussion to be having, with one's husband, no less! "No," she answered.

At his laughter, she dropped her hands.

Oh, this was a consolation indeed. Perhaps they could be friends!

"Dev told me of your plan," she said, suddenly serious. "I don't want you to do it if you feel it is too dangerous, or if you doubt your ability to come out of it unharmed."

The look on his face echoed her doubts.

"Are you afraid?" she persisted.

"It's been over a decade since any of us has done it." He began plucking at his coat again. "Dev said he will do it first, inspect the formation and document the tides precisely. I don't think he'd let me do it if it isn't safe."

Oh, yes, she'd assumed as much. Dev would not allow Harold to go into any danger that he himself would not investigate thoroughly beforehand. Thank God, she'd not known him while he'd been away at war. She would have worried every day, every hour, every minute.

"You will be giving up a great deal — your family, your heritage, your very place in life — here in England." All rather daunting. "You are courageous to even consider doing this."

"I can hardly think of anything else. And yet, feeling the specter of the law hanging over me does not come without a fear all its own." He glanced at her quickly. "I could be hung for who I am. Stewart could be hung. It is referred to as an unnatural crime and is punishable by death. Some rumors as to my... predisposition have made their way back to my mother. More specific ones than those which had been spread before. I must admit, Sophia, that I was surprised no one mentioned anything to you when we became engaged."

"Your parents are worried for your life." This revelation brought on a greater understanding as to why they would be so heavy-handed with the marriage contracts. They wanted Harold safe. Believing marriage to Sophia would protect him, neither of his parents had been willing to delay the wedding. No wonder the duchess had welcomed her so warmly.

Harold nodded. "My father demanded that I end things with Stewart, well, not Stewart specifically, but he demanded that I not act upon my feelings in the future. Ever. My marriage to you was my concession to him. I could not send Stewart away."

This explained so much. Sophia pondered that there was always so much more to a situation than one might see initially.

And complicated problems usually required complex solutions.

"What does your... What does Stewart think?"

"Stewart has felt the threat of hanging as well." He stared out the window for a moment before he spoke again. "As ugly, as unnatural and grotesque as I always thought of myself, and these perverted desires I have lived with, I cannot help but think humanity has it backwards. They want to kill me for it. They wish to kill me for something God has put inside of me! What kind of god is that, Sophia? I ask you, what kind of god would make me this way and then put me in this world?"

His words were passionate. These thoughts, these questions, were as foreign to her as anything she'd ever heard and yet, a part of her understood perfectly.

Shame.

He'd felt shame. Shame for something he could not change about himself. Shame about something very, very private. And along with this shame, came fear.

And then all fight seemed to leave him. "Out of all of this, the one person in this world who I would never wish to bring any pain or sorrow, suffers."

"Stewart?"

"My mother."

People are so much more complicated than we ever consider. Over the past few months Sophia had considered Harold simple and safe but a little unfeeling, and then she'd thought him uncaring and manipulative. Last night, she'd realized he would likely have to hide a part of himself from the world for the remainder of his life. And today, she learned of a depth of affection he held for his mother.

"First, there was her disappointment, the sadness I knew she felt when she suspected I was not the same as Lucas — and when she realized I'd never take a wife, give her grandchildren. And then, her attempts to help me, a series of subtle attempts to save me from myself. But more recently, I see worry in her eyes. Every time she hears even the hint of a rumor, I watch that worry grow. Occasionally, articles show up in the paper telling of a public hanging. I know she sees them and imagines it could be me. And she is right! It well could be! Or Stewart!"

"You said that our marriage was partly a concession for your father. It was also for your mother, then?"

"Yes, anything to bring her some peace." He leaned forward, resting his forearms along his knees as the carriage bumped along. His posture, one of despair. "God, Sophia, she has never stopped loving me despite it all. My father, I think, has given up on me as a human being. But my mother…" He blinked a few times as though surprised at his own thoughts. "…sometimes, I think she loves me all the more for it."

"She will be devastated after your… accident." He simply could not do this to the duchess.

Sophia remembered the walk she'd taken with her grace along the portrait gallery and felt horrible.

"But, in a way, Sophia, it will bring an end to her suffering. Ever since this morning… I've had an idea. My mother was over the moon thinking that you and I had… that we were… I'll hate to see the disappointment on her face again when she realizes it was only an illusion."

Sophia watched him. "None of this can end well."

Harold nodded. "I know. But which is worse, waiting for me to be caught, tried and then hung? Or believing me to be at peace… in death?" It was a solemn question indeed. "I wondered if perhaps it would not give her some happiness if she believed you and I had fallen madly in love. If it might give her some comfort to believe that I'd died a happily married man. A natural man."

"How do you feel about that?" Sophia asked.

He tipped his head back against the plush upholstery and closed his eyes. "I feel like it would be the least I could do for her, after all of her support, all of the times she's defended me to my father."

Sophia wondered how Dev would feel about it.

"What does Stewart think?"

"Stewart loves my mother nearly as much as I do. She has welcomed him into our home. She has never treated him as a servant, or as a villain. He would have me do whatever I could to ease her suffering."

Sophia considered what he was suggesting. "Penny, my maid, is awfully observant."

At that, he chuckled dryly. "Apparently so."

"Knowing this, there are things that can be done... acts that could be staged..." Sophia's mind was already considering how it could be accomplished. Was she really considering this? "But there would be more to it than that. While we needn't make spectacles of ourselves, it would be necessary for us to act affectionately toward one another, specifically, when we are in the presence of any servants. For they truly are the backbone of the really good, juicy gossip."

"You would not mind?"

Sophia contemplated all that he would be sacrificing, if he went ahead and staged his death. A few weeks of play-acting was nothing compared to that. "I do not mind, Harold. You do realize, however, that this will require we share a chamber at night."

"You've nothing to fear on that front." Again, that dry, cynical laugh. "It will be like sleeping with my sister."

Sophia groaned and then laughed a little too. At his jest,

but also at the ironies of life. But that her own stepbrother had been similarly inclined as well.

* * *

PRETENDING to be in an intimate relationship with Harold proved easier than she'd thought. For she did feel a rather, well, sisterly affection for him. And since Harold had never been considered an outwardly emotional person anyway, not much would be expected of him even if he did have an affection for his wife.

While sitting in their private dining room the first night, when the driver slipped inside to ask a question of him pertinent to the following day's travels, Sophia made the most of the interruption. Recalling her night with Devlin, Sophia picked up a particularly succulent piece of an orange and reached forward, placing it against Harold's lips.

And Harold understood her motive immediately.

He opened his mouth and ate the slice right out of her fingers. He then, even managed to send a hooded and sultry look her way. She'd barely been able to contain herself until they were alone again before she burst out laughing. "Where'd you learn to do that, Harold?" Oh, such a foolish question. Perhaps he and Stewart had…?

"Perhaps I ought to have been born to the stage?" He laughed back.

They'd other similar moments, but not too many. Sophia and he had discussed that too much of a difference in their behavior could give the charade away just as easily as not enough. They would be subtle, and yet, not.

The most awkward hurdle they faced, of course, was sharing a chamber. She wondered who was the most uncomfortable when he followed her back to the large suite reserved for them. It did, in fact, only have one bed. Harold had gone downstairs for a nightcap while Penny attended to Sophia's bedtime needs.

"Brush it at least one-hundred times," Sophia told her. And then she asked, "Did you remember to bring my perfume?" Sophia imagined how she would feel, what she would say, if she'd known that it was to be Dev, instead of Harold, coming to her tonight.

Penny merely smiled and then pulled the vial of perfume from a cloth sack. "Of course, my lady," she said.

Whenever Sophia was alone with her thoughts, her mind returned to Dev.

What was he doing right now? When would he come to Priory Point? Sometimes she thought she missed him *too* much. She felt she would die if she didn't see him soon.

Which was ridiculous, of course. And melodramatic.

When he was with her, anything seemed possible. On the same hand, the longer she went without seeing him, the more impossible the situation felt. Oh, she loved him though. She did not doubt that any longer.

And he loved her.

She would not allow herself to distrust him again.

He'd knelt beside her on her bed and made the same vows Harold had made in a church of God.

But they'd meant so much more.

She'd not asked him to do so. And he'd not asked her to reciprocate. He'd wanted to give her reassurance, comfort... love.

Yes, he loved her.

She worried about him. He was strong, yes, and fit, and healthy. He'd been honed for defense, a military man for over a decade.

But he was also flesh and blood. He was a mere man, after all, besides all of his confidence and abilities. He'd said he would do something about Dudley, but what did he have in mind? She chastised herself a million times since for not demanding he keep himself from danger.

Oh, Dev, but that I could hear your voice today. But that I could catch one glimpse of your smile.

Penny finished braiding her hair and tied it off with the same ribbon she'd used the night before. "It's like spun gold." She sighed. Penny's own hair was tucked under a cap. She was a pretty brown-eyed girl, with plain clothing and nothing to draw attention to herself.

Sophia was going to have to become better acquainted with her. Some lady's maids stayed with their mistresses for life.

That was a very long time.

"Do you have a beau?" Sophia asked her impulsively.

Penny blushed but shook her head side to side. "I don't, but the master's valet is a fine-looking gentleman, that's for sure."

Sophia would have groaned at this sentiment if she could have. But she could say nothing, for Stewart and

Harold's secret was hers now, too. She must protect it as such.

Harold and Stewart's lives depended upon it.

UNABLE TO DEPART Town that first day as planned, Dev returned to Prescott House to spend one more night before leaving London. He missed out on the family supper but later, found St. John alone in his uncle's study.

Several members of the family had chosen to attend the theatre and would not be returning until after midnight.

Lucas, though always a bit remote, seemed slightly more melancholy than usual. He held a tumbler of whisky in one hand and a book in his lap.

The book was closed, though the glass nearly empty.

Feeling the loss of Sophia more than he'd like, Dev poured himself a drink and dropped into a nearby winged-back chair. "Not squiring Miss Mossant about tonight?" He pulled over an ottoman and swung his booted feet upon it.

St. John half smiled and shook his head.

"Not tonight," he said. "Pleasant chit, but I'd best watch my step with her. She'll be expecting me to declare myself soon, no doubt."

Sophia had mentioned that Miss Mossant was developing a tender for St. John. She'd mentioned that the young woman *was*, in fact, hopeful of a declaration. A slight resentment at his cousin's caviler attitude arose inside of him, but he quickly dismissed it. What was the matter with him? Had he turned into a bloody matchmaker now? Now that he'd fallen himself?

For he'd fallen.

God, how he'd fallen.

Crazy, madly, wildly in love with Harold's wife.

Except that she was not.

She was his — body, heart, and soul. She was his, by God, and yes, he was hers.

A few... complications simply needed ironing out.

"You've no intentions in her direction, then?" Dev spoke casually. Sophia would want to know. She'd want to warn Rhoda to protect herself.

Between the two of them, and their friend, the Countess of Kensington, they'd reason enough to distrust men.

St. John glanced at him sideways. "Miss Mossant is like a long, cool, glass of water on a hot day. She is bright, witty, and really, quite a looker. She will make some gentleman a fine wife someday. But not mine."

Dev wondered. "Why not?"

St. John merely crossed his legs and reclined deeper into the chair. "You know as well as I, Dev. Nothing less than the daughter of an earl for me." Dev hated St. John when he did this. When he turned aloof, and arrogant. Dev knew it to be a mask of sorts. He'd known Lucas as a boy. They'd shared their hopes and dreams too often as children for Lucas to get away with it now.

But that didn't mean his cousin didn't try.

"That you speaking, Luc, or your father?" Dev challenged.

"The voices are the same these days, echoing inside my head."

Dev nodded. "If she isn't the one, then she isn't the one. But don't blame it on Prescott. You're your own man. You're nobody's puppet."

At these words, a devious gleam lit St. John's eyes. "I'm currently being diverted by a particularly long-legged redhead. One with whom the constraints of Society do not apply. God knows, I'm in no hurry to curtail such activities. And why rush into setting up a nursery? My father is hale and healthy, as is yours. We bachelors must stick together, Dev. I don't see you lining up with the latest crop of insipid debutantes."

They both took a few drinks, neither apparently willing to extend the subject at hand. And then St. John turned to him. "Do you think it's possible that Harold actually bedded his pretty little wife? Mother is convinced, and I've never been one to question the information she obtains, nor her opinion on such matters. What a godsend that would be. Little Miss Babineaux would be worth her weight in gold if there is any truth in it."

"Harold's pretty little wife and her activities in the bedroom," Dev wanted to say, *"were not a matter for discussion."* And as to her value, he would grab St. John by the collar most convincingly and assert that it could never be measured against silver or gold.

Instead, he stared into his half-full glass. "I haven't the faintest. For your mother's sake, though," he said half-heartedly, "we can only hope."

He'd be with Sophia this moment if it were possible.

God, it felt as though he were missing an arm, a leg, a part of his heart to have her taken away from London, away from him today.

"My own flesh and blood," St. John took another sip of the strong amber liquid. "I'd give my life for him, and yet, he sickens me. He could have so easily put all of this to rest. No decency at all. No self-control."

Ah, yes, the family shame. Dev did not understand Harold's manner of loving; he would not pretend to admit that he did. But he did know that this was not something Harold had given into easily. He'd fought it. On one occasion, Harold had told him after the fact, he'd been tempted to take his own life over the matter.

No, it was not about decency, and it was not about self-control.

Poor Harold.

Yes, poor Harold, miles away with Dev's own lovely Sophia.

Devlin would complete his tasks and go to her as soon as humanly possible.

CHAPTER 16

*I*t wasn't until their second night on the road that Sophia began to wonder that her maid was not so much a gossip as a spy.

Because as she went to descend the staircase before supper, Sophia overheard her maid speaking directly below her to the innkeeper.

She wished to send a missive to the Duchess of Prescott.

Sophia had not even been aware that Penny could read and write.

But listening to her speak with such authority and direction, she realized that the maid was not at all what she seemed.

Sophia considered this new information carefully and then noisily cleared her throat and continued her descent.

Penny glanced up with a start, but Sophia merely smiled. Let the girl believe her mistress was a birdwitted ninny-hammer. "Did you see which way my husband went, Penny? We're to dine together in the private room."

It was the innkeeper who answered. Stepping out from behind the counter, he was all excellent manners and obsequiousness. "My lady, yes, right this way. A special meal has been prepared for my very special guests." He led her down a short corridor and into a private room. "Lord Harold awaits you." He bowed slightly and backed away.

Oh, good Lord, Sophia thought. Even he would cover for the maid — who worked directly for the duke and duchess — who would pay the innkeeper's bill. Of course.

This was how all of this worked. How naïve she'd been! It had been the same with Mr. Scofield. She and her mother had never really known independence.

Harold rose to his feet as she entered the room and walked around the table to take her hand in his. "My lovely wife," he said. "I was beginning to miss you already."

He performed magnificently. Almost too well. She imagined he'd had many occasions to practice similar deceit.

Sophia lowered her eyes and curtsied demurely. "And I, you."

They waited for the footman to finish serving them before saying anything further.

Once alone, Sophia worried at their lack of real privacy. Feeling as though they were being watched, she collected her plate and walked around to Harold's side of the table. Let them believe she merely had a desire to be near him. He looked a little surprised but made room for her utensils helpfully.

"I think my maid is a spy for your mother." She leaned into him and whispered. "I've just overheard her sending a letter, although she does not know that I know."

Harold reclined in his chair and then nodded. "Of course, my mother would not truly send us off, completely on our own, without having a means of observation." And then he laughed. "It is simply not the Prescott way."

"I didn't realize the extent of her... intrusiveness."

They both heard some shuffling outside of the door and shook their heads at one another. They had each been speaking softly, so most likely no one had overheard their conversation, but their suspicions were solidified.

They would need to be doubly careful.

First, in their playacting to convince her grace of Harold's miraculous recovery, and second to be on high alert as to what they said regarding the plan to fake Harold's death.

For the ten-thousandth time that day, Sophia wished Dev were here.

"The first thing I'd like to do when we reach Priory Point..." She spoke loudly and cheerfully. "...is seek out the beach. It's been ages since Mr. Scofield took us to Brighton, and I absolutely love to swim." If the servants overheard her wishes, it would seem natural then, when she and Harold explored the cliffs and caves. She'd already informed Harold that she wanted to see this secret cavern they'd discussed.

"You enjoy swimming?" He seemed genuinely surprised by this information.

She did, in truth, love to swim, although she'd only swam

in the ocean a few times. She'd learned the skill initially in the still waters of the lake near Mr. Scofield's country home.

A footman stepped forward to refill Harold's wine glass. At the same time, Harold reached a hand forward and covered hers with it. "Anything you wish, my dear. And I'll take you walking by the cliffs. We'll take picnics, and our bathing costumes, and enjoy our time together before the rest of the family arrives."

"Just the two of us?" She fluttered her lashes at him.

"Just the two of us."

The footman stepped back, and with a nod from Harold, left the room. Harold drew close and whispered in her ear. "Stewart can divert your maid. We should arrive tomorrow around noon. I'm beginning to feel anxious about the cave's condition. Did Dev tell you when he thought he might arrive?"

Sophia giggled, as though he'd whispered something flirtatious.

"No, I didn't know we would be traveling alone until after he'd left me. But I cannot believe he would dawdle." She reached up and pushed a lock of hair out of his eyes. "Penny thinks Stewart to be quite handsome."

At which, Harold chuckled. "All the ladies do, Sophia." And then he shocked her further by leaning in and whispering again. "But he's mine."

* * *

THE WEATHER CONTINUED to cooperate the next day, and as

Harold had predicted, they arrived at Priory Point just before nuncheon.

It was a most impressive estate. The steep and winding road that led to the ancient castle was narrow and more than a little harrowing at times. Sharp white cliffs and rocky formations made for breathtaking scenery unmatched by anything Sophia had ever seen. Occasionally, she got a glimpse of the beach below. She was anxious to explore and swim. If only this really was a simple holiday.

The castle itself had been built over two centuries ago but had been renovated and modernized often. The Prescotts were not a family to allow their properties to fall into decline, Harold explained. Foundations were continuously inspected, as were roofs, windows, and exterior coverings. The estates' budgets required these items to be in constant repair, and if any was left over, only then could the interiors be improved upon.

The Prescotts were a diligent family with what they'd been given.

As they entered, Harold introduced Sophia to some of the staff, and then the two of them made arrangements to go exploring. She was to enjoy a quick lunch, change, and then meet her husband in the downstairs foyer. Stewart, Harold had told Sophia earlier, would keep an eye on Penny. He would make certain she did not get anywhere near the caves.

And so, shortly after they arrived, Sophia, in half boots and one of her older dresses, and Harold, wearing well-worn riding clothes, set off together, hand in hand along a well-tended path.

This footpath led to the main beach. It descended gradually, she could see. But Harold veered her off it onto a trail, if one would even call it such. She could never have found it on her own. It climbed steeply, before leveling and then descending behind what appeared to be a huge pile of rocks.

"Watch where you place your feet, Sophia. The rocks can be unstable." Harold stepped a little tentatively himself.

She could not see the ocean, but she could hear it.

And then, "Over here, Soph. We piled rocks around the opening so others wouldn't find it." He bent over and moved a few smaller ones, and then together, they rolled back one of the larger rocks.

Cool, humid air wafted from the opening they'd revealed. She couldn't see much inside, but when she peered in, the sounds of water splashing below sounded ominous.

Sophia shivered.

She couldn't imagine why any sane person would ever have any desire to explore such a cave. The thought of being trapped inside could give a person nightmares.

"It's level for a few feet and then drops practically straight down. We used ropes to climb in and out." Harold knelt beside her, and she gave him some space so that he could crawl inside. "Yes, the ropes are still here. We'll want to replace them." A little sheepish, he ducked his head back out. "I'm a little heavier than I was back then."

In truth, Sophia was not happy about the condition of

this so-called cave. It was dreadfully small, and the earth around it did not seem all that stable.

"Show me the lagoon," she demanded, standing up.

They replaced the rocks, hiding the cave once again, and he guided her around the outcrop. A few fledgling trees and bushes grew, slightly protected from the winds blowing in from the sea. They climbed the nearby rise, and just as Harold grabbed her hand, she caught her breath. For a sheer cliff dropped hundreds of feet down to a swirling cauldron of water. Rocks hung over the edges precariously, but some had fallen and poked up when the sprays of froth ebbed away.

"The water never empties. It's never a beach like the other side," Harold said. He was slightly breathless from their climb.

She could not imagine swimming in such a perilous pool.

"Oh, my God, Harold" was all she could bring herself to say.

She looked over at him.

Whereas he'd looked a little flushed before, he had suddenly gone white as a sheet. "I don't remember it being this…"

"Formidable?" she asked.

"Horrifying," he answered.

DEV WAS PLEASED with the condition of Dartmouth Place and found it necessary to order only minimal repairs. He left instructions with the man who'd been acting as steward and then made his way directly to Priory Point. It was a two-day ride, and he was glad to have good weather for the journey. Although it was always safer to travel with a companion, it was not always practical or expedient. He almost always travelled alone.

He was nowhere near the first of the family members to arrive. If he hadn't spotted some of Harold's younger cousins running about on one of the lawns, he would have been alerted by the constant coming and going of various tradesmen and servants.

Ah, yes, the house party had commenced.

It had been five days since he'd seen her.

He was not the sort of fellow to pine. He'd been infatuated a few times, but never had he felt such a... connection... such a bond as this. What was it about her?

As he neared the castle, his heart seemed to skip a few beats. Neither she nor Harold were on the lawns with the other guests.

Five nights had passed since he'd held her. Since he'd left her, drowsy from his lovemaking, wearing nothing but a sheet.

He dismounted and then affectionately patted his mare before handing her over to one of his uncle's stable lads. His aunt, of course, would have his room set aside and readied for him. Of all the ducal properties, Priory Point was Dev's favorite. He even dared to feel somewhat at home here.

He didn't wait for a maid to bring up a basin of warm

water. The cold water in the pitcher was sufficient. He washed and changed out of his dusty riding clothes.

The newlywed couple was down at the beach, he'd been informed. They'd swam every day since arriving.

Harold must be practicing. Hearing that his cousin was swimming was encouraging.

Sophia had told him she enjoyed sea-bathing. She'd not done it often, she'd said, but had learned the skill in a lake as a young girl.

He followed the well-worn path down to the beach almost without thinking. Everything about this place elicited youthful memories — racing along the trail, hiding from his uncle, playing pirates with Lucas and Harold.

Cutting across the last switchback, Dev landed easily as he jumped down to the hard sand. At first, the beach appeared to be empty but for a few gulls and a pile of driftwood. But, no, not far from the shore, a blanket was spread out on the sand near a basket, and two people were in the surf.

One of them was face down, swimming out to sea, and the other stood watching the swimmer, in nothing but a chemise, plastered to her wet skin.

She must have sensed his presence as she glanced over her shoulder for no apparent reason and raised her hand to her eyes to shade her view.

Dev lifted one hand and waved.

"Dev!" She didn't hesitate before turning back toward the sea and yelling once again. "Harold! Dev is here!"

She'd been playing in the water with the exuberance of a child. It reminded him of the enthusiasm she'd had while making love. When Sophia discarded her prim and proper manners, she did so with uninhibited gusto.

Her sleek, wet hair had worked itself free of her coiffure, her chemise was sliding off one shoulder, and an exuberant smile stretched across her lips. Struggling against the water, she lifted her feet high and ran toward the shore. Harold had caught sight of him as well and, standing in chest high water held up one hand in greeting.

But Dev had eyes only for Sophia.

Her pale skin had taken on a sweet honey tone, and her eyes burned brighter than the sea.

Coming to a sudden stop where the white foam of the waves still rolled over her bare feet, Sophia stood not five feet from him. He knew she wanted to throw herself into his arms, but she checked herself suddenly.

Perhaps they were being watched. Yes, it was likely that some family member or another could come upon them at any moment.

But for now, they were alone.

"You look more beautiful than ever," he said hungrily.

She looked down at her toes and then back up again. She bit her lip, nervously. "I've been working with Harold on his bathing technique."

It was not what he'd expected her to say, but since when had she done what he'd expected? Dev felt himself grinning for the first time since she'd left London.

"How's that working out?"

She laughed. "Well... he's doing much better now. I hadn't realized that a person could completely forget how to swim. But apparently, that's what Harold had done.

Rather, he said his mind had not forgotten, but his body had."

Dev eyed her curves from head to toe. Her chemise, in that moment, did little to hide her charms. He was glad no one but him could see her — in close proximity, anyhow — and witness her state of dishabille. She shivered and wrapped her arms around herself, clasping her elbows at her sides.

"So, you have not been pining for me?" He laughed at her sudden shyness, but his voice was tender as he removed his jacket. Stepping into the surf, he dropped it on her shoulders and led her toward the dry sand. She leaned against him as he did so.

It was the most they would get away with.

"I am so glad you are here." Her words were muffled as she spoke into the jacket. Although no one else but Harold was in sight, and the wind and surf would drown out any words they spoke, she was cautious.

But it was obvious she'd known that he would come. She'd not doubted him.

"You cannot imagine my disappointment when I came downstairs for breakfast and discovered you had left." He'd not kissed her goodbye. He wanted to kiss her now, but that was out of the question.

"So, you know what the duchess believes?"

He nodded his head. "The world has gone insane with glee over it — rather, the Prescott world, anyhow."

She sat on the blanket and looked up at him. "It is a Prescott world in which I now live." She sounded a little forlorn. "It's as though the servants' sole duty is to spy on us. Harold and I are followed almost everywhere." Her eyelashes dropped, but then she boldly gazed back up at him. "I've missed you."

How had this happened? "God, Sophia." The physical urge to take her into his arms, to make love to her right here on the sand, was nearly excruciating. "What am I going to do with you?"

Harold had reached the water's edge and approached them slowly.

"Harold!" Dev shouted over the sounds of the waves. "You are looking well! Married life appears to suit you."

At which his cousin rolled his eyes, and Sophia laughed ironically. Dev felt something warm inside his heart. They had become friends, Sophia and Harold. Two people he realized he cared for deeply.

Harold took a seat on the sand, a few feet from Sophia. She handed him a second blanket, glancing around surreptitiously. Dev dropped onto the sand as well, putting some distance between himself and the newlyweds.

Sophia then opened a nearby basket and pulled out a few bottles of wine. As she handed Dev his own bottle and an apple, Harold proceeded to tell him what they'd been doing since they left London.

Watching his cousin and Sophia interact now, he was happy to see that they'd made peace with each other. Harold's awkwardness with her was gone. Of course, her sweet charm, her compassion and understanding, had most likely gone to work on the way Harold saw himself. For she knew his secret and had not treated him with any ill will.

Sophia glanced over and caught Dev's eye.

He'd thought he would be able to leave her alone until after Harold and Stewart left the country. But in that moment, as she smiled at him warmly, he couldn't remember why.

CHAPTER 17

"So, you are going to climb to the bottom, swim out through the tunnel and then back into the cave and climb back out, up the rope?" Sophia had insisted on coming along today and would not be shielded from any of the pertinent details. Ignoring Dev's instructions for her to step aside while he and Harold cleared the rocks away from the cave, she continued picking up some of the smaller stones and tossing them to the side.

Dev had not been able to go to her the night before. Nor the night before that. For the newly married couple had established that they slept in the same bed, and to do differently, might signify that they'd lost interest in one another.

And Harold was determined to leave his mother with a favorable memory of her second son. He'd told Dev he would not back out of this stunt. He'd been swimming every day, growing stronger and more agile, at Sophia's urging.

Today, they were to investigate the condition of the tunnel.

It had eroded considerably. Dev saw this right away, as they moved the rocks back. He only hoped that the underwater channel would still present a clear passage. Pulling the last of the larger stones away, Dev then turned to the sturdy tree nearby. Sophia opened the picnic basket and pulled out the rope.

As she handed it to him, his fingertips brushed her palm. Her hand felt especially soft. He hesitated just a moment before relinquishing her touch.

The rope she handed him was thick and heavy. After testing the weight of it, he tied it around the trunk of the tree methodically and then tugged. It would do.

At the tunnel, he dropped to his knees and went to crawl forward, but suddenly felt a hand on his shoulder.

"Dev…" He looked back and saw bright blue, concerned eyes. Sophia would not try to stop him, he knew, but neither would she pretend no danger existed. "…be careful." And then, despite Harold's presence, she leaned forward and pressed her lips against his.

He'd not had an opportunity to touch her intimately at all since arriving. And he would have prolonged this kiss but for, well, Harold was but a few feet away, waiting for him to climb into the tunnel. Dev allowed his lips to linger on hers, though. He missed her taste. He missed her essence.

"This shouldn't take long," he assured her.

She touched his face and then sat on her haunches, away from the cave's opening. His brave Sophia. She would not cling to him and cry. He would return to her. He would find a way to go to her tonight.

Dev was not afraid.

He did, however, respect the elements involved in what he needed to do. He imagined that this edge of unease was akin to fear but refused to dwell upon unproductive emotions. Instead he sharpened his mind to the task at hand.

Except…

Impulsively, Dev withdrew from the opening once again, pressed another quick kiss against her lips, and then ducked back into the cave. The ground extended just a few feet and then dropped off. He remembered this now. Even the musty scent was vaguely familiar.

Water splashing against the rocks below echoed off the cave walls. Good then. The fissure in the rocks hadn't been blocked.

The rope was coiled loosely, and without hesitation, Dev tossed it into the darkness below. After a moment, it made a thud against the rocky side wall, and then a less emphatic clunk onto the floor. He carried with him a flint. Harold was to toss down the torch once Dev reached the bottom.

Sliding on some fitted gloves he'd worn in combat, Dev proceeded to climb, hand over hand, down the slick rocky wall. The memory of doing this as a boy gradually returned as he found footholds, and various outcrops on the way down. Just as his muscles began to burn, his feet landed at the bottom.

"I'm down!" he shouted up. The small amount of

sunlight that had illuminated his way was temporarily blocked.

"Are you ready for the torch?" It was Harold, watching him from over the edge of the drop.

Dev lit the flint and held it out away from him. "Go ahead. Drop it!"

He saw the torch for a moment, and then an instant later, it was in front of him. Not even thinking, he grabbed it out of the air with his empty hand before it could hit the ground. The flint had stayed lit, and so he held it to the torch. Much better.

Turning around, he waved the fire toward the water. It looked much the same as it had, all those years ago — only smaller. As a grown man, how much more confined would the underwater tunnel feel? His own shoulders were slightly broader than Harold's. That was good. If he could fit through, then Harold ought to as well.

Waving the flame around, he found a ledge where he could prop the torch to illuminate the room. Ah, yes, he remembered the importance of the illumination. When swimming back through, he would need to follow the light from the fire. Very important.

He then pulled his boots off and slipped his shirt off over his head.

As he did so, he took slow, deep breaths.

The light at the top shadowed again. "Please be careful, Dev." It was Sophia.

He smiled. He'd never appreciated the concern of a woman before.

He hoped to hell this worked. He hated the secrecy, the

deceit. He could only imagine how Harold had felt for most of his life, hiding who he really was.

"Don't worry, love." He spoke casually and then dove cleanly into the pool.

It was cold, but not overly so. This was England, after all, and the ocean was always cold, summer or not.

He acclimatized himself to the water by diving under several times before returning to the pool's edge to slow down his breathing. Going out was not the difficult part; coming back in would be trickier. "I'm going to head out shortly!" he shouted upward. "Once outside, it will take me a few minutes to return." He closed his eyes and took deep relaxing breaths. As he did so, he felt his heart rate slow. He'd gone over all of this with Harold, but it wouldn't help much in the long run. Harold would have the waves to deal with. And the rocks.

As would Dev, after he'd slipped out the other side.

God, they'd been daredevils as children. He'd have his own sons' hides if they ever attempted to do anything so dangerous.

If he ever had any sons, that was.

One long, slow breath, and Dev purposefully submerged himself in the direction of the tunnel.

It was still there.

It did appear smaller but not impossibly so. He resurfaced again and then, taking another deep breath, dove decisively toward the fissure.

His head and torso entered easily, and he intentionally pushed all thoughts of turning around out of his mind. The water had an ebb and flow to it.

When it ebbed, it sucked him into the tunnel farther.

He kicked his feet and pulled at the rocks with his arms toward what he could now see was the other side.

The water at the end was not black, but a lighter blue, aquamarine.

He maneuvered around a few outcroppings of rocks and carefully kicked his feet.

When his lungs began to burn, he merely focused on the lighter blue water.

He was almost through.

A tug, a pull, a painful slash along his side, and he felt himself pulled out of the tunnel.

Now up, up, up…

Air.

He inhaled a few gulps of air and then laughed.

This was why they'd done it as young adventurous boys. This sense of danger and then an even greater sense of triumph.

Dev treaded water for a few moments as he took in the dangers around him.

Some rocks to his left had not been there a decade ago. They must have fallen during a storm, or perhaps centuries of the surf, pounding below them had finally taken its toll. Either way, they now presented a definite danger.

He watched the swirls of the water and swam away from them accordingly.

The positioning of the rocks and the moving water prevented a swimmer from resting. Climbing the cliff was impossible as well. The only way out of the cove was back through the tunnel.

It was perfect for what they'd planned.

Relaxing into the waves, he rested for a moment and then, taking a deep breath dove back under.

It took him five tries before he could reach the tunnel again. He felt his heart begin to race faster and emptied his mind to decrease its pace.

He knew exactly where the tunnel was now. He emerged from the water, took in a great breath, and submerged himself once again.

He headed straight for the opening.

Almost impossible to see, he found it with his hands and pulled his body inward. On this attempt, he avoided the rocks that had slashed at him before.

But the water worked against him now.

As he used his arms and legs more, he knew his body would require extra oxygen. He emptied his mind and continued pulling at the rocks and kicking, and pushing off them with his feet.

A weak glow caught his eye.

It was a glimmer of light from the torch.

He focused on it and pulled and pushed and tugged his body through.

The difficult part was that the water wanted to expel him back into the lagoon again. He could not let it get ahold of him.

A great lunge with one foot, though and…

Yes… that sense of triumph once again.

He took a few breaths and then swam over to the other side of the pool.

"What do you think, Dev?" Harold must have heard him

return. "Is it much the same?"

Dev did not want to scare Harold, and yet he didn't wish to give him a false sense as to the level of difficulty the stunt would require.

He knew that Harold's heart rate was going to increase dramatically as soon as he hit the water from above. It was a long, exhilarating, jump. Perhaps if Dev could mark the tunnel somehow... "I'll be out in a moment." He was non-committal.

SOPHIA HAD NEVER HEARD a sweeter sound than Dev's voice when it echoed out of the top of that blasted cave. She and Harold looked at each other in relief. And then, Harold was backing away, and Dev's water-slickened head poked out.

He was like a seal, with black sultry eyes and a power-ful, well-defined physique.

Her Dev.

He winked at her before turning to Harold. "It's much the same, Harold. I think it was always tricky. We simply were too foolish to recognize the dangers."

"But you recognize them now," Harold said grimly.

Dev nodded. "I do." Standing up, he gestured for both of them to follow him.

They were headed for the cliff, and when he stepped into the sunshine, she noticed the large crimson stain on the side of his shirt.

Dev was explaining something to Harold, though, and

pointing downward. "There would have been a rockslide since we last dove. If you look down there…"

Harold was nodding. "I thought it looked different. Do you think the jump still possible?"

Sophia felt her heart squeeze. Harold's determination and courage were admirable, but she would not wish him to be harmed… or worse…

Dev had pulled his dry shirt on carelessly, most likely not even realizing that he had been hurt. It was not tucked in and hung long past his waist. Sophia wanted to rush forward and examine Dev's wound, but she knew it was not the time.

"If we jump from over here, we miss them," Dev said walking about ten paces to the left. He then pointed again. "See that outcrop of brush, with the large rock just below it?"

Harold was nodding.

"The tunnel is about four feet to the right of it. It's dark when you go down, so you need to search for it with your hands. And be prepared for the pull of the cove. You must not allow it to take hold of you once you are inside of the tunnel." He then began swinging his arms back and forth as though to loosen his muscles. "The tide is still high. What do you think? Shall we do the jump together a few times, while we have the chance today?"

Sophia wished she would faint.

But she'd insisted upon coming and would not become a liability now. Dev was grinning at Harold, and she realized he did this intentionally. She knew he'd already spent a great deal of time discussing techniques and problems to watch for. Now, she knew, he was ready to share his courage.

Gritting his teeth, Harold nodded.

"Here." She stepped toward Harold, taking the lead from Dev. "I'll hold your waistcoat." If Harold was not ready to do this, then now would be the time to back out.

She also knew that Dev would not lead his cousin into an impossible situation.

As did, apparently, Harold.

Harold handed Sophia his coat and then sat on the ground to remove his boots. When he stood up, he began moving his arms back and forth as well, and jumping from one foot to the other. "All right, then, Dev," he said. He flashed his cousin an impulsively wicked grin. "On three?"

Dev merely shook his head and took a running leap. As his body flew off the side of the cliff, he tucked his feet beneath him into a tight human missile.

Not waiting even another second, Harold followed him enthusiastically into the churning cauldron of the cove's murky depths.

Sophia covered her face. She knew what she needed to do now. She was to return to the cave and wait.

CHAPTER 18

*A*ll in all, Harold jumped three times And Dev twice.

She could imagine them, as boys, spending warm afternoons, throwing themselves into the sea, over and over again until they'd worn off their adolescent restlessness. It hadn't taken them long to swim back into the cave, thank God. Sophia had heard Harold's laughter just moments after she, herself, climbed back to the opening.

When she'd heard it, she couldn't help grinning. Dev's voice was casual, matter-of-fact, as though he'd not doubted Harold's abilities for a moment. The greatest challenge for Harold had been climbing back out of the cave itself. With a few pointers, though, and encouragement from Dev, he'd eventually emerged, full of confidence, ready to do it again.

"At first, I thought I wouldn't make it through that tight part, in the middle, Dev," he said as he stepped gingerly through the rocks back toward the cliff, "until you shoved me from behind. This time I'll do it without your assistance."

"I'll let you do it alone this time, then," Dev said. "I could see that once you found your handles on the rocks, you would have made it through without my help."

"You think so, Dev? I thought so too. But I wasn't certain. I'd forgotten how important the torch was. We'll have to have it set in place when I jump in. Blazing bollocks! That water was cold as I hit it. Nearly drank a gallon of saltwater when I went under." And then he smiled at Sophia. "Excuse my language, ma'am." He looked sheepish for all of two seconds. "Couldn't have done it if you hadn't encouraged me to do all that swimming this week, Sophia. I'd give you a hug if I weren't all wet…" He looked down at his shirt front. "…and covered in mud."

On Harold's second jump, Dev waited with Sophia. Both of them watched as Harold threw himself into the water and then dove for the tunnel.

This was progress, indeed. Up until today, this part of the plan had been an uncertainty.

After Harold disappeared into the tunnel, Dev glanced over at her, grinning. But his gaze held an intensity.

His hands landed on her waist, and he pulled her up against him.

"I'm soaked, and I'm just as covered in mud," he growled into her neck, "but I'll not let this opportunity pass."

"It's been forever," Sophia agreed, closing her eyes and tilting her head to give him better access to her nape. His skin was warm beneath the wet fabric, which reminded her. "You cut yourself, Dev. You're injured."

But he made no move to release her. "It's nothing, a scratch." His lips trailed her cheek before settling upon her mouth.

Oh, yes. He tasted of salt and man and sunshine. Sophia wanted to stay in his arms forever. She wanted to explore every inch of his skin, inhaling his scent as she did so. Their time together the night of her wedding had been like an explosion. They'd gotten a taste of one other, but not been able to savor and delight. She dug her fingers into his scalp and hair, pressing herself closer to him in the process.

Breathing harshly, Dev broke away and again buried his face on her shoulder.

For although Harold knew of their relationship, the situation demanded restraint. The three of them were too close to success to jeopardize it now.

And so, after a moment to regain their composure, Dev turned her, draped one arm around her shoulder, and led the two of them back to the mouth of the cave.

Harold could be heard climbing the rope.

"Dev, are you out there? I will do it one more time, but I need to make it look as though I truly am falling. I'm thinking," he said, his face appearing at the opening, and he addressed Sophia, "I must look as though I've lost my balance. When I jump this time, I want to make it look as though perhaps I'm teasing you, you know, showing off, and then I can appear to have underestimated the proximity of the cliff. Any witnesses, hopefully, will be too far away to see how I land in the water."

Sophia's heart squeezed. Harold really was going to do this. She and this brave young man had grown surprisingly close over the past week. And he was going to go away.

Forever.

She was going to play the part of his grieving widow.

Dev seemed to read her mind. "You are going to have to be something of an actress, Sophia. I'm going to wait in the cave, with the light burning and a disguise for Harold. It will be vital he get away from Priory Point and Dover unrecognized."

Harold was leading them back to the cliff once again. Now that he'd experienced some success, he seemed to not be wavering at all. "Stewart is going to join me after my memorial service. It would look strange if he, my valet, were to leave without attending."

Joy could be heard in Harold's tone. Not the words themselves, but in that he could speak them openly before Dev and Sophia. This was why he did this. All he wished for was the freedom to love. The same thing Sophia and Dev wanted.

Only for him it would come at a much greater price.

He must give up his home, his family, his birthright... everything.

The risks of him not doing so, but continuing to live as he did here in England, were too great.

Now that Harold had proven he could perform the stunt, other realities of what they must do came into play.

Sophia mostly dreaded deceiving his mother into believing her youngest son had perished. Although she now knew that the duchess had likely taken part in the manipulation of her marriage, she'd also learned that it had been done out of fear for the son she loved dearly.

And now Sophia was going to perpetrate a horrible falsehood upon her. With a dawning horror, she stood back and pondered all the ramifications of their deceit as Dev and Harold considered varying techniques for Harold's fall.

She'd not been listening to them closely, caught up in her own thought, so when Dev seemed to slip, and then lose his balance and fall into the water, she ran to the cliff's edge in a near panic.

"Dev!" She could not stop the cry that was dragged from within her.

Harold laughed, catching her by the hand.

"I'm going to try it now. You tell me afterwards if I'm as convincing."

Her heart raced, her emotions becoming more unsettled as the planning proceeded. She nodded, nonetheless and watched encouragingly as Harold pretended to jest for her, lost his footing, and then tumbled over the side of the cliff.

We are most certainly all going to go to hell for this, she thought as she traversed back to the cave.

* * *

DEV KNEW Sophia was beginning to have doubts. He could see it in her eyes every time they referred to the deception required after Harold's *death*. Ironically, it seemed, the more confidant Harold became, the less certain she was.

If Sophia later regretted any of this, if she could only come to him filled with guilt, Dev would never forgive himself. Therefore, they all must be absolutely certain Harold wasn't feeling coerced or pressured in any way.

And so, later that day, while Sophia took tea with her mother-in-law and a few of the aunts, Dev pulled Harold aside for a private discussion in the library. The other men were enjoying the billiards tables this afternoon, and so he did not think they would be interrupted.

Harold, too, had a few things to say.

Before Dev could even pour a splash of whisky, Harold approached the subject of Sophia.

"I've grown rather fond of Sophia, Dev," he said. "She's not at all the sort of lady I'd thought she was before I married her." This was an intriguing notion for Dev to ponder. He realized, then, that Harold had never had a close relationship with a young woman. All he'd ever known were those who had been presented to him by the *ton* –– the seemingly endless parade of laced-up, parasoled, empty-headed debutantes. And Harold had had no reason nor inclination to pursue any of them.

Until Sophia.

And, hell, Dev, himself, had thought Sophia was one of them when he'd first stumbled upon her trapped behind the lion with Peaches. "There is more to her than meets the eye," he agreed.

"I do believe that being with her this past week is what it would have been like to have a sister," Harold continued. "I suppose you realize how clever she is. But even more than that." He frowned as though searching for the right words. "Without having to convince her, without explaining to her my frustrations with myself... it is as though she understands a great deal of what is in my heart." Harold took the glass Dev handed him and then raised it to his lips. "And she does not judge me." He shook his head side to side. "She's not once acted disgusted by..." Seeming to realize how intimate his words were, he turned his head and stemmed the flow of words. "She gives me hope, Dev," he said instead of whatever he'd been thinking a moment before.

Dev could not help but smile at this. Could he find the words to express all that she'd come to mean to him in so short a time? Brave, compassionate, forgiving, sensual...

Dev was happy to learn that Harold felt hopeful. He would be even happier when he could see some optimism in Sophia again. Perhaps after Harold took the fall and made his safe getaway.

"She's afraid for you. She's afraid you'll regret giving up your family," Dev said.

"I know." Harold set his glass upon a coaster. "It's why I wanted to speak with you. She and I, together, we've had long discussions, on a few occasions, when one of us has been unable to sleep. And I've tried to tell her how much my freedom means to me. But I don't think she realizes..." Looking a little uncomfortable, he glanced back up. "Afterward, will you tell her for me, that she well may have saved my life? Tell her that, aside from my own mother, she's the only woman I've ever felt close to? But mostly, tell her thank you." He choked a little at his words.

Dev took a sip of his own drink. "I will."

Harold waited a few minutes before he spoke again. "I've also been thinking about St. John." He never referred to his brother by his first name. At some point, the wedge of separation had grown so great between the two of them that Dev wasn't certain it could ever be removed. "St. John is going to remember the cave."

Dev nodded. Back to the details. This was more comfortable ground for both of them. "We need to bring him in on the plan."

Harold spoke into his glass, deep in thought. "He's never accepted me for who I am. I will forever be a deviant to him. A reminder that all is not perfect in this great ducal family."

"But he worries for your safety," Dev felt compelled to add, although Harold had the right of it. St. John would always worry most for the reputation and dignity of the Prescott legacy. "Would you speak with him about it, or would you prefer that I do?"

Harold took another sip of the amber liquid. "Would you think me a coward if I said I'd prefer you do it?"

"You're no coward." Dev would put that notion to rest forever.

"Yes, he needs to know. And he will understand why I wish to leave. He'll agree with it, in fact. Dev," he added, then, with furrowed brows, he returned to the earlier subject, "when I'm gone, you are going to marry Sophia, aren't you? Because something is wrong with her family. Something about them that frightened her. She hasn't told me anything, but I don't want her sent back to them, just in case I am right about this."

Dev could put this doubt of Harold's to rest quite easily. "I am, Harold. You need not worry about her safety."

And hearing these words, Harold nodded. "You love her."

Dev would leave his cousin with no doubts whatsoever. "I do." And then, "I'll speak with St. John tomorrow. When do you wish to stage the accident?"

"If St. John doesn't pose any difficulties, the day after. The sooner we do this, the better."

This was Dev's opinion as well.

"I'll tell Sophia tonight. It will be the last night that we pretend to sleep together as a married couple. She has informed me that the night before the accident I ought to be with Stewart..." Harold flushed. He'd likely not intended to reveal something so intimate. But then he added, "She promised to *handle* her maid."

Perhaps, tomorrow night, Dev could go to her. She would need reassurance. She would need comfort.

Hell, Dev was simply mad for wanting her.

And then out of nowhere, Harold winked at him, almost as though he had read Dev's thoughts. They both burst out laughing. Harold was in a particularly uncharacteristic mood. Life was never simple.

Dev spent the remainder of the afternoon reminiscing with a cousin he'd practically written off years ago when he entered the military. Conversing with him today, knowing what he faced, Dev was glad he'd taken this chance to know him as an adult. As youths, they'd practically been brothers.

He would lose him again, he realized. Due to the gravity

of the situation, it would be just as though his cousin were to die, in truth. Harold could not return to England. Ever. It would be dangerous for him to write, to send word. He was even going to have to take on a different name.

Dev laughed at a particularly embarrassing memory Harold had brought up.

He would enjoy his cousin's company today.

Tomorrow he would speak with St. John.

SOPHIA WAS NOT, in fact, taking tea with the duchess and her sisters that afternoon. For Rhoda had only recently arrived, and Sophia was eager for the two of them to catch up in private. They'd conversed briefly that morning, but with Rhoda's mother and sisters present, and then later, in Sophia's chamber, Penny had hovered. They'd been able to talk about silly, inconsequential matters, but they could not really share. And since Sophia had been spending so much time working with Harold on his swimming, she'd missed out on her afternoon walks with Peaches.

That afternoon, then, was the perfect time to devote to Rhoda and Peaches. They would avoid the beach. Sophia'd had enough of that to last a lifetime. She didn't wish to think about Harold's jump today. It was becoming too morbid, too depressing, too deceitful…

Too real.

Sophia removed Peaches' leading string, allowing her pup to scurry about unimpeded. Unless they came upon a rabbit, Sophia knew Peaches would stay nearby.

Sophia was curious… "How have matters proceeded… with St. John?"

At this, Rhoda clasped her hands beneath her chin. "I don't wish to jinx it," she answered, "but I believe he has become somewhat enamored of me."

Sophia's brows rose. It was possible, she supposed. She'd previously considered the man to be somewhat cold and too condescending to be attracted to her friend. Rhoda was keenly intelligent and liberal-minded. But, perhaps she was the perfect woman for St. John. Perhaps he needed a wife who could complement his traditional ideals with an ounce or two of progressive thinking.

"He is attentive? He shows you and speaks of affection?" she asked.

A smile drew the corners of Rhoda's full lips upward. "He is, and yes, he does." She took a few steps and then hugged herself a little self-consciously. "Sophia, he calls me his flower. He touches me in such a way, on occasions… I cannot help but imagine them over and over again in my mind."

"Mmm…" Sophia understood this. Over the past two days, she'd cherished the memory of Dev touching her arm, brushing her hand, leaning in and allowing his breath to linger near her nape. It was all the more evocative since they'd been forced to keep their distance from one another most of the time.

How long would they wait… after?

Except she did not wish to think about this.

"Has St. John mentioned speaking to your father?" This

was important. This was how a gentleman revealed his true intentions.

"My father has not traveled to London, yet." Oh, yes, Rhoda's father and mother rarely resided in the same city — let alone house — at the same time.

"He is still in Bristol, then?"

Rhoda scowled. "He is." They stopped and watched Peaches dig into a particularly fascinating section of earth, before continuing their meandering walk. "I suppose, though," Rhoda began, "Bristol is not the end of the earth. If Lucas is serious about me, it would not be unreasonable for me to expect him to travel to my father, would it?"

Lucas, indeed? Sophia agreed whole-heartedly. "It would not be. He is a marques. He can do as he pleases, travel where he wishes." Oh, she hoped Harold's older brother was not planting false expectations in Rhoda's heart. Rhoda deserved a husband who loved her, one whom she loved. Just over a week ago, Sophia had given up on this possibility for herself.

But Dev had not.

Warmth blossomed in her heart.

Dev had not given up on her.

"I am happy to see you so content with Lord Harold, after all. I'd not thought he would ever appear so... demonstrative, in front of others, no less."

Sophia flushed at these words. She wished — oh, how she wished — she did not have to keep this secret from her friend. It would be such a relief to share this burden with Rhoda.

But she could not.

And so, she must perpetuate the lie they'd begun since the wedding.

"Harold is a sensitive and thoughtful gentleman." Best to stay with the truth as much as possible. "I realize, now, after coming to know the person he is, that he is a very special man. It's silly, really, Rhoda, how we think we understand a person, know what's in their heart, after sharing a few dances and a turn in the park. Courting, within the *ton* anyhow, does not allow a lady and a gentleman to comprehend one another at all."

"Except," Rhoda smiled enigmatically, "for when they slip away together, unseen, along a dark garden path or behind, perhaps, a well-placed fern."

Sophia shook her head and smiled. But she would kill St. John if he was merely dallying with her friend!

They changed directions to keep up with Peaches, who seemed to be navigating this journey, and now had a lovely view of the sea. "Lord Harold and I have swum in the ocean every day since we've arrived. This estate is situated perfectly."

"Once one has safely arrived," Rhoda added. "The drive leading up to the castle is daunting. I could barely look out the window at times, what with all of the turns, and climbing, and cliffs below."

Sophia wrinkled her nose. That had not bothered her when they'd first arrived. She'd had other things to worry about at the time. So much had changed. She felt years older than she had a month ago.

"Mama is looking well." Sophia changed the subject. "Wouldn't you agree?"

Rhoda nodded. "You've made her so happy. Dudley did not join them for this visit?"

Sophia sighed. "We are lucky to be spared his company." And then, "What have you found, Peaches?" The little dog carried a large stick between her teeth. "You wish to play, do you?" She wrestled the stick out of Peaches' teeth and then threw it as far as she could. Dev had told her Dudley was in Brighton. The mere mention of his name caused her stomach to churn. He'd lied about an exam. He would gamble himself into debt again. Dev was right in that her stepbrother might not limit his transgressions to herself.

What if he'd hurt others already? Dudley needed to be brought under control somehow!

Yes, Dev was right.

"What of Captain Brookes?" Rhoda's words jolted her. It was as though her friend could read her mind. "I had thought the two of you had developed an affection for each other."

Oh, how Sophia hated keeping her feelings, her fears for Harold and her relationship with Dev, from her closest friend.

"It is better this way." Sophia chose her words carefully. "Better to accept what is and move forward. And really, Harold has been a dear."

Rhoda played with the seam on her glove. "Do you love him then? As a woman loves a man? As a wife loves a husband?"

Focusing on the first question, Sophia did not have to lie. "I do, Rhoda." Like a brother, the brother Dudley had never been. "He is funny and clever, and sensitive. He is a wonderful man." She felt no disloyalty in her words as she spoke them. She loved Harold as a friend and also as a dear relation. It was just as Dev would wish.

She knew this because she'd seen the sadness in his eyes today. He'd been proud of Harold's success, but he felt a sadness as well.

"Do you love St. John? Could you ever love him, do you think? As a woman loves a man, as a wife loves a husband?" She turned the question back upon her friend.

Rhoda, rebellious, decisive, fearless Rhoda suddenly looked bashful. Of the four of them — Sophia, Emily, Cecily and herself — Rhoda'd always been the most flirtatious. But she'd never fixed her attentions upon one particular gentleman, not longer than a week, generally. But today she was different.

Rhoda's cheeks were slightly flushed, her eyes shining and her lips turned up in a mysterious smile.

Admittedly, Rhoda had found Dev attractive for a few days, but who would not? This thing with St. John, however — this was different.

He'd paid court to Rhoda now for nearly a month.

St. John was a marques. He was a highly desirable bachelor.

And St. John was especially high in the instep. He could afford to be. For he was much sought after. Perhaps too much so.

"I could be, I think," Rhoda practically whispered the words.

Sophia took Rhoda's arm and patted her. "He should be so lucky."

At which words Rhoda laughed. "He is a marques!"

"And you are one of my dearest of friends who happens to be even more beautiful on the inside than you are on the outside. You are loyal and true, compassionate and intelligent. He will not find anyone better to take as a wife. If he does, well, then he is a fool!"

Rhoda stared into the distance. "Have you heard from Cecily or Emily?" She changed the subject, obviously uncomfortable contemplating both St. John's intentions and Sophia's sincere compliments.

"Both, actually." Sophia was happy to report. "Mother brought letters with her yesterday when she arrived. Emily..." She sighed. "...cannot wait to return from Wales. Her aunt wants her to stay on as a companion, but her parents have told her she may have one more Season first. And Cecily is melancholy, as can only be expected."

Poor Cecily did not have a Captain Devlin Brookes to extricate her from a loveless and arranged marriage. Before leaving London, after Lord Kensington's *accident*, Cecily had done her best to convince them all that she was content with her situation. But Rhoda, Sophia, and Emily had seen behind her cheerful declaration. Cecily was unhappy and would be for as long as Lord Kensington lived.

"Has her father not returned yet then?" At one time, they'd all believed Cecily's wealthy father could remove her from the catastrophic marriage, but they'd yet to hear anything promising in this regard.

Rhoda shook her head. "I would be devastated to discover such dishonesty in St. John. Of course, with my near non-existent dowry I'll not ever have to wonder if a man marries me for my money."

They both chuckled ironically.

"But," Sophia warned cautiously, "we have learned that people don't always represent themselves honestly. Stay watchful, my friend. Stay watchful."

"When did you become so cynical and grave?" Rhoda patted her hand reassuringly but then added, "Without a doubt."

CHAPTER 19

The air was cool, and a fine mist hung over the sea when St. John and Devlin rode out from the castle. The house party had grown to a much larger family gathering than anyone had intended and so, to avoid the possibility of interruption, Dev arranged for an early morning ride with his older cousin. This conversation would demand absolute privacy, and this way, he could be assured of it. St. John, sensing something of import, had agreed readily.

Initially, they allowed the horses to set the pace, racing across the field, but after less than a mile, they slowed to an easy walk. At this point, Dev got right to the point. He would not hedge around the subject with St. John.

"Harold is going to leave England. He is going to stage his own death, and then he and Stewart are leaving the country."

And as Dev suspected, St. John showed little emotion at

the news. "So, it has all been a ruse then? The happy loving couple? For mother's benefit, I presume."

"Of course, Luc." Dev patted his horse on the neck. "I've promised to help him. He plans to do it tomorrow. He's quite determined, but we have need of your assistance."

St. John brought his mount to a halt and stared out to the sea. The mist was burning off already. It looked as though today would bring with it another clear blue sky.

"I should have known. It was too much to hope for, too good to be true." Glancing at Dev, he narrowed his eyes. "Why did he not come to me himself?"

Dev did not want to get into any of this. "He knows you too well. He knows your feelings on the matter."

St. John glared back at him but then apparently dismissed his disgust with a careless shrug. "What does he need of me?"

Thinking St. John had more to say, but would not, Dev paused a moment before explaining the plan, occasionally answering the few questions his cousin had.

St. John hated scandal. If Harold was going to do this, it would be in the family's best interest for him to do it successfully. "Justin arrived yesterday," St. John interjected. "He will make an excellent witness."

"He is a vicar now?" Dev hadn't seen Justin White for ages. He was a cousin on the duchess' side.

"Yes, and less likely to have his observations questioned. Miss Mossant, I think. She is not squeamish and will be a credible witness as well. I imagine you plan on assuring yourself of Harold and... well, that Harold escape unharmed and unobserved."

Dev nodded. "I will be at the cave with a mount for him and his disguise." He would drag Harold out of the water if necessary, alive, of course. He would be certain Harold was as successful tomorrow as he'd been yesterday.

"Lady Harold knows, I presume," St. John said, looking about, acting restless and bored with this conversation already. He was thankfully not opposing Harold's plans, but with no apparent concern over the loss of his brother, either, which was slightly disturbing to Dev. Not surprising, but disturbing. A small amount of brotherly protest would have been admirable.

"She does."

"I imagine this will be a picnic outing?" At Dev's nod, he continued. "She will want to have even numbers then. Tell her to invite Lady Caroline. Aunt Lucille has brought her along, and I would not mind such genteel company."

Well now. That would be pleasant for Miss Mossant.

They had St John's cooperation, however, and that was what mattered most.

And so, it was set. The final pieces of the puzzle were falling into place.

Tomorrow, Harold would set both him and Sophia free. Dev grimaced. It was unseemly. It was devious and sinister even. He hoped in his heart that this did not cast a shadow on his and Sophia's future. He would have her free of guilt, free of any shame or sorrow. But one did not always have control of such things.

He knew one thing for certain, though.

He would have her.

* * *

Sophia informed Penny she would most likely ask her husband to abstain from joining her that evening. She was expecting her courses, she told her, which was the truth but not the real reason.

From what Harold had divulged, Stewart was nervous nearly to the point of making himself ill. In addition to this, as a twosome, who had been used to spending a great deal of time in one another's company, they'd hardly had any time together since the wedding. They would wish to give each other courage. To reassure one another.

Stewart had been forced to keep company with Penny on several of the afternoons when Harold and Sophia had gone swimming. Furthermore, he'd been alone during the nights. Not that this was so terrible, but, she supposed, when one was used to sleeping with one's lover, well, the absence of him would be a considerable loss. Even if only for a few nights.

Sophia would give him and Harold a parting gift, per se. They would not be traveling together until they both reached the crossing. It would be nice for the two of them to bolster one another. And one night would not put any doubt in the duchess' mind.

After sending Harold away for the evening, Sophia found herself feeling a little lonely. What was Dev doing? They'd not been *alone* together since those stolen moments on the cliff. She missed him. Fraternizing with Dev and his family, dining together at the same table, and not being able to act upon her natural instincts toward him disheartened her.

Was she childish to need his reassurance? To need his comforting touch, his encouraging voice? Tonight, she felt the emptiness of it all the more. For these past several evenings, Harold had been here to distract her.

Alone in her chamber, she was free to dwell on her worries and guilt.

Where was Dev tonight? She needed him. She'd not heard anything save a terse missive with instructions pertaining to the outing scheduled for the following afternoon. In bold straight handwriting, he'd told her who was to be invited and what hour they ought to leave. Those details seemed inconsequential now but would matter greatly in the end.

She'd handled them to her satisfaction and then found herself at loose ends.

Even Rhoda was nowhere to be found.

Sophia was dispirited, rather, as though Harold was, in truth, going to die.

It was what she'd wanted, to be free of this marriage. It was also what Harold wanted. But with such a tremendous price to pay!

She'd hardly been able to look the duchess in the eye when she'd spoken with her before dinner. Sophia shivered and stood looking out the window. God, the view was spectacular — rocks, cliffs, and the sea. Her window revealed everything that made Priory Point so very beautiful, and yet so very dangerous.

She contemplated that she would forever have mixed feelings of her time here.

A tear escaped. She must find something to distract herself. Sophia picked up a book of poetry and tried to lose herself in some verse.

It was useless though.

She could not sleep. She'd be lucky to sleep at all that night. Even Peaches seemed more agitated than normal. Sitting on the floor, Sophia took a small toy and played hide and seek with her pup. She welcomed any diversion that might feel ordinary.

When would her life feel normal again? If it did — when it did — she vowed she would never take it for granted.

Sophia snatched the chew-toy out of Peaches' mouth and hid it behind her back. But Peaches was not interested. For Sophia had failed to notice that they were no longer alone.

Peaches noticed though.

The pup welcomed Dev as though he were her long-lost best friend.

Smart dog.

Dev shushed Peaches affectionately and locked the door behind him.

He was dressed formally, as he had been at dinner. But seeing him in her bedchamber like this caused her heart to skip a beat and a flush to warm her cheeks. Even so, she drank in the sight of him. His jacket and breeches fit perfectly, almost too perfectly. Freshly shaven, with his normally unruly hair tied back and boots polished to a high shine, he brought with him a masculine energy foreign to her very feminine abode.

Sophia had already changed into her nightgown and dismissed Penny.

"I could not remain downstairs any longer." Sophia spoke apologetically.

Harold had felt the same. The guests had been playing a game of charades and it had been impossible to summon enthusiasm to pretend enjoyment.

"I presumed as much." Dev reached down and helped her to her feet. Without hesitation, she moved into his arms.

"I feel as though my selfishness is to blame for all of this," she whispered into his chest. "I'm frightened for him."

"Sophia," Dev said, "you haven't a selfish bone in your body. It is Harold who has been pushed into taking such drastic measures. He's admitted to me that he would have done something like this regardless. He and Stewart have been dreaming of leaving England for a long time. This gives them an opportunity to search for a place where they can live their lives without fear."

"I know," she said. "He's told me this too. I just wish..."

"So do I." He rubbed her back. "He couldn't have done this without you, you know — the swimming, the encouragement, the friendship..."

"Harold is a good man, a good person. Her grace is going to be distraught with grief. Is there no other way?" She knew there was not. She'd pondered endless possibilities and dismissed all of them for one reason or another.

"It is what Harold wants. He is pleased that in doing it,

he can set you free as well."

A muffled sob escaped her. "I cannot imagine what would have happened if I'd never met you..." Peaches began jumping at Sophia's feet in concern. The pup did not like it when her mistress was upset.

With her cheek pressed against the linen of Dev's shirt and his arms stroking her hair and back, Sophia released the tears she'd held back all evening. "I've missed you so much. And now that you are here, I never want you to leave." She sighed and wiped her face with the sleeve of her nightdress. "I'm being ridiculous. Penny will return eventually to check on me. Having a lady's maid and governess, I have discovered, are disturbingly similar."

Dev did not release her. Instead, he nuzzled her ear. "I once had a valet, just before I bought in. He wanted to follow me to war, attend me on the battlefield."

Sophia tilted her head to listen but moaned softly at the sensations his lips ignited.

"But *he* had not enlisted. I did not wish him to put his life in danger simply because I chose to. I found other employment for him before I went away. Since I've returned, my father has been telling me I ought to hire myself a valet..." Dev chuckled. "...if I intend to live as a proper gentleman."

Throughout his narrative, Dev had been inching them toward the door. She didn't realize what he was up to until he reached behind her and tugged at the knob, testing the lock.

"She will sit outside and wait," Sophia whispered.

"It's no matter. I can work with that." He winked at her

before swinging her up and into his arms and then carrying her into the other room.

"She may even listen at the keyhole."

"We'll keep you silenced then." He laid her on the bed, kissing her in various sensitive places along the way. His body pressed against hers the entire time.

Except for the split-second it took him to pull the nightgown over her head.

The texture of his formal clothing against her naked skin aroused her in a most wicked way… the leather of his boots against her legs, a button here, a pocket there.

Exhilaration filled her. She needed this release. She needed his passion.

She'd held herself back from him for so long it was as though after taking her first breath, she'd nearly forgotten how to live.

Oh, but her body had not forgotten.

Her body warmed instantly to him.

Sophia gasped at the sensation of Dev's hot mouth on her breast. With each tug, he demanded more.

They did not have much time. Sophia hated that Penny might be eavesdropping. "Dev…" A moan escaped her.

He placed his hand over her mouth, a devilish glint in his eyes. His other hand had moved lower, between her legs, fondling and exploring.

She returned his impudent stare boldly. He seemed to delight in watching the emotions she could not hide.

When he slipped one finger inside her, her eyelids drooped shut. She could not restrain the cry she'd kept in check until then.

But his hand blocked the sound.

"Look at me, love," he commanded. His voice was low, caressing.

She did so but with heavy lids. He pressed into her with another finger, sliding and pumping slowly. A heat, a liquid, rushed to her core.

Being with Dev was like breathing, or eating, or drinking fine wine, like sleeping and waking.

Keeping her gaze focused was difficult, nearly impossible, but his own would not allow hers to waver.

She licked the palm of his hand.

Now it was she who watched his eyes cloud with arousal. "Wench," he whispered, removing both of his hands to unfasten his falls.

And then he was free, pressed against her, sliding along the slickness that her body had prepared for him.

She pumped her hips upward. This, she wanted this. One night with Dev had not been enough. It had only ignited a hunger in her she'd never known existed.

And now, to have him so close, so ready, she couldn't wait a moment longer.

She pushed her hips higher.

Tense and focused, he met her thrust.

She would have cried out, but his hand silenced her again. He filled her, and yet she wanted more. She wanted him to stretch her, conquer her. She wanted him touching her womb, her heart, her soul.

He pumped into her again.

And then he removed his hand, and his mouth caught her next whimper.

It was as though the world, everything she'd ever known, had come together and created her for the sole purpose of being with this man in this way.

In every way.

She would have him consume her completely.

They moved together slowly at first, and then gradually, a frantic pace took over.

Dev's hands pinned hers above her head. His mouth pressed into hers, tasting, taking, giving.

They breathed the same air.

She wrapped her legs around him and clung tightly; all the while he never ceased thrusting, pushing, finding the very center of her being.

It could have been an hour or a minute. She wanted it to be forever, with Dev all around her.

When the waves of pleasure crashed, she reveled again as he found his satisfaction, and the heat of his seed warmed her.

And then they both collapsed into one boneless heap of man and woman.

After lying motionless for several minutes, Dev slid off to lie beside her. "Is this how normal people make love?" Sophia asked as she burrowed her face in his chest.

He chuckled. "I don't suppose I'd know."

"Mmm..." She sighed. "Maybe later, when we are an ordinary couple." She wondered again. When would that be? It seemed impossible right now. And yet...

She was alive again.

They would live through this, together.

CHAPTER 20

$\mathcal{T}$he group outing, planned for late in the morning, consisted of a nature walk and an early picnic. Half the participants embarked upon it with a carefree manner and the other half with a sense of dread.

Sophia knew Harold was taking breakfast with his mother today, his last day as Lord Harold Prescott. He'd arranged to do so in as casual a manner as possible, but it would be his last moments with her.

Sophia would not think about it. It made her too sad.

Dev had snuck out of her chamber in the early hours of the morning.

Not knowing if Penny still waited outside Sophia's door, the silly man had insisted upon climbing out the window and down the trellis. Before she'd even realized what he had in mind, he'd pressed his lips against hers and then disappeared into the darkness.

She'd not slept much after that.

Upon tossing and turning for hours, terror and relief

swept through her when dawn finally arrived. She pulled the bell pull and unlocked the door. Naught could be done but go about her morning as though nothing were amiss. Most of the details would be taken care of by Dev and Harold. She wished they'd left something for her to do — something that would have occupied her nerve-ridden mind.

Once she was dressed, and Penny had finished with her coiffure, it was Peaches who finally provided her with a welcome distraction. Looking mournful and scratching at the door, the pup needed to go out. Grateful for some way to pass the time, Sophia opted for a walk in the garden. The gardens were not on the ocean side of the castle. She could pretend for a little while, anyhow, that today was the same as any other.

Four guests had been invited to serve as witnesses. Sophia and Harold had met with his cousin — Mr. White, Justin White, the vicar of the family — yesterday, and Harold had invited him. And then Dev had asked her to invite Lady Caroline.

She wasn't family, well, not direct family, anyhow, but a distant niece of one of the aunts. The other two members of their party would be Rhoda and St. John.

When Sophia arrived back at her chamber to hand Peaches into Penny's care, Harold awaited her there. Pale but confident, he offered his arm. "My lady." He bowed low and formal. "Shall we?"

He was being brave this morning.

Sophia forced herself to be cheerful. "I suppose we should, my lord." She curtseyed and then took his arm. As they made their way to the foyer, she glanced up at him. "You are certain, Harold?"

And with those words, he nodded. "Scared to death, Sophia, but more certain of this than anything I've ever done."

She swallowed hard.

He was going to go through with it.

The baskets, along with a few blankets, had been delivered to the foyer. Mr. White, dressed in a country suit, was already gathering one of the baskets up to carry, while Lady Caroline flirted with St. John.

Rhoda arrived behind them and scowled at St. John's attentiveness to the other lady. Sophia knew Rhoda was confused and angry, but for all of her own anxieties, could barely register the hurt in Rhoda's eyes.

Her own terror, yes terror, was so great that she later would not remember a single word spoken as they strolled along the path toward the beach. Mr. White offered Rhoda his free arm, and the three couples seemingly meandered aimlessly toward the cliffs.

Of course, nothing was being done aimlessly.

Even St. John had a determination about him.

They would not hike down to the beach.

No, of course not.

The plan was to take the alternate path, the one which just a few weeks before had been overgrown and unused.

Avoiding the area near the cave, Harold and Sophia led the group to the overlook, near the drop-off into the sea.

It was precisely where they'd planned to set up the picnic.

Playing hostess, Sophia mechanically distributed breads and cheeses and wine. The sun shone perfectly from above, and waves could be heard crashing into the rocks below.

Lady Caroline was shameless with St. John, preening and smoothing out her skirts on the same blanket as he. Mr. White was polite and considerate with Rhoda, but Rhoda had gone quiet. All in all, the luncheon began uncomfortably.

But that they knew how it would end…

If only it didn't have to end.

If only time could stand still.

But of course, it did not. The wine was drunk, the food consumed, and sighs of satiation mingled in between the occasional conversation.

And then it was to begin.

After eating, as designed, Harold rose to his feet and began shuffling around. He looked so very natural, but Sophia knew better.

He threw a few rocks off the edge of the cliff in something of a restless manner.

She was supposed to tell him to please be careful. *"Stay back from the cliff, Harold,"* she was supposed to say.

But she was unable to speak because once she said those words she knew, she knew, the sequence of events would be set into motion.

Once spoken, she could not take back the words that were to be Harold's cue.

"Stay back from the cliff, Lord Harold!" It was Rhoda, not Sophia, who set things in motion.

But Harold acted upon them as though Sophia had given the order. He walked up to the edge.

"It is not so steep," he said. And then he made some silly falling motions with his arms.

"Don't scare the ladies, Harold," Mr. White admonished him. "It isn't kind to give your new wife such a fright.

And then Mr. White glanced over at Sophia and winked. He was a kind and attractive gentleman.

But St. John goaded his brother. "Harold won't go near the edge. He's always been afraid of heights."

St. John knew!

Of course, he would have to know.

He'd jumped off the cliff with them long ago. Dev and Harold had not had a choice but to bring Prescott's heir into the plan.

And he was goading his brother. As though he really would have Harold fall to his death. As though he really did wish Harold gone from his life.

Her dear, dear friend looked over at her and then began walking backwards.

She would remember his sweet face.

The challenges he'd endured.

"Heights be damned!" he shouted. And then he looked as though he lost his footing, and a flicker of true horror seemed to sweep over his features. Was he changing his mind? Did he wish to change his mind?

And then he was gone.

Sophia jumped to her feet and tried to scamper toward the cliff. Mr. White, however, acted quickly and grasped her from behind, keeping her from the edge.

"Good God, St. John! Is he all right? Good God!" Mr. White's voice vibrated harshly behind her.

Sophia could not wrench herself out of the vicar's arms, and then Rhoda was there, holding her as well. Sophia wanted to look down into the water. She knew she would not see anything. For he would have dove by now and found the tunnel.

But she still had the urge to look for him.

To know that he was safe.

This was such a nightmare. Had Harold changed his mind?

Had he jumped safely?

"Oh God, Oh God, Oh God." She did not realize it at first, but she was saying the words aloud. "Oh, God, Harold." Her face was now pressed into Mr. White's jacket.

To make matters worse, Sophia could not block out the screaming. An incessant screaming had emerged from Lady Caroline the moment Harold disappeared.

St. John abandoned the hysterical lady to look over the edge. "I don't see him." His voice was stoic, emotionless. He sent Lady Caroline an irritated frown and then turned again to peer off the edge of the cliff. "Justin," he said, his voice breaking now, for all of a split second. "It's impossible... the rocks...the tide... And there is no way up... no way for him to save himself."

Perhaps the danger of Harold's actions had affected him, even for only a moment. They were brothers, for God's sake!

Sophia could not break free, even when Mr. White

ANNABELLE ANDERS

loosened his grip slightly. "Hold her." He pushed Sophia into Rhoda's arms. "I'll see if I can climb down."

"No!" Both Sophia and St. John shouted the words at the same time.

It was then that Sophia was able to drop to her hands and knees and crawl to the edge. "Harold!" she called, "Harold!" Her tears were not feigned. Her cries were not forced.

"It is too steep," St. John said even as the vicar removed his jacket.

"Please, don't. Oh, please do not!" This from Rhoda.

Mr. White stood beside Sophia and studied the water and then crouched down beside her. "Don't give up hope, my lady," he said. "We will bring out some ropes, more men. We can go down and see if he has perhaps found some safe place to swim to. Perhaps he can swim around to the beach." His hand landed on her shoulder. "Please, don't give up hope."

But she heard the hopelessness in his voice.

Sophia was then led back to the castle by Rhoda and Lady Caroline, who'd finally stopped her constant screaming. Mr. White provided escort while St. John went in seek of help.

The vicar was adamant a search begin as quickly as possible. St. John agreed, but seemed to do so reluctantly. He maintained that Harold could never have survived the fall.

A virtual army went out shortly after that, of servants, relatives and neighbors.

Sophia was taken to her room.

* * *

THEY WANTED Sophia to take a dose of laudanum, and although she'd refused at first, Penny finally convinced her to drink some of the distinctive-tasting liquid.

Already she regretted it.

And so now, here she sat, fighting sleep and waiting to hear from Dev.

Waiting to hear if her dead husband had made it out of the county safely.

They'd done it. They'd managed to fool everybody so far.

She was absolutely disgusted with herself.

She wondered if Harold was as well.

And Dev.

* * *

LESS THAN TWENTY-FOUR hours had passed since she'd last sat alone in this room, the eve before the accident. Even less time had passed since Dev had taken her to the brink of heaven and breathed new life into her.

Nothing was the same.

It was quiet, yes, the same as it had been last night, but even Peaches seemed to sense the sadness within the household.

Sophia felt as though somebody, somebody dear, truly had died. She'd had to watch as sorrow swept over her grace's face, into her shoulders, and gradually throughout her entire body when St. John delivered the news.

And then she'd endured his mother's embrace.

Harold had become something of a prodigal son over the past two weeks.

New hope had blossomed for him, for his life.

For the family that Sophia and he would supposedly have.

And now the prodigal son had been ripped away.

The duchess had not wept at first. Instead, she'd comforted Sophia. And Sophia had not had to feign tears.

This was horrible!

Tragic!

So very wrong!

She'd been unable to stifle a sob. And this had released her grace's tears.

But along with the sadness, the deep, heart-wrenching sadness, overwhelming guilt covered her. It almost felt as though she'd killed him herself.

When Harold's adjoining door opened, Sophia glanced up hopefully. It would be Dev — or Harold.

No, it would not be Harold. The laudanum's effects had befuddled her already.

But Dev perhaps… he would have news and encouragement for her.

Only it was not.

She should not have stopped locking her doors.

Dudley walked in.

"Where is everybody?" he demanded in a snide tone. He wore traveling clothes. "What's this? The servants are speaking of an accident? Have you killed off your husband already, Sophia? I never would have thought you had it in you."

Sophia was glad Peaches was not present. She'd gone outside with Penny for a constitutional. Hopefully, their errand would be quick, though. Hopefully, Penny would return any minute.

"What are you doing here?" she asked. Her tongue felt thick and fuzzy. And then she sniffed. "Get out of my room, Dudley."

Penny sometimes dawdled with Peaches. She would often stop and flirt with a house boy or chat with the cook until she could weasel a treat.

Sophia knew she was not safe. She was never safe alone with Dudley.

She needed to do something, anything to protect herself, but her limbs felt lethargic and heavy. She blinked, unable to summon any resistance. This was not good. Why was her stepbrother here? When had he arrived at Priory Point? She ought to scream, shout for help, but her mouth seemed disconnected from her brain.

"Your mother said the invitation had been extended to the Scofield family. Am I not your brother, Sophia? Oh, but no, you are Lady Harold now, are you not? But I am still your brother." He went to the door to the foyer, she assumed to lock it, but before he could do so, a light tap preceded Rhoda's head peaking in.

Rhoda had been devastated along with Sophia and had spent much of the afternoon comforting her.

What would she have done without her friend?

The instant Rhoda caught sight of Dudley, Sophia knew

she would be safe. Rhoda knew of Dudley's treachery and would make him go away.

"Mr. Scofield. I am *so glad* to have found you," she gushed. "The gentlemen are searching yet for Lord Harold. There is still hope. You are needed at the cliffs. All able-bodied gentlemen must assist in the search."

Dudley shrugged dismissively. "I can be of no help, Miss Mossant. I wouldn't know where to go."

But Rhoda was adamant. "I will show you." She extended her hand, as though she would guide him physically, if necessary.

Looking rebellious, but then apparently realizing he could not protest the request for his assistance, Dudley acquiesced reluctantly.

"I'll return shortly," Rhoda told Sophia, looking over her shoulder as she led Dudley away.

With a watery smile, Sophia nodded.

Oh, thank God! Oh, thank God!

Summoning the last vestiges of wakefulness inside of her, she managed to stumble to the door and lock it behind her friend. As she returned to the bed, she glanced out the window and barely caught sight of Rhoda leading Dudley toward the cliffs, along the path they'd taken earlier. The sun had begun to set, and shadows were already long and dark. It did not take long for them to disappear. An edge of fear for Rhoda touched her, but Dudley would not attack her friend out in the open with so many gentlemen nearby.

Thank you, Rhoda. Oh, thank you.

She stumbled back toward the bed.

She would lie down for a moment. When Dev came back, she would unlock the door for him.

But her will was not stronger than the drug she'd been given, and sleep overcame her within moments.

* * *

AFTER ASSURING himself of Harold's safe escape, Dev returned to discover a full-out search in effect. Several of the estate's manservants as well as gentlemen neighbors had climbed down as far as they could safely do so, and others were discussing taking a small craft into the cove.

Dev would kick himself if he could, for not considering this aspect of their plan.

This *accident* they'd pulled off would become all the more deplorable if someone attempting a rescue were to be hurt... or worse.

St. John was in his shirtsleeves and had already climbed down twice. He was doing his best to keep the vicar from doing so from a different angle.

The two of them had a fine line to walk. Making efforts to *rescue* Harold without allowing anyone else to put themselves at risk unnecessarily. The only way Dev could do this, as St. John had already done, was to take on the most dangerous aspects of the recovery effort himself.

And so, the rest of the afternoon was spent in a small craft, maneuvering himself and St. John around some deadly rocks in an *attempt* to find Harold... or, as many now conceded... Harold's body.

Sophia would be in turmoil if she knew of this.

They'd been unable to keep Justin from climbing partially down the cliff from various points, until only a little while ago. He'd finally been convinced by St. John that the family needed him back at the castle — for spiritual and emotional guidance.

He'd reluctantly acquiesced to their wishes.

He'd not been unaffected by the loss of their cousin. Many of those who'd come out to search for Harold grieved. Seeing this warmed Dev's heart, but it mostly made him ill at the deception of it.

Dev dreaded facing Harold's parents.

The duchess would be the worst.

He wondered how Sophia fared.

Left a few moments alone, St. John had briefly described how she'd truly seemed devastated when Harold went over. He also admitted that bringing Lady Caroline had been a mistake.

Oh, yes, even Dev had heard the screaming from below, inside of the cave.

It had gone on forever.

Miss Mossant had been the voice of reason, St. John had admitted. She'd comforted her friend in a calm manner and somehow prevented Justin from diving in after Harold.

They waited until sundown to call off the search.

It was too dangerous, they said. If Harold had survived, he would have been found by now.

Damp from spending so much time on the water, Dev entered the castle from one of the side doors. His arms and back ached from rowing. Blisters were forming on his palms.

He would assure himself that Sophia was holding up, and then he would go to his aunt and uncle.

When he entered the foyer that led to her room, consternation filled him. Both the maid and Miss Mossant sat outside. "Is Lady Harold well?" he asked Sophia's friend.

The protective maid glanced up at him and then toward her mistress' chamber door, but it was Rhoda who spoke. "She's locked the door. I think she's asleep from the draught the doctor gave her."

Dev did not like to think of Sophia drugged and locked inside alone. Removing a knife from his boot, he approached the lock and picked around inside of it. It was ancient and simple. It clicked open easily.

He could not go to her now, but at least she would not be alone. Glancing at Sophia's friend, he realized that the day's events had not been easy for anybody. The normally vibrant young woman looked pale and drawn. A haunted look lurked in her eyes. When he looked down at her hands, he realized they were shaking.

He kneeled in front of her and took both of her hands in his. They were freezing. "You must rest as well, Miss Mossant. Lady Harold will sleep. Allow me to escort you to your chamber."

"He was there, Captain. One second he was there, and then he was gone." Her lips looked almost bloodless. The shock of the accident must have been delayed. This was not the woman St. John had described earlier.

He assisted her to her feet. "Where is your chamber, Miss Mossant? Do you have a maid to assist you?"

She nodded but did not seem to hear him.

Penny pointed to the end of the hallway and spoke up. "Miss Mossant's room is at the end of the foyer, Captain Brookes." And then with a curtsey, she disappeared into Sophia's chamber.

Dev escorted Sophia's dearest friend to her own chamber and then turned to seek out his father and his aunt and uncle.

This devastation was not Harold's fault.

It was not Sophia's fault.

Dev would accept much of the blame as his own.

He had ignored the struggles Harold had endured all these years. He'd separated himself from the prejudices and not allowed himself to become involved. Perhaps, he could have done something. He could have said something...

Anything would have been better than this.

Slumped behind his desk, his uncle barely resembled himself. Tonight, he was not the Duke of Prescott, but a grieving father.

This surprised Dev.

At times, Harold had obsessed over the disappointment he'd been to his father. He had spoken of how their relationship had deteriorated to perfunctory greetings and encounters. Nonetheless, Dev should not have assumed his grace would be unaffected by his *son's death*.

It had been stupid of him.

Of course, his uncle believed he'd lost a son today.

A son with whom he'd failed to connect, a son whom he'd all but shunned, but a son, nonetheless.

And he not only *believed* he'd lost his son, he *had* lost him.

Harold and Stewart could never return.

As Dev walked across the room, his aunt rose from her chair and stepped into his arms.

He knew that she'd wept, but also that she would attempt to keep her dignity about her. She was a warm and loving woman, but she was also a duchess. She would not wish for her close family, even, to see her lose control.

"Oh, Devlin," she said as he embraced her, "thank you for trying to find him. But Lucas was right to call a halt to the search. It is too unsafe. These damn cliffs are too dangerous." She pulled away and dabbed at her eyes. "Poor, dear Sophia. She was inconsolable, I think. She loved him so dearly, and Harold loved her. At least he found love in his lifetime. My sweet Harold."

Dev swallowed hard.

"I'm so sorry, Aunt. What of you? You must be exhausted." He led her back to the chair and assisted her as she dropped into it. She seemed frailer this evening than she had been the night before; smaller even.

His uncle rose. "I will assist you to your chamber, my dear. Arrangements can be made tomorrow. Perhaps his body will wash ashore tonight…"

There would not be a proper funeral.

Mr. White and Dev's father remained, sitting across from one another at a table near the end of the room. Dev wondered if the other guests would stay for long. A memorial service would be in order. The entire household would fall into mourning.

His father approached him then and, without warning, wrapped him in a tight embrace.

It was nearly too much to bear. This deceit they'd all perpetrated. This involved more pain than they ever could have imagined.

They should have imagined it though.

Perhaps Sophia had. She'd shown more reluctance than any of them.

Thank God, she was upstairs, sleeping. He would do his best to shield her from some of it, if possible. But as the grieving widow...

Oh, hell, what had they done?

CHAPTER 21

A modiste arrived the following morning, not Madam Chantel, but a lesser-known seamstress from Dover, to make up several mourning dresses for Sophia, her grace, and a few of the family relatives who were staying on.

After that, the days passed in a blur.

Mr. Scofield and Sophia's mother departed for London shortly after Harold's services. Dudley must have left as well. Perhaps he'd decided the goings on at Priory Point were not festive enough for him. She wondered even, if seeing him had been a drug-induced nightmare. She'd meant to ask Rhoda but never got the chance. She, Mrs. Mossant, and her sisters had left Priory Point the day after Harold's accident. Sophia couldn't blame them.

Sophia was to remain with her in-laws.

It had been decided that she would travel with the duchess to the ducal country estate, Eden's Court, in Kent and remain there indefinitely. The duchess had need of her often and demanded much of Sophia's time.

The duchess, it seemed, found a special solace in spending time with her new daughter in-law. It was as though by talking with Sophia, speaking of her younger son's final days, she could keep him with her somehow. She often asked questions about Harold's last days, memories he'd shared with her. And then sometimes, she'd ask Sophia to repeat them again.

And so, Sophia spent hours with her mother-in-law, speaking of a man as though he was dead, knowing he was not, to a woman who mourned him greatly. It was the least she could do.

She'd crossed paths with Stewart on just a few occasions before he departed the estate. She knew plans had been set for him to rendezvous with Harold soon. But he, too, carried a look of sadness about him. Others would consider his melancholy his show of mourning. But Sophia recognized it far too easily. For she carried it with herself every day.

It was guilt. Plain and simple guilt.

She only wished she could flee as well. She wished she could run away with Dev, forget all of this had happened, and move on with their lives. But even if this was possible, she sensed a change between Dev and herself. An odd barrier of sorts had developed. To worsen matters, what with the duchess' kindly demands, Sophia had difficulty finding time for herself, when she might seek him out.

When she was not needed by the duchess, Penny hovered. The constant companionship was stifling.

It had been ten days since Harold's services, and the last remaining guests, as well as the duke's entourage, were scheduled to leave the next day. Sophia felt a sense of panic at not knowing Dev's immediate plans.

Was he going to return to Eden's Court with them? Would he go to Surrey, or London perhaps?

Wrestling with such uncertainties, Sophia gave into her restlessness and went on a walk with Peaches in the small garden behind the castle, the side that faced the moors. Penny was busy packing, and her grace was taking a nap following tea.

Sophia needed to find Dev but did not know where his chamber was. And she could not exactly ask after it. That would be most improper.

Newly widowed ladies did not seek out a gentleman in his quarters. If she were to ask after him, surely, it would be reported to her grace. Her grace was privy to all details pertinent to her family's well-being.

Oh, Dev!

As though her thoughts conjured him, she nearly burst into tears when she rounded a corner and saw him sitting on a conveniently placed stone bench.

They'd not been alone together for days.

And yet she felt hesitant.

It was Peaches who jumped at his legs until he lifted her onto his lap.

It was Peaches who reached to kiss his chin with her tiny tongue.

Dev tolerated the dog's energetic affection for a few minutes, smiling and patting her on the bum, before setting her back onto the ground. He looked sheepish when he glanced up at Sophia. Not one to forget his manners, he rose from the bench and gave her a half bow.

That was the moment she knew that he too, in fact, felt this… distance… between them.

It was not her imagination.

He took her hands in his.

"Sophia." He stared down at their entwined fingers as he spoke her name.

His hands were dear, so slim and beautiful, but so very strong and capable as well. She dipped into a half-hearted curtsey. With a sense that she was constantly being observed, Sophia glanced around nervously. "Dev," she said. Her heart beat anxiously.

Did he regret all of this? Was he already lamenting the promises he'd made?

Allowing him to pull her down to the bench with him, she searched his eyes for answers. "He did make the jump safely?" The thought had occurred to her that Harold had been hurt, or worse, and that this was why Dev seemed so distant.

"Oh, yes, of course." Dev set her fears to rest. He then rubbed her fingers for a moment before raising both of her hands to his lips. "I did not imagine in my wildest dreams how devastating this would be."

Sophia's eyes burned. "The duchess is overwrought at losing him."

Dev nodded. "She is, but Sophia, you must remember the risk Harold would have faced if he'd continued his relationship with Stewart, here in England."

"I know," she agreed. "I only wish the duchess could know that he lives."

"Harold and I discussed this. She could not have kept the truth from Prescott."

"I know." Sophia sighed. And then, "What's going to happen now?"

Dev finally looked her in the eyes. "We wait." He surprised her with what he had to say next, though. "I cannot remain in the same house with you any longer, unable to be with you, unable to speak to you freely… to touch you." Passion burned in his obsidian eyes. "And yet, it is too early for me to publicly declare my intentions. The family wounds are raw. I think you've realized this as well." Dev was quiet, and then he looked off into the distance. "I'm torn, Sophia, by my love for you and this sickness inside of me, this sickness at what we've done."

His words were terrifying. Was she losing him? She knew they were going to have to wait, but how long? Six months? A year? Forever?

She needed to say it first. "I think we ought to wait at least a year. No promises, Dev. No commitments to each other. Neither of us could have predicted the devastation of… all of this. After a year, then perhaps, if we both feel the same as we did… we can see…" Her heart split in two as she spoke. He was her true love.

A year would not change that.

Dev raised her hands to his lips once again.

"We will, Sophia. I'll prepare my estate for the two of us. We'll be together then…"

But Sophia shushed him. "We will see."

His eyes, which had been clouded in grief, suddenly burned clear and black, filled with intensity. "I will prepare my estate for us." And then he pulled her toward him and his lips pressed against hers.

This kiss was more a promise than a token of passion or affection. His hand had taken hold of the back of her head. When the kiss ended, he dropped his hands but pressed his forehead into hers.

Meeting his gaze, she realized that this man, this brave man, was holding back tears.

She did not want for him to make promises to her that he might not wish to keep. "Prepare your estate, and then we shall see." But she could not help but take hold of his hands. She pressed into him.

Perhaps her body would say the things she could not say out loud. Perhaps her body knew the words that her mind did not.

They sat this way for several moments. Sharing one another's essence.

"Sophia!" A voice in the distance caused them to pull apart.

It was the duchess.

With one last kiss, Sophia silently said goodbye.

She then scooped Peaches up and rushed away. "I'm coming, your grace!" she shouted. She would not look back. She could not look back. For if she were to do so, she would most likely burst into tears.

* * *

THE WEATHER the next day was not ideal for a journey. A drizzle had begun during the night, and by morning had turned into a full-force gale.

Sophia and her grace would wait another day but the duke, St. John, and Dev's father would depart as planned. They must attend to some business in London before joining Sophia and her grace in the country a few days later.

Normally, they would ride mounts, but, due to the weather, today they would travel by carriage. Dev had departed on horseback just before sunrise. The duchess had casually mentioned that he'd left for Dartmouth Place.

Sophia tried hard not to dwell on the physical distance he was putting between them, but that was nearly impossible. And the weather increased her anxiety. How could anyone travel in such a storm?

As her grace's knitting needles clinked rhythmically, lightning occasionally flashed in the room. Rain pelted the windows.

Perhaps Dev had been able to get ahead of this storm.

She hated to think of him out in the open, vulnerable to the elements on horseback. She hoped he would have the good sense to stop at an inn and not allow himself to get soaked and then chilled. She already felt his absence greatly.

"Sophia…" Her grace's voice interrupted her worrisome thoughts. "…I haven't wanted to bring this up, as it's something of a personal matter. But your maid hinted to me… Sophia, is it possible that you are increasing? Is it possible that you are carrying Harold's child?"

Damn Penny and her lack of discretion! Sophia had considered this.

She had missed her courses.

But upon consideration, Sophia was not overly concerned about it. For she had often been irregular, and it was not unusual for her to skip a month or two altogether. Stupid, blabbermouth Penny had merely given her grace hope for something that was highly unlikely. And Sophia was certain to disappoint the poor lady once again.

She smiled sadly. "Although, I suppose, it is possible, it is unlikely, I think."

But the duchess was persistent. "But it is possible? You have missed your courses, then?"

Was nothing to be kept private?

"This is not an unusual occurrence for me, your grace," she said gently. This was not something she'd ever expected to discuss with anyone. "And I've not sensed any other... changes."

Her grace dropped her eyes. Sophia had not realized the duchess would even consider such a thing. Although, what with the charade she and Harold had enacted, she ought to have realized such an expectation might exist.

"I know it must seem awfully presumptuous of me to bring this up with you, but when I thought it might be possible, I could not help but hope..."

Sophia dropped her book and moved to sit beside the older woman on the long sofa. The fire was warm and cozy. The room invited such confidences.

"No, no, I understand completely." And then for good

measure, "I, too, cannot help but hope... but I don't wish to raise expectations when I think it unlikely..."

Her grace nodded and leaned into her. "You have been such a comfort to me, Sophia. I cannot imagine what I would have done without your steady presence, without the knowledge that you made Harold so very happy in the end."

Sophia wished for the one-millionth time that she could tell the duchess the truth. That she could tell her Harold still lived and that he was happy as he was. That he'd not needed to change in order to find happiness and comfort. That he'd found love. That he was merely searching for place where he could have a life with Stewart, the man he loved.

But the lie must endure.

And then, in the distance, she heard the slamming of a door, anxious voices, and then quick footsteps running up the stairs. Without knocking, Priory Point's most ancient butler, Mr. Girard, pushed open the door looking rather flushed from his exertions.

Bowing, he entered, seeming somewhat at a loss. And then, "Your grace, my lady." He swallowed hard and then spoke again. "There's been a horrible accident. His grace's coach... it didn't make it down to the main road."

"Are they returning to Priory Point then, to the castle?" her grace asked, looking up from her knitting.

But he was shaking his head. His expression almost one of bewilderment. "That's just it, my lady. The coach fell into the sea."

* * *

THE REALITY of what the butler was saying washed over Sophia before her grace could contemplate the full extent of his words. "The... coach alone? What of the horses?" her grace asked curiously.

"Did the passengers escape?" Sophia jumped up. "What of the passengers?" she asked. But the somber servant continued shaking his head side to side.

"The outrider downstairs... he has traveled from the wreckage on foot to get here. He says none of the passengers could escape. He says he and the driver barely managed to leap off before it went over."

"His grace's carriage?" The duchess had apparently finally comprehended what the butler was trying to tell them.

And then the butler gathered his wits about himself. "The outrider is resting downstairs. Shall I send out more servants to verify what has happened?" And then he stood straight and thrust his chest out slightly. "I, myself, will travel down to see what has happened."

But Mr. Girard was elderly, and the roads were wet, and muddy, and slippery...

The duchess hadn't moved, and so Sophia answered him. "No, Mr. Girard, send Richards and Quimbly on horseback." They were the outriders who had stayed back to travel with the women tomorrow. They were burly, physical men of the world. They were employed as much for their protection as for any duties they might perform on a regular basis. "Tell them to be cautious of the stability of the road — we do not want any further calamities — but to discover what has happened. We will send down a few additional footmen to assist in a rescue, if that is possible. And to send for a magistrate so that—" What did magistrates do? They dealt with legal issues. They investigated crimes. "—to see that the accident is investigated properly and to ensure all is done that can be done."

Surely this was not happening. It was not possible!

Sophia touched her forehead. She was in fully uncharted territory. Oh, Lord, she wished Dev were still here. Oh, God, or Harold, even.

Who had been in the duke's coach?

The duke, of course.

And she believed St. John had chosen to keep out of the rain as well.

Good, God! And Dev's father.

They needed to locate Dev. "And Mr. Girard. Send… send…" Oh yes, the stable master. He was familiar with Dev. He would know the route Dev had been going to take to Dartmouth Place. "Send Henry after Captain Brookes. He left for Surrey early this morning and must be notified immediately."

"What if the road is impassable, my lady?"

What if the road…?

"Tell him to find a way around it. Dev — Captain Brookes — must return at once. We need answers right now. We need to know exactly what has happened, and if those gentlemen need assistance, we must get it to them as soon as possible!" Good Lord, she'd go herself if she had to!

God help her, she hoped assistance would be of some benefit at this point.

"Very well." The butler seemed relieved to have been given instructions. He bowed stiffly and disappeared as quickly as he'd entered.

Sophia did not move for several minutes; rather, she just stood there frozen and listened as the household stirred into action.

It sounded as though an army were being deployed.

Only when the sounds died down did she turn and face the duchess.

"Sophia, can this possibly mean what I think it does?" The duchess was white as a sheet. Her eyes were glassy as she shook her head side to side.

This could not be happening.

Sophia clasped her hands together to keep them from shaking. "Let's wait to see what Richards and Quimbly discover. The footman could well have been mistaken. What with the fog and the rain..." But what if it wasn't a mistake?

The duchess had dropped her knitting into her lap and stared straight ahead, eyes unfocused. This proud, compassionate woman had already endured so much recently.

This cannot be happening.

Forcing her feet to move, Sophia walked over to sit beside her mother-in-law. The emptiness in her grace's eyes was frightening. Sophia took the duchess' hands in hers and, finding them ice cold, rubbed them for warmth. "We mustn't jump to any conclusions at this point, your grace," she said firmly. "You and I, we must be strong together. We will pray, and we will hope. Please, your grace, do not give up hope."

And then the duchess looked into her eyes. "If they are gone, then Sophia, you are my only hope. I will pray every day that you are carrying Harold's child. For if you are not, then I truly will have lost them all. My entire family."

Sophia swallowed hard.

CHAPTER 22

*L*eaving Sophia was one of the hardest things Dev had ever done.

Her eyes had pleaded with him, and yet her words had pushed him away. She'd told him she did not want a commitment from him. She was fearful their feelings might change with the passage of time.

His would not. He'd been with other women, even thought himself in love a time or two. But he'd never felt for anyone the way he did for Sophia. It was as though when he found her, he'd discovered a part of himself that had been missing his entire life.

No, his feelings for her would not change.

But he could not be so confident in her feelings. She was young, beautiful, and, for the first time in her life, would be free of her family's manipulations. Although the duke and duchess hovered over her now, she would eventually be allowed a sense of freedom. She would meet new and interesting people, new and interesting men, and be allowed liberties she'd not known as a debutante.

The mere thought of this nearly had him turning his horse back toward Priory Point to lay claim to her.

But he would not.

He'd made decent time despite the rain and the poor conditions of the road. The journey was not a comfortable one, though. He traveled alone, but with a second mount to carry his bags. Rain crept under his collar and into the clothing he wore beneath his coat. If he tilted his head just so, a pool of cold water dribbled off the brim of his hat.

The horses, he knew, were nearing their limits. With no sun to tell the time of day, he guessed it to be late in the afternoon. He would stop at the next inn. The mud was not only dangerous for himself, but for the horses. Rather than simply changing them out and attempting to travel late into the evening, he would stop early for the night.

If he came across a suitable inn, that was.

He was already becoming soft, out of the army for just over a month.

He laughed ironically at himself.

Before he could ruminate over what he was going to do without Sophia in his life for an entire year, a sign for an inn ahead beckoned. Turning his head, water poured off his hat down the front of his coat.

He would stop.

He turned off the highway toward the two-story building and rode around back to the stables. Fortunately, a hostler, who was handy to care for Dev's cattle, was able to inform him that rooms were available to let.

Although his heart was heavy, he would be grateful. Harold was safe, Sophia was free, and time would soothe matters over. And he had easily found a bed in which to sleep, which wasn't always the case in such poor travelling conditions.

A hot bath, a good night's sleep, and Dev would cover a greater distance tomorrow. Perhaps, if the rain stopped and the roads dried up... Dev scraped the mud from his boots outside and then stepped inside to pay the innkeeper.

Coming out of the rain reminded him of the day he'd met Sophia in the park, of ducking into the gazebo with her. Would she ever be far from his thoughts?

Was he doing the right thing? He could not swoop in so soon. He hadn't much choice, really.

After a tepid bath, Dev climbed into the bed and determined to put such thoughts aside.

Surprisingly, he slept.

"Captain Brookes! Captain Brookes!" A pounding at the door roused him in an instant. It was not the voice of a friend or reveler who shouted. It was panic-stricken and anxious. He knew that sound all too well.

Jumping up, he pulled on his breeches and opened the door before the entire inn was awakened.

Henry stood before him, covered in mud, quite literally. The only clean part of him was the whites of his eyes — which held a foreboding message of bad news.

"You are needed, sir, at Priory Point," he rasped in a loud whisper.

Some of the other guests had stuck their heads out of their doors to shush the late-night messenger.

Dev beckoned for Henry to enter his room. Mud trailed after him. Dev's night of rest was not to be. If he was needed at Priory, he would leave as soon as the horses could be readied. Glancing at the window, he was at least relieved to see that the rain had ceased. They would only have darkness and mud to contend with on the journey back.

Was it Sophia? Had something happened to her? Or had Harold returned? He could not imagine what disaster had befallen so much so that his immediate presence would be called for. It must be Sophia.

"Tell me what's happened." He lit a few candles in the room and then pulled the door closed behind him. Not much light came in from the windows as the moon was still enshrouded in clouds.

Henry looked at the floor and then shook his head. "There has been another accident, sir," he said. But the words did not flow easily.

"What kind of accident?" Dev's chest tightened. God, not Sophia.

"The duke's coach, with St. John and also your father, sir." And then Henry looked up at him with an abundance of compassion on his face. "They've all perished. The road washed away, and their carriage fell into the sea."

Dev replayed the words in his mind to be certain he had not misunderstood what the stable master was trying to impart to him.

This hardly seemed possible.

And yet, Dev considered the conditions when he, himself, had set off earlier that day. Soggy, wet… even on a bright and sunny day that road had always seemed more than a little precarious.

Nothing like this had ever happened before, however, and the castle had sat perched on the point for hundreds of years.

His father?

He swallowed hard. Henry would not have come all of this way to give him such news if it were inaccurate.

"Is the road passable now?" It must be, if Henry had made it through. "Did her grace send you?"

Henry was shaking his head. "Not passable by carriage, barely by horses. We have workers shoring it up with rocks now." The obviously exhausted man paused and then remembered Dev's second question. "It was Lady Harold who sent for you."

Sophia… was alone at the castle. She was alone with his aunt — a woman who was under the impression that her youngest son had died not two weeks ago.

"All of them?" He could not help but to ask.

Henry's face expressed regret and sadness. "The only ones to escape were the driver and one of the outriders. Even the horses went in."

At these last words, Dev thought the man might lose control of his emotions.

Henry had cared for the duke's cattle his entire life. Those horses would have been like children to him.

His father was gone. His uncle. His cousin. "All three of them were in the coach?" Somehow, he needed to hear it again. It did not seem possible. "The duke, St. John, and my father? None of them were on horseback?"

Henry continued shaking his head. "The rain was heavy. They said they'd ride in comfort until the storm passed. They were going to London and then on to Kent. The ladies remained at Priory Point and planned on traveling tomorrow."

Dev ran his hand through his hair. Thank God, the ladies hadn't been with them. It could so easily have been Sophia. He pushed such a thought out of his mind.

Still... this... this... loss. It was nearly inconceivable. He could not dwell on his personal emotions right now.

The women were virtually trapped at the castle.

Her grace would be beside herself.

And Sophia... sweet, innocent, loving Sophia... would be caught in the middle of it all.

Devil take him, he needed to contact Harold.

Harold was the duke now!

That had to change everything. Wouldn't it? Wouldn't the death of his father and brother be cause to return? To stage some miraculous reappearance?

Dev looked up and realized that Henry awaited instruction.

The man needed to get some rest before taking to the road again. Dev pulled on his shirt and gestured toward the basin. "Clean up and rest a little, Henry. I'll have the horses readied and see about locating sustenance for the journey. I need to attend to a few matters before we leave, and then I'll send a maid to wake you." After pulling his boots on, he forced himself to sweep away the pangs of loss threatening to engulf him. "Are you up to it, Henry, or do you need to wait until morning?"

But Henry would not wait. "Practically morning already. Send the maid when you are ready." He grimaced. "At least the rain is stopped now. I'd not let you travel alone, you being the new duke and all."

Oh, hell!

He needed to reach Harold! And as quickly as possible. For if Harold and Stewart's packet had set sail already, it could take months — years possibly — to track them down.

"Don't say that," Dev said. "Don't call me that."

He could make no explanations to the lifelong retainer his uncle had employed. But he was not the duke. Had not ever really even considered it.

He stuffed his belongings into his knapsack and pulled on his jacket. Thankfully, it had dried by the fire the chambermaid had lit before he'd lain down. "I'll be back within an hour."

Looking at him with sympathy, Henry nodded.

The innkeeper was angry at first when Dev woke him, but after he heard about the tragic accident, his demeanor changed from that of annoyance to obsequiousness.

"I need a messenger to travel to Dover. The matter is of the utmost importance. Time is of the essence."

Dev had written a message in code to the false name he knew Harold had taken on. Dev wanted to punch something, the wall, a door. He realized that most likely, Harold and Stewart's ship had already sailed. His only hope was that the weather might have delayed it.

They could not continue to perpetuate the lie of Harold's death now, could they? With explicit instructions, he sent the message off in hope that it reach his cousin in time. He could not even begin to fathom the implications… What with the guilt he and Sophia had experienced, he could only wonder at how Harold would handle news of this very real tragedy.

It was nearly four in the morning, and most of the inn's staff were yet abed. Dev exited the inn and made his way around to the outbuildings. He would assist the hostlers who'd been awakened when Henry arrived. It would give him something to do with his hands, with his restlessness, while he allowed the other man some rest.

THE OUTRIDER HAD NOT BEEN MISTAKEN.

Everything he'd originally reported had been verified.

Since the road up to the Priory was still considerably dangerous, Sophia could not send for a physician to tend to the duchess. Instead, she'd directed the housekeeper to locate some of the laudanum that had been given to her shortly after Harold's *death,* and had a dose administered to the duchess. The magnitude of the woman's loss was unfathomable.

Nonetheless, a doctor could not be called in.

Without getting any sleep herself, Sophia found herself called upon to attend to the magistrate who arrived early the next morning. He'd asked for the duchess, but Sophia explained to him that her grace was indisposed. He could discuss matters with her. He'd met her once before, when she'd described to him how her husband had fallen off the side of a cliff.

The pity that gushed from him was not welcome.

She did not deserve pity. She did not welcome his compassion.

She was a fraud, a villain even. She invited him to enter and be seated, and then asked Mr. Girard to bring tea.

It was all rather civil really.

The magistrate pulled out the notebook she remembered from the last time he'd spoken to her and began reading off some of the details he had scribbled earlier.

Apparently, all of the bodies had been recovered.

They'd managed to attach a hoist to the wreckage, detach the front axle, and pull it to a level area above the water. Some rescuers had been lowered, and the bodies had then been lifted out. He assured her that the deaths occurred quickly; he was mostly certain. The impact had done most of the damage. He did not think any of the gentlemen had drowned. The bodies had been pulled up on the village side where the road had collapsed. He asked her if she had any instructions as to what the duchess would have him do with them, since they could not be brought back to the castle.

"Eden's Court," she said. "They must be transported to the duke's estate in Kent." The family plot was in Kent. The duchess had lamented to her several times that they could not bring Harold home with them, where he belonged. "Whatever the cost, I am certain that is where the duchess would have them laid to rest."

"Do you know where we can locate Captain Brookes?" he questioned her then. "Our records show he is the heir. What, with your husband gone, and the marques, as well as the duke and his brother. Captain Brookes must be notified immediately. We've deployed messengers to London in order to begin all necessary legal proceedings."

Sophia's head spun.

Dev? Dev was the duke now?

Oh, dear God, but he wasn't.

Harold was.

In that moment, she was severely tempted to tell the magistrate everything. Harold must be found. He must be intercepted before leaving England for God knew where. He was all his mother had left.

"I've sent for Captain Brookes already," she heard herself say. Suddenly, for the first time, tears threatened to escape from behind her eyes. What a quagmire they'd created. This poor, poor, family had been decimated, and all because of her!

If she hadn't married Harold, none of them would have come to Priory Point.

If she hadn't assisted Harold in staging his death, they would not have been on the road yesterday.

And if they hadn't been on the road yesterday, they would not have been killed.

Even now, she worried for the duchess' health. Although her grace was by no means an elderly woman, the toll of all of this was enough to cause even a young woman to become frail and despondent.

Could a person die of a broken heart?

Sophia wondered.

Would it never end?

"My lady? My lady?" The magistrate was speaking to her still.

"I'm sorry. Pardon me?" She sat up straight and schooled her features into impassiveness.

The housekeeper entered after softly tapping on the door. She carried a setup with tea and morning victuals.

Sophia nodded as the servant set the tray down on a nearby table.

Sophia was supposed to do something now.

Oh, yes. It was her duty, as hostess, to serve the tea.

She stood, for all the world as though this were any polite call, and then poured the magistrate's tea. She remembered from his other visit that he took his tea with just a splash of milk.

She methodically prepared the familiar beverage and placed it on the table beside the magistrate. Then, lifting the plate of pastries, she offered it to him as well.

He thanked her profusely as he took three of them from the platter. When Sophia turned to pour her own tea, for just a moment, she forgot how she took it.

Hot, she said to herself. Like the depths of hell would be when she arrived.

"I believe the road can be made somewhat passable for horses and such, if my lady and her grace wish to depart for Eden's Court as well. Would you like me to make arrangements for a carriage to collect you both there, on the other side of the landslide?"

The bodies would need to be buried quickly after

arriving in Kent. They would have to be transported with ice, a great deal of it, as matters stood. To delay the funerals would be... unpleasant. No time could be wasted.

Sophia and her grace must leave right away.

"It was a landslide then? Is that what they call it?"

The magistrate grimaced. "The mud gave way, causing land above and below the road to collapse into the sea. I imagine it would be accurate to refer to it as such, yes." He answered her and then put the entirety of the last morsel he'd procured for himself into his mouth.

It truly was amazing, she thought, that the bodies had been recovered. A morbid part of her wondered in what condition they had been. "Their necks were most likely broken when they fell," she said softly, answering her own question.

Chewing, the magistrate nodded in agreement.

And then she made a decision. "Leaving for Eden's Court will be best for the duchess."

Would Dev arrive soon? She hoped Henry had been able to locate him. It was a long road to Surrey. With many inns along the way he could easily be missed.

But she could not afford to wait.

She needed to get the duchess away from this horrid, horrid place.

She needed to get herself away from it.

She did not think she would feel an ounce of regret if she were never to see the sea again.

Or the cliffs.

The bodies would need to be put into the ground as expediently as possible.

The bags had been packed earlier, before, when they had planned to meet up with the duke a few days later, at Eden's Court. But what of the duchess? Would she be able to get down the road on horseback? How would she react to passing the carnage that had stolen her husband and his heir away from her?

And Dev's father.

She mustn't forget Dev's father had perished as well.

And aside from the protocol of following the bodies to their final resting place, Sophia had a pressing need to flee the castle. If only for her own sanity.

"We will meet you there at three in the afternoon." She spoke more decisively now. It was early in the morning yet. She would rouse the duchess and persuade her as to the necessity of their departure. "Thank you, for your thoughtful consideration," she added. "Would you be so kind as to make any other necessary arrangements with Mr. Girard?"

The man nodded and then stood, apparently knowing he'd been dismissed.

As he excused himself, Sophia looked out the windows at the craggy cliffs that marred the horizon. If it was up to her, she'd have the castle fall into the sea.

After they'd all left, of course.

Sophia arranged for tea and breakfast to be sent up to her grace and then waited half an hour before tapping on the duchess' chamber door. As the maid invited her in, she was more than a little relieved to see the duchess up and dressed. She seemed much more alert than Sophia had thought she'd be.

Yes, her mother-in-law had regained control of her emotions, for now, at any rate. The duchess had hundreds, thousands of empty days and lonely nights in her future. For now, she wore a black crepe gown and sat on a chaise lounge with a cup of tea.

Her posture was rigid and her eyes somewhat dull. "Sophia, you will forgive me, dear? For abandoning you to the magistrate this morning? As soon as I heard he'd been here, I realized I'd already neglected my duties, leaving you to cope with them all alone."

Sophia was quick to reassure her, although she did feel a tremendous sense of relief, knowing the duchess was not, after all, incapacitated by her grief. "Not at all, your grace."

"I was told you arranged to have the bodies taken to Eden's Court, but I've corrected your orders. A service will be held in London, at St. George's Cathedral. It must be held in London. His grace loved London and considered it his home more than anywhere else in the world. St. George's, of course, will be packed. The streets will be lined with mourners. It must be in London.

"And then, afterward, we'll proceed to Eden's Court where there will be another service, and the burial of course."

As Sophia listened to the duchess' detailed plans, she realized that maids were efficiently collecting items from around the room. The duchess was preparing to leave Priory Point. Sophia could have cried, knowing that all of this was not to be her burden to carry alone. And as soon as she thought that, guilt set in again. Such a burden would not exist but for her own selfishness.

"I told the magistrate we would meet him at the... land-slide... so we could transfer to carriages there. At three o'clock this afternoon. Does that meet with your approval?" she asked, realizing that the duchess was once again, fully in control.

When the duchess had stopped talking, she'd gotten a faraway look in her eyes and had been gazing across the room, unfocused. Sophia's words had seemed to spring her back to life again. "That will be fine. The magistrate will know that we require several carriages. Thank you, again, dear, for accommodating him earlier today. Did you sleep last night? It is my greatest wish that you not overtire yourself. A lady in your condition must take special care. If you feel uncomfortable, or ill, at any time during our jour-ney, you must tell me. We will stop. The dead shall be honored and buried, but now, we must look to the future. We must protect the new life you are carrying."

At these words, Sophia drew her brows together. "But your grace—"

"Sophia, dear, until you are given evidence indicating otherwise, we are going to move forward as though you are, in fact, increasing."

"But—"

"We mustn't waste any more time. It is nearly noon already, and I've a list of instructions to dictate and have sent ahead of us."

Sophia rose.

She had been excused.

Not in any mood to argue with a determined duchess, Sophia left the room more confused than before. She no longer would be expected to handle the details of the crisis. No, because, apparently, she was now with child.

When a duchess declares you with child, does that make it so?

She touched her abdomen with her right hand. It felt the same as it always had. She felt the same as she always had.

Was it possible?

But, oh, the duchess believed any child would be Harold's! Even if she were increasing, the child would be Dev's! With black hair, most likely, and black eyes! Harold had blue-gray eyes and light brown hair. Sophia's hair was blond and her own eyes blue. How could one explain such a discrepancy as that?

Surely it would be obvious.

Oh, dear Lord, what a mess she'd made.

This was what lying did.

The cock and bull story they'd told had led them into all of this.

She entered her chamber and looked around, certain she would never return. Not if she had any choice in the matter, anyhow.

Peaches was napping on a chair and opened her lids lazily for just a moment before returning to her slumber.

Closing her own eyes, Sophia recalled the lovemaking she'd shared here with Dev. Their passion had burned, like a raging wildfire, for a brief time in the high, four-poster bed. She truly believed that those moments had carried her to the pinnacle of happiness.

Had they been worth it?

Oh, yes.

And that first time, in London, on her wedding night.

They had spent two nights together in exchange for the demolition of an entire family.

Had they created a baby?

Sophia studied herself in the mirror. She had the same face, the same hair, the same eyes and lips and cheeks. But she was not the same girl who'd gotten engaged this summer.

Her eyes were haunted, her lips not so easy to smile, and her heart now filled with secrets and despair instead of hope.

But she was also now a woman who had loved. A woman who had known the heights of passion.

She was a different person now.

"I've everything packed, my lady." Penny had somehow slipped inside without Sophia hearing a sound. This was not the first time she'd done that. The Prescott servants were all that way, like a camp of sleuths and spies, loyal in all matters to the duchess.

"Very good, Penny," Sophia said. How on earth had she and Harold and Dev managed to fool all of them?

"Do you wish to change into traveling clothes? Your riding habit, perhaps, since the first part of the journey is to be on horseback?" Sophia glanced down at her dress. It was made up of a stiff, black crepe material. It had none of the style of any of the new gowns Madam Chantal had made up for her before the wedding. Her new habits were all made up of bright colors — yellow, one red, and one an emerald green.

"I will wear black," she said. "I want you to burn everything else. Better yet, leave them here."

"Of course, my lady, but I've already packed—"

"Leave them," Sophia said forcefully. "Bring only the mourning gowns. I never want to see the other dresses again." Her voice forbade any argument.

Her maid looked aghast. Sophia knew it was a common practice to hand down one's unwanted gowns to servants, but she did not wish to ever see any of them again. They were reminders of her selfishness, her own greed to manipulate life in her favor.

"Leave them," she said again. And then on a sigh. "You can retrieve them for yourself the next time you are here." Let her maid believe they would not be going to waste. Sophia, knew, though, that she would never return to Priory Point.

Ever.

Penny grimaced. Perhaps the maid wished to never return either. Of course, the servants experienced their own grief.

Grief was everywhere.

CHAPTER 23

One would have thought that the private, collapsed road was the height of London traffic, for all of the carriages and horses and activity. Dev arrived just as the duchess and Sophia were being carefully led around the landslide.

Of course, they would be going to London. He'd passed the caravan of coffins a few hours earlier. The coffins had been packed in ice and the coaches covered in black.

The duke and St. John.

And his father.

Dev dismounted and made his way around the awaiting vehicles. His aunt, he recognized easily by her posture and the dignity with which she carried herself.

Behind her, he'd had to search behind the black veil, in order to recognize Sophia. Peaches was tucked beneath her chin.

Burly servants escorted the ladies around the nearly non-existent road.

This was where it had occurred.

The dried mud preserved the marks where the wheels had slid over the side, and others, from the rescue effort — until the next rainstorm anyhow. Apparently, a large rock had given way from below, destabilizing the road above it. They hadn't stood a chance.

His aunt, he noticed, avoided looking in the direction of the sea. She stared forward, and therefore, saw him first.

"Dev," she said.

He rushed toward her and took her hands in his.

"Oh, Dev. Such a loss, such a devastating loss for us all!"

He bent forward and kissed her cheek. She stood rigid. She had dawned the mantle of the duchess. "Aunt, I am so sorry, so very sorry." For everything. God, how sorry he was.

He turned toward Sophia, who had finally torn her gaze away from the large gap where the road had once been. "My lady," he said. He tried to speak to her with his eyes, if ever he could. *"This is not your fault,"* he would have them say. *"I will find Harold,"* he would want her to know.

I love you.

He could barely see her eyes, hidden by the black veil. She curtseyed in his direction. "Captain," she said softly.

"We are headed for London. There is no time to waste..." His aunt spoke again, all decisiveness. "...as I'm sure you must perceive."

He'd expected this. The duke's servants who had been traveling with the bodies had informed him of her grace's plans.

"I am here to escort you," he spoke formally. He would

not allow the ladies to undertake such a journey alone. Not in these circumstances. Not as long as he breathed.

And then his aunt touched his sleeve and leaned in to speak to him more privately. "We wish to arrive in a timely fashion, of course, but will stop if Sophia is overtired. A lady in her condition must endure as little discomfort from travel as possible."

He could not help but widen his eyes at her words.

A lady in her condition?

A lady in her *condition?*

Dev glanced over at Sophia. She'd not heard his aunt's words. She merely stood, looking out at the sea, patiently waiting to move along, it seemed.

If Sophia was in a delicate condition, why then…

He could hardly bear considering…

She was so tiny. Would she bear a child easily?

Suddenly, the only emotion that even bore consideration was a tremendous fear and worry for her health. It was his child she was carrying in her very precious body. Everything in life that mattered to him was embodied in the small woman shrouded before him in black.

Sensing his stare, she glanced at him. For the first time, Dev could see clearly into her eyes, in spite of the black transparent material.

"I love you," they seemed to say. *"It's hopeless though."*

But he would ignore the despair.

"Ladies, let me assist you into your carriage and let us get off the side of this damn cliff."

At his words, his aunt actually chuckled. Dev took her

arm and led her to the waiting carriage. As a footman opened the door, she released his arm and climbed in. He then turned toward Sophia and took her by the elbow and hand. She wore long black gloves, despite the warmth of the day. He would have kissed her hand, but the duchess watched. So instead, he tipped his head forward and inhaled her fragrance.

"My heart is yours, Sophia" was all he had time to say. But he'd needed to tell her desperately. He'd needed to give her the only thing that he could.

Oh, God, was she truly carrying his child?

Before he knew it, he'd assisted her into the carriage and closed the door.

All around them, servants cautiously crossed the ravaged road with trunks and cases filled with the duchess' and Sophia's belongings. Dev recognized Sophia's lady's maid as a footman assisted her into a different coach nearby.

It was with an abundance of caution that the long caravan of ducal vehicles rolled down the remainder of the cliffside road.

HE'D TOLD her that his heart belonged to her, and then he'd said her name. Sophia. It always sounded like a whisper when he said it. She had his heart, but she would never have him. It was impossible now!

Sophia did not sit beside the duchess, instead choosing to ride with her back facing the horses. Peaches was on her best behavior, as though even she realized she must show respect while traveling with a duchess.

Sophia had grown to love her mother-in-law, and yet, she felt more stifled than ever. The duchess had closed the curtains covering all of the windows, casting the interior in darkness.

When one traveled with a duchess, one did not expect explanations. If she had been traveling with Rhoda, or with Emily or Cecily, they would have discussed with each other. Should we close the drapes? Do you mind if I close the drapes? A duchess simply closed them.

Sophia rested her head against the seat-back and closed her eyes.

"My heart is yours, Sophia."

Oh, his touch, his nearness had been so brief. How could she crave him with such intensity, knowing what the two of them had done? The duchess was not two feet away from her, and all Sophia could think of was how much she desired to be caught up in his arms.

Emptiness filled her.

And yet, his voice had awakened her again.

Sophia hugged herself with her arms and was surprised to feel a tenderness in her breasts. *Dev... oh, Dev.*

"You should try to sleep, my dear. You will find a pillow stored under the seat if you pull the cushion up." The duchess' suggestion was spoken in such a way that brooked no argument.

Sophia slid sideways and pulled out the pillow. If she slept, she could escape all of this for a short while. The uncertainty, the fear, the guilt. She plumped the velvet-covered cushion and tried to make both herself and Peaches comfortable. She dared not remove her shoes or pull her feet up onto the seat. She was riding with a duchess, for goodness' sake.

But the pillow was soft, and she'd not slept much the night before.

And.

And she knew that Dev was nearby, watching over them as they crossed the countryside to London.

Nothing terrible could happen with him watching over them.

She slept soundly for the first time since they'd gotten the horrible news.

* * *

Upon hindsight, Sophia was astonished at how naïve she had been when she'd told the magistrate to transport the bodies directly to the duke's country estate.

She'd failed to consider that her father-in-law, as cold and manipulating as he'd seemed with her, and as cruel and unaccepting as he'd been to Harold, was one of England's most powerful and beloved dukes.

This had become more apparent as they passed through one village after another on their journey back to London. For as the news of the tragedy spread, onlookers and crowds periodically lined the road to watch as their coach rolled through. And as they neared London, the crowds grew larger.

It was nearly as frightening as it was humbling.

ANNABELLE ANDERS

When they arrived at Prescott House, after two long days on the road, death in the household was readily apparent by the black wreath upon the door, and the black crepe-covered windows.

Mr. Evans informed the duchess upon arrival that the funeral furnishers had cared for the bodies, and for this one night, they had been laid out in a room in the front of the house. The funeral proceedings would be tomorrow. It went without saying that the room would be kept cold.

Dev had stoically supported the duchess and made all arrangements for their rooms, their meals, and the care of the cattle, servants, and coaches while travelling. He'd often ridden ahead, the duchess had told her, to give instructions and confirm that her grace's orders were being carried out properly. His military training and habits were evident in his natural leadership and self-discipline. Sophia knew he'd rarely rested.

Entering Prescott House, Sophia immediately covered her nostrils with her handkerchief. That smell... must be the oils used to care for the bodies. It grew stronger as they approached the drawing room.

Sophia followed, uncertain as to what she should do. And then the duchess, leaning heavily upon Dev, paused and turned around. "You mustn't, Sophia. Your condition. It would be too upsetting."

But Sophia saw something on Dev's face. Emptiness, pain. She could not leave him alone. Even if all she could offer was her presence.

"I am fine," Sophia insisted.

When, in fact, she did not feel well. She felt tired, and

faint, and hungry, yet not. But how could she abandon him at a time such as this? She could not, of course.

She motioned for them to continue. After a moment's hesitation, the duchess pinched her lips and then nodded.

They first stepped up to view the duke.

Someone had dressed his grace's corpse in a resplendent uniform consisting of an abundance of lace, golden embroidery, and jewels. His beringed, clay-like hands crossed one another upon his chest.

His face had been powdered and painted.

He did not resemble the man she'd nearly hated while he had been alive. Despite the powder and rouge, his face was slack, his skin sallow. Sophia turned away and took a deep breath from inside of her handkerchief.

When she did so, she was confronted by the sight of St. John, similarly resting.

Rhoda!

She'd not had even a moment to consider that her dearest friend had developed an attachment to one of the men who had been killed. Did Rhoda know? Of course, she must!

She would be devastated! She'd practically admitted to being in love with him. Oh, dear, poor Rhoda. Sophia choked back a sob at the thought. Now was not the time to show such distress.

St. John's corpse appeared eerily similar to that of the duke. Less wrinkles, yes, and no graying hair, but the bone structure of the face resembled the duke's almost perfectly.

Sophia had always thought Harold took after his

mother in looks. Viewing these two men, confirmed her opinion.

And then, a third body.

Dev had abandoned the duchess standing near the duke and moved toward his father.

Sophia wanted badly to follow him, to wrap her arms around his waist and give him what little comfort she could.

She took a few silent steps away from St. John and stood behind Dev. It was all she could do. She hoped he understood. She hoped he could feel her comfort, her love, in such a tiny, insignificant gesture.

The duchess had stepped away from her husband and turned to view her firstborn son.

The room was so very cold.

A clammy sweat broke out on Sophia's forehead as another, stronger wave of nausea swept over her.

And then a few familiar elderly ladies slipped into the room, approached the duchess, and embraced her quietly. Sophia remembered them from before the wedding, and later, as guests at Priory Point. Both had departed before the road washed out. They were cousins or sisters or somehow related to the duchess.

They whispered their condolences and encouraged the widow to lean upon them. "Come, dear, you must be exhausted." They led her from the room, only to be halted at the last moment.

"Sophia, dear, you must rest as well."

But Sophia could see that the duchess was distracted by her family.

"I'm going to say a few prayers, your grace, if you do not mind. I will find my own way to my chamber." The one she had supposedly shared with Harold. The place where she'd discovered a passion within herself that she'd never known existed.

The duchess considered her for just an instant and then nodded.

Prayers? Ha! Surely Sophia had secured her place in hell thrice over by now.

When the large door closed behind them, Sophia moved to stand beside Dev.

She took his hand in hers. At first it was lax, and then, after a brief hesitation, he squeezed hers back.

"I'm so sorry."

She'd known he loved and respected his father. His father had been all he'd ever known. He'd lost his cousins, his uncle, and now his father. Not ever knowing his mother, he was truly all alone now, but for his aunt... and herself.

"My father would have approved of Harold's decision. He was convinced Harold was in increasing danger the longer he pursued his relationship with Stewart." Dev's voice was flat. "I've always trusted his judgment, and he believed your marriage was for the best. He was Prescott's conscience. He has always been my touchstone. But now..."

He seemed to swallow hard before he could go on. "Sophia, I must contact Harold. He cannot remain in hiding. He is all the duchess has left. He is the duke."

Sophia did not want to hear any of this right now. She

wanted him to turn and embrace her. She wanted to give him comfort.

She placed her other hand over the one she held and massaged it, as though for warmth. "Have you written to them?"

"I have. But I don't know if it was soon enough. In fact, I'm almost certain it was not. I've no way of being assured he will receive my letter. He is going to learn of his father's and brother's death in some newspaper in a distant land. We can only wait, and hope he sends word back to us soon."

Sophia had never been at a loss of words with Dev. But, upon the thoughts he'd voiced, she did not know what to say.

Harold needed to return. She'd known it all along. The complications of their situation were becoming more real with each passing day.

Her courses were yet absent.

This could be due to the traumatic events that had occurred over the past month, but even Sophia was beginning to doubt such reasoning.

This was not the time nor the place to discuss such a possibility with Dev…

And then he turned to her. "Is it true? Are you…?"

…or so she had thought.

Lacking privacy in her life was becoming intolerable. If it wasn't the housekeeper, it was her maid; if not the maid, then the duchess. She was going to have to rectify this situation somehow.

But, she could do nothing about it now. "I am not

certain. But the duchess is hopeful — more than hopeful — desperate for me to be."

Her words must have held a hint of resignation, for he leaned closer to her in concern. "You're all done in, aren't you?" His tone softened. This was her Dev. This was the voice that would be her undoing.

"I'm well enough. It has been a long journey... I never would have thought anything like this could happen. Everything, Dev, has spun out of control, and I... I miss you so." She could not contain it. Just as on that first occasion, when she'd told him she loved him.

When had that been? How soon had she known?

From that first instant, when he'd dropped into the corner behind the lion's cage with her, she'd known.

She'd known he was safe.

She'd known he would protect her.

She'd welcomed his nearness even then. And now, at the worst possible time, she needed him more than ever.

"Sophia, I cannot take Harold's birthright." He pulled her into his arms. They must be ever so careful. The door was not locked. They could be interrupted any moment. "And yet, you may be carrying my child."

He had the right of it, for certain. They needed to locate Harold and bring him back somehow.

She pressed her face into his chest and rubbed her hands over his back. "Dev," she said and then tilted her head back.

It was as though neither of them could stop it, this connection, this need. His mouth was there, waiting for hers. Their kiss was tender, comforting, two people afraid to release their emotions, afraid to allow anything more.

Sophia knew it would end, any moment, any second.

She pressed herself into him, as close as was humanly possible. She'd pulled back her veil when they'd entered the house, and now it covered only her hair. His hands searched beneath it until he found her nape.

Sounds from outside the door penetrated their need, and they pulled away from one another abruptly. Sophia turned from him, and found herself facing the duke.

Her mother was here!

Dev had turned back toward his father and ignored the newcomer.

Her mother seemed flustered, but to Sophia, appeared familiar and comforting. "Darling, oh, darling, such a horrible time for us all." She pulled Sophia into her arms. The tears Sophia had been holding back finally escaped.

"Mama," she said. Her mother's sympathy was her undoing. A wanton woman one moment and a weepy child the next.

"Come, dear, let's get you to your chamber so that you may rest. The duchess has told me everything. I'm going to assist you into your bed, and you are going to have a well-needed night's sleep before leaving for Kent tomorrow." Her mama did not acknowledge Dev as she led Sophia out of the room.

CHAPTER 24

*D*ev was duty-bound to assume the burdens of the dukedom until matters of the estate were settled. As he was the closest living male relative, his responsibilities were social, legal, and financial in nature. No one questioned that any other person ought to step into the ducal shoes his uncle had left behind. Most, in fact, looked to him as though he'd already inherited the title, for the moment, anyhow.

He drew the line, though, and snapped at anyone who dared address him as *"your grace."*

No legal declaration as of yet had been made and would not be for an undetermined length of time.

Two issues remained in doubt, first the question as to whether or not Sophia was carrying, and the second, the fact that a death certificate had not yet been issued for Harold, as a body had never been recovered.

Dev was diligent in focusing on immediate matters as

they arose and deliberately chose to put off any decision that would affect the dukedom long-term.

Initially, the most pressing concern he faced was to support his aunt through the funerals. The duchess had insisted upon attending the full pomp and circumstances of the services but refused to allow Sophia to join her.

It was unusual even, for her grace to be present.

She did, however, lean heavily upon Dev.

The long, drawn-out ceremony concluded with a formal procession transporting the bodies to Eden's Court for burial. All of this took over twelve hours and made for an exhausting day. Her grace remained poised and stoic through it all. Dev was only grateful Sophia had been sent ahead with her maid to Kent. She fretted too much already. None of it could be good for the baby she might be carrying.

His presence at the funeral was only the beginning of Dev's new responsibilities.

Over the next weeks, he'd had to abandon all thoughts of working Dartmouth Place, instead focusing his energies upon resolving the quagmire he'd landed himself in. He'd yet to hear from Harold, in code or otherwise.

Meanwhile, the solicitors were most concerned with an issue Dev was quite reluctant to address.

"Your grace — sir," the man corrected himself. No one knew how they ought to address him.

"Captain Brookes," Dev supplied.

"Captain Brookes, then." The short balding man cleared his throat. "Many issues could be resolved if we were allowed irrefutable determination as to the, er, condition of Lord Harold's widow. It is my understanding that she has not yet called in a physician, and yet it has not been reported that she is… not with child."

Dev did not suppress his annoyance. "Lady Harold will inform us when she is ready. I'll not press her on this matter."

The solicitor failed to hide his frustration at Dev's response. Nonetheless, he pulled out another document and moved to his next item of business.

"The other matter can be considered resolved, however," the solicitor said as he handed an official-looking document to Dev. It was titled, Certificate of Death. Dev assumed it was a copy of some sort, of either Prescotts', St. John's or his father's, but when he looked down, he read Harold's name.

Glancing up at the solicitor, he raised his brows in question.

The solicitor jumped to answer. "It seems, your… er, Captain Brookes, that what remains of Lord Harold has been recovered. The magistrate assumed you would wish to have what's left of his body brought here. He asked me to deliver this to you and inform the duchess as well."

A ghastly mistake had obviously been made. "Who identified the body?" Dev asked.

The solicitor frowned. "Well, you see, the body was virtually unrecognizable and not completely intact, what with the sea, and fish and whatnot. Three of the servants at Priory Point, however, confirmed that the ring discovered with the body belonged to the deceased –– belonged to Lord Harold."

Dev had not expected that.

Harold had safely escaped Priory Point.

Would not Stewart have contacted him if Harold had failed to show? Of course, Stewart would have returned as well.

The body could not possibly be his cousin's.

He'd assisted Harold out of the cave, himself. He'd watched as he'd rushed away on foot, in order to rendezvous with the mount waiting for him a short mile from the cliff.

Dev's heart dropped into his shoes at the possibility of Harold meeting up with some sort of catastrophe when he departed. But Stewart would have contacted him; Dev was certain.

"The remains are being sent here?"

"They are outside on the coach, sir."

Dev took in a deep breath.

The solicitor pulled a small cloth sack from his jacket pocket and handed it to Dev. Inside was a ring Dev had known Harold to wear for most of his adult life. "The remains are not... something any refined person would wish to examine. They have been transported as a courtesy. You will present the ring to her grace and to Lady Harold?"

Dev nodded. "Of course."

"And the other?" The solicitor looked at him hopefully.

"Will be known in due time." Dev clamped his lips together to keep from biting the man's head off. When the solicitor went to withdraw another form from his pile of paperwork, Dev stopped him. "We'll continue tomorrow. All of you may return then."

The man paused and then looked to his colleagues and shrugged. It took a few moments for all of them to collect their belongings and leave.

Ignoring them, Dev sat behind the oversized desk and waited for the room to empty.

It must be a mistake.

He did not wish to contemplate more death. But whose body had the solicitors brought to them? And why had the person been wearing Harold's ring? It could not possibly be Harold's. It could not!

This had all been done so that Harold could live a life without fear, so that he could live!

It had been done for Sophia, and for himself, yes, but mostly, they knew, it had been done for Harold. Had it not? And if Harold had not survived, if some tragedy had befallen him somehow, then all of it had been for naught!

He was saved from further contemplation when, with a short knock, the door opened again.

"Dev." It was the duchess. She looked more herself, these last few days, apparently finding some hope in Sophia's condition. "I would have joined you with the solicitors earlier but did not know they had arrived."

The duchess, even more so than the solicitors, was concerned with the matters of ascendancy. As well, any duchess would be.

Dev rose and waited for her to sit down.

Once she'd settled her gown around her, he handed her the certificate. It made no sense to hide this from anyone, especially, with the body on hand as well. He placed the ring in front of her while she perused the document. If a mistake had been made, she might clear it up rather quickly.

But Dev was quite certain this was Harold's ring.

"A body was discovered near Priory Point. This was discovered with him."

His aunt blinked away tears and reached for the ring. "Prescott gave it to him when he reached his majority." She confirmed Dev's opinion. "And so, for now, you are Prescott."

Dev did not want to hear that. He ran both hands through his hair. "But Lady Harold—"

The duchess interrupted him. "I wish to speak with you about her."

"Is she all right?" Sophia had looked pale as of late and had seemed to lack her normal energy. She'd been watched over closely, however, by both his aunt and her maid. He knew she was not happy. Despite residing in the same house, they'd not been alone together since before the funeral.

"She is fine." His aunt smiled softly. "I am certain she is carrying. I think she is fearful something will go wrong. I believe that is why she is so reluctant to make a declaration. But her maid assures me…" She shrugged. "It has been over a month since his passing, and nearly two since they wed. It is the only logical conclusion."

Dev waited. She'd said she wanted to discuss Sophia with him. Was there more?

"I think, Dev, that you and Sophia should wed."

* * *

IT TOOK a minute for Dev to absorb his aunt's words.

It was the desire of his heart to take Sophia as his wife. He already considered them wed, which made no sense, and yet, all the sense in the world. But this was not something he'd expected to hear from the duchess. Had she seen something? Had she heard something? Had Sophia spoken to her?

"She is in mourning," Dev reminded his aunt, as though she would not have considered something so blatantly obvious. "We are all in mourning."

"She is mourning, Dev, but she is also increasing. And I think she is fond of you. I think she is lonely and frightened."

But if Harold lived, and if he returned, Sophia would be a bigamist. Dev was torn in that he wanted more than anything to take her under his protection, to be able to give her affection without hurting anyone, without hurting his aunt. It was as though the duchess were handing her to him on a silver platter. Giving both of them what they'd wanted all along.

He needed, however, to hear from Harold.

But would he? Ever? Frowning, he glanced at the certificate sitting on the edge of the desk.

If the body that had been recovered was not Harold, then exactly who was it, and why had he been wearing Harold's ring? Despite what the solicitor said, he was going to have to make some attempt at identifying the deteriorated remains. But for now, the duchess awaited a response from him.

Dev knew his aunt all too well.

That would be rather neat and tidy, would it not?" If Sophia gave birth to a boy, then Dev, as trustee, would raise the young duke. And if Sophia gave birth to a girl, then Dev would become the duke, Sophia the duchess, and Harold's child would be raised as the daughter of a duke.

His aunt merely shrugged. "It would warm my heart to know that the two of you could comfort one another. To know that Harold's child would be raised by two parents."

Why was he resisting this? Marrying Sophia was something he'd wanted all along. "Have you spoken to her about this?" He doubted it. And on that thought, he understood why the suggestion bothered him.

More manipulation.

He did not want his relationship with Sophia, marriage to her, to be determined by his aunt, the dukedom, or anything other than the love he and Sophia had for each other.

"I had thought to run the matter before you first," she answered.

Dev had sent coded messages, with the name Harold had told him he would take, to every possible location he could imagine Harold might be. But locating him was going to take time.

"With all due respect," he began, "I insist you refrain from suggesting any such thing to Lady Harold. She is not even willing to admit to herself that she is increasing. The last thing she needs is to be pressured into another marriage."

"But—" his aunt began.

Dev held up one hand to stop her. If the duchess wished to treat him as though he were the head of the family right now, then he would use his power to reign in some of her machinations.

"There will be no further mention of it." He would not be crossed on this matter.

She looked at him in frustration before relenting. "Very well, Dev, for now, anyhow. I'm going to revisit this with you once Sophia admits to her condition." She then stood up, as though to let him know that she was still the duchess and was the one who would end this meeting. She smoothed her dress and turned regally before leaving the room.

Dev felt some small satisfaction in that he'd been able to protect Sophia in this one small matter.

For once.

SOPHIA NOTICED the unusual coach behind the solicitor's from her chamber, which overlooked the large open lawn spread before Eden's Court. One did not forget what such a conveyance was used for. If it had been carrying ice for the kitchens, it would have been driven around to the servants' entrance.

No, such a conveyance signified death. She set aside the

letters she'd been about to open, one from Rhoda and another from Cecily, and called for Penny.

After having her hair pulled into a tight chignon and donning one of the newer black dresses she'd had made, Sophia stoically headed downstairs toward the foyer. As she did so, she came upon the duchess, who was just emerging from the study where Dev spent most of his time. "Is something amiss? Your grace..." Sophia reached out and touched her mother-in-law's arm tentatively.

Without speaking, the duchess led Sophia into a nearby drawing room. Once they entered, she pulled her down onto one of the sofas beside her.

"What is it?" She began again, unable to contemplate what could possibly have happened now.

"Sophia," her mother-in-law began. But then, seeming to reconsider her words, she turned her fist and then opened it for Sophia to see what she held.

It was Harold's ring.

Sophia had seen it on him often enough; in fact, she could not remember a time when he had ever removed it. "Where did you get that?" she asked, her mind quickly trying to ascertain whether or not she'd seen Harold wearing it on that last fateful day.

She was almost certain that she had not.

Perhaps her grace now wished for Sophia to have it. But Sophia did not want it. His mother ought to keep it.

"Sophia, dear..." The duchess spoke tenderly. "...the ring was taken from Harold's body, which was found washed up on one of the beaches near Priory Point."

Sophia frowned. But this was not possible.

"His valet did not give you the ring when he packed Harold's possessions?" The ring had not come from Harold's body. She was certain of it. It could not have been. Harold's body was off somewhere in a distant land, starting a new life.

The duchess patted Sophia on the arm. "No, dear, he has been found and returned to us. I will plan a small burial service for him. He will be laid to rest with his father and brother."

Sophia scratched the side of her face. Who had been wearing Harold's signet ring, if not Harold?

And a suspicion arose within her.

Dudley.

CHAPTER 25

*A*s soon as Sophia could make her excuses to the duchess, she stepped into the foyer and took a deep breath. She needed to speak with Dev.

They'd not been alone together since that day before the funeral at Prescott House.

Feeling tired, out of sorts, and sickly, Sophia had avoided him by remaining in her chamber much of the time. This way she could keep herself from reaching out to touch him, from moving close to inhale his scent. When they were in the same room with one another, usually only during the evening meal, she found it difficult to keep her gaze from following his every move.

But the duchess was always nearby, watching her carefully, urging her to eat, ready to take her for a brief stroll through the gardens for some fresh air.

Sophia entered the study quietly, her heart fluttering when she caught sight of his dark head bent over the sheet of paper he studied. "Dev," she said in a near whisper, closing the door behind her. "Where is the body?"

"It's not in any condition—" he began.

"It's not Harold," Sophia said. She had a feeling about this. "I need to look at it. I think I know who it is."

Dev's eyebrows rose at her statement.

Her stiff crepe skirts rustled as she crossed the room toward him.

Dev stood, belatedly observing his manners. "But how can you?" He must have thought she'd gone mad, for really, how could she have any idea as to the identity of a body that had washed up weeks after their departure.

When Sophia reached the desk, she put both of her hands on the polished wood and leaned across it so that he would hear her words. She would whisper them, for she was coming to discover that the walls of the Prescott estates had ears. "It may be Dudley."

Dev indicated for her to sit before dropping once again into his own chair. "But he was never at Priory Point."

"He was! Well, I believe so anyhow. On the day of Harold's accident, after Penny gave me some sort of sleeping draught. When I awoke, I didn't see him again, and I'd come to believe that perhaps I'd dreamed it. I used to have these nightmares, you see… But I think that perhaps it was not a dream after all. I think Dudley came into my room, using the adjoining door from Harold's chamber. I was surprised, and the drug was already affecting me, but Rhoda interrupted him. She entered the room, realized what he was about, and took him out to assist in the search.

I did not see him after that, and nobody ever mentioned his arrival. But he'd been in Harold's chamber, and I would not put it past him to steal a deceased man's possessions."

"So, you think he might have stolen the ring and then met with an accident of his own?" Dev leaned back in his seat, considering what she told him. "Did Miss Mossant ever mention seeing him again after that?" He frowned.

Sophia shook her head. "No, Rhoda and her mother left before the funeral. There was no reason to discuss it with her, and really, at that point I considered I'd imagined it or dreamed it."

"The ice carriage is being driven around to the back of the house. I will view the body first, and if there is anything about it that could possibly be identifiable, I will allow you to view it as well." He looked grim. "The last I'd heard of young Mr. Scofield, he'd gone down to Brighton for a few weeks. Your recollection would explain why he's not yet returned to London."

Sophia appreciated that Dev took her suspicion seriously.

"What with the danger he presents, I feel it is as important to establish whether or not the body is his, as it is to verify that the body is not Harold's. Only one way to do this." He stood and offered her his arm. "As much as this goes against my better judgment, I think it best we address this unpleasant task this afternoon."

Tucking her hand into his elbow, Sophia tilted her chin up stubbornly. "Let's get this over with then."

They'd removed the body from the carriage into a building that was half-buried behind the stables. It was tucked away, dug partially into the earth, and most likely normally used as a cellar of some sort. Dev suggested Sophia wait outside while he disappeared down the dark steps.

Waiting patiently, Sophia noticed for the first time that the sunlight was no longer the bright white light of summer. It had that subtle golden tint to it that signified the onset of autumn. When had this occurred? Where had summertime gone?

She breathed in deeply, preparing herself for death to enter their lives once again.

When Dev reappeared, a scowl marred his features.

Brushing dirt from his hands, he announced, "I'm somewhat confident that the body down there, whoever it may be, is most definitely not Harold."

"So, it is intact?"

Dev did not answer her question directly. "It must have been in the salt water for a considerable length of time, preserving various fragments. However, his flesh was not immune to creatures of the sea, and it suffered further decomposition most likely after washing ashore."

"But were there any identifiable features?" Sophia persisted.

Dev finally nodded reluctantly. "Tell me if you feel faint at any time, and I'll get you out at once." Taking her hand, he assisted her down the earthen steps.

The interior smelled of decay but not death. Sophia had her handkerchief ready. A few candles cast enough light so that she could see the wooden casket, opened and situated on a long table.

She approached it cautiously, as though something might jump out at her at any moment. This was the stuff nightmares were made of. She stifled her imagination and stepped closer so she could peer inside.

Why, it was not much of a body, at all.

It was really just a pile of bones, with some hair and a few pieces of ripped clothing on it. "The ring was not discovered on his person," Dev said, "as you can likely see. But the iceman said it was in his pocket."

What remained of the deceased's hair was darker than Harold's. The thin tufts were indeed the color of Dudley's and curled just slightly. The clothing seemed familiar as well, but it, too, was discolored and practically reduced to threads. And then she caught sight of the location where a mouth had once been.

A large gap split the upper front teeth just as Dudley's had.

Harold's teeth were almost geometrically perfect.

Sophia cringed as she remembered her stepbrother's menacing smile all too well. One did not forget such a significant feature of one's tormentor. "He is Dudley, Dev. I'm ninety-nine percent certain."

Surprisingly, she was not nearly as bothered by this body as she had been by the others. It exuded no odor at all.

No putrefied flesh was left to emit any.

"Who discovered him? I would not think it likely that many people would be so honest as to return such a valuable ring." She was a little in awe that it had survived when most of the body had not.

"One of the older servants at Priory Point, I believe. He will be rewarded justly, be assured," Dev said. "Are you finished?"

Sophia nodded. "Oh, yes, yes. Let's get out of here." She could easily imagine all manner of spiders and crawly things having at what was left of her stepbrother's body.

As she climbed the stairs, Dev's hand on her back comforted her.

If that was Dudley in the cellar, then Harold was still alive somewhere.

And if Harold was still alive, then he could easily return at any time.

"We have plenty of daylight before sunset," Dev said once they were again above ground. "Would you care for a stroll?

Oh, yes.

Oh yes. It would be lovely to be alone with him for a while. To be free of the duchess' overly concerned and watchful gaze.

"I would." She took hold of the arm he extended. "What will you tell the duchess?"

They walked a short way before she realized they were on a path that would wind them around a more densely overgrown section of the garden. They would have some privacy.

"The truth, I suppose. Your parents ought to be notified."

She walked quietly. She did not wish to reveal to her parents that Dudley had come to her room. That he'd likely stolen from her *deceased* husband. "What if Harold does not wish to return, Dev? Would it not be... comforting... for your aunt to believe he's been found and brought home?"

"Are you suggesting we leave matters as they are?" He did not dismiss her opinion outright.

"I feel as though some explanation will be required, regarding Dudley. Explanations I'd rather not go into with anyone." She also wanted to speak with Rhoda. What had happened that night? "If Harold returns, we can have the body exhumed. But if he does not..."

"Will your parents not be concerned for your step-brother's whereabouts?" Her dear, sweet Dev had yet to object to her suggestion.

"I think that so long as he is not up to mischief and spending their money, they are well enough to have him out of their lives." She knew her mother would be happy without him, anyhow. Dudley had never been pleasant company. He had been something of a menace.

"If you think that is what's best, then I cannot argue with you. I'd planned upon curtailing his activities anyhow. This way, your parents will not be exposed to any scandal, and neither will you."

Sophia relaxed. Beneath her hand, Dev's arm felt solid and warm. She leaned into him, and he kissed the top of her head. It was as though she had come home from a long and lonely journey.

What an unusual day this had become.

Locating a granite bench in the sunlight, Dev steered her toward it and pulled her to sit down. Turning, he searched her eyes meaningfully.

"How are you feeling today? Are you faint? Do you still feel ill in the mornings?"

These were the things she would share with him daily if their fates had not become so twisted. But here, now, she was alone with him for once.

She nodded slowly and allowed a secret smile to curve her lips. She was finally convinced that she was indeed, increasing. But she had wanted to tell Dev first. She'd not wanted all the world to know before him. "I'm a little queasy every morning, but other than that, I have more energy today."

He stilled at her expression, as much as at her words. And in case he was left with any doubt on the matter, she shrugged a little sheepishly. "The world has turned upside down, and it would seem as though we've made one mistake after another. But in my heart, I cannot regret any of it." Her words were truer than she could have thought. "I'm going to have your baby, Dev." And she could not regret it now. Out of the uncontrollable passion they'd experienced together, they'd created a life. And appropriately, the child would be born in the springtime.

Was it possible they could have just a few minutes together to celebrate, even though uncertainty abounded everywhere?

Dev's features softened, and then he jumped up restlessly. He paced back and forth several times before finally returning to sit down beside her. A new vitality seemed to come over him.

"Do you think, Sophia," he said, "that the two of us will

ever carry on a normal conversation?" He smiled as he spoke the words, teasing her.

She could not resist his mood. "You mean about the weather? Or about bonnets? Or about whether our child ought to have a governess or go away to school?"

He nodded. "Instead of who died, when, and how we are going to bring people back from the grave?"

And then she felt serious again, just as quickly. "I wish, oh, how I wish that by some miracle, all of this could work out. I want for Harold to return. It seems only right that he should return. And yet, if he does…"

Dev took her hands and raised them to his lips. "I feel the same, Sophia. All we can do is wait."

She relaxed into him and sighed. "It all seemed so harmless, when you first told me about it. About Harold going away to live his life the way he wanted. No one was supposed to be hurt. I'd imagined St. John proposing to Rhoda, you and I finding our way together, and everyone living out their lives peacefully. Everything has turned to ashes! Who would have thought it could ever come to all of this?"

Dev let out a dry chuckle. After so much death and sadness the past month, a little laughter, a little sunshine, was exactly what they needed.

"We will give Harold until after the holidays. If he has not sent word by then, then you and I will marry in the New Year. My child will have my name, regardless of who everyone else believes the father to be."

At his words, Sophia remembered the night he'd first

made love to her, when he'd recited the wedding vows to her by candlelight.

"So, we wait until the New Year."

Dev pulled her to her feet. "Just after the holidays."

That seemed a lifetime away. So much could happen between then and now.

But suddenly, hope was alive again.

CHAPTER 26

*S*ophia waited one more week before informing the duchess that she had sent for the local midwife. She told her that, although she'd gone several weeks before without having her courses, she'd never gone this long. In addition, she said she was experiencing a few pronounced symptoms consistent with what would be expected of a lady in an interesting condition.

The duchess was overjoyed, of course.

"But not the midwife, dear. We will have a physician from London attend to you. I shall keep him here on retainer so that you receive the best of care around the clock." The duchess stood and clasped her hands in front of her. "Oh, I knew it, Sophia! I am so happy! You are giving me the greatest gift any daughter-in-law could ever give. You are giving me back a part of my son!"

Sophia would have grimaced at this but kept a placid expression on her face. Before imparting this news to the duchess, Sophia had considered her position within the household carefully and was determined to affect some changes.

"That is not going to be necessary, your grace," Sophia said softly, but firmly. "I have already sent for the midwife and would find myself quite... uncomfortable having a physician here." She paused.

The duchess raised her brows nearly into her hairline at Sophia's disagreeable statement.

"I have also hired a new lady's maid. I appreciate Penny's efficiency and dedication, but I find she and I are not... completely sympathetic to each other." No, Penny's loyalty had always, and would always be, to the duchess first. Which, as the duchess' employee, was perfectly acceptable, but Sophia decided she needed to put an end to the constant monitoring on her grace's part.

While meeting with the solicitors a few weeks earlier, Sophia discovered that, as Harold's widow, she could freely access her own accounts. She would pay her maid from those funds. The girl she'd hired from a nearby village, Gilly, would be exclusively employed by Sophia. Although she would be expected to give deference to the duchess, there would be no question as to where her loyalties would lie.

In a secretive interview, Sophia had discussed her need for privacy with the girl. And although Gilly was not as refined and educated as Penny, Sophia felt an affinity with her. She would be arriving at the estate to take up her position later this afternoon.

The duchess' eyes narrowed. "You know, Sophia, that I

have always had your best interests at heart in everything I do." Her tone imparted disappointment and hurt.

Sophia touched her mother-in-law's hand. "And I have appreciated your care and concern…" She wanted to be honest. She wished to establish a sense of independence with this conversation. But she did not want to build a wall between herself and the duchess. "…I can no longer abide having the most personal details of my life shared with others. It makes me feel… uncomfortable, exposed." Sophia was determined to have a maid with whom she could trust the most intimate aspects of her life. "You would not tolerate such a lack of privacy, would you?"

The duchess pinched her lips together tightly. "The solicitors prefer a physician confirm your condition," she persisted.

But on these matters, Sophia was adamant.

Emily, who was so well read as to practically be considered a bluestocking, had once explained to herself, Rhoda, and Cecily, that the difference between a physician and a good midwife could be life or death for the woman and her child. Although the physicians were well educated, they could not understand the woman's body as a midwife could. Emily had advised her friends, on one particular occasion as they'd sat amongst the other wallflowers, that when they were with child, they ought to find a midwife who'd attended numerous births, and then investigate each of their mortality rates.

Sophia had already asked Dev about this, and he'd taken the task to heart. He'd located a woman from Kent who was highly recommended. She would come and see Sophia later that day.

"The midwife's opinion will have to be good enough," Sophia declared. She would hold her ground. "She will be here later today."

The duchess considered Sophia with pursed lips for a long moment before surprising her by turning and tugging at the bell pull. "Well then…" She seemed to have come to a decision. "…we might as well have some tea."

Other encouraging aspects materialized that day as well. It seemed that as soon as Sophia decided to take a modicum of control over her life, good things followed.

First, the midwife declared Sophia's womb to be the size of a woman who had conceived perhaps eight weeks earlier. It was mostly filled with water, she told Sophia, the baby barely the size of a bean. Sophia wondered how a person could know this.

Mrs. Fletcher, the midwife, asked Sophia several questions about how she was feeling and then gave her advice as to how to cope with some of the ailments of her condition. All in all, she announced, Sophia and the baby seemed perfectly healthy.

Gilly had arrived just before the checkup and was taking to her position quite instinctively. She'd a prior acquaintance with the midwife, in fact, and this helped remove some of the awkwardness from the examination. And, although likely not as educated as Penny, Gilly was able to write down Mrs. Fletcher's instruction and even asked a few questions.

Sophia was pleased, all in all, with the afternoon.

Even more so when she received Cecily's letter!

Cecily was free of Lord Kensington forever! Even so, she had not stayed a single lady for long. She'd married Mr. Stephen Nottingham, the earl's cousin, whom Sophia had known Cecily loved. Of course, Cecily had told them adamantly that she did not, but Sophia had not believed a word of it. And now Cecily herself was expecting a baby just a few months earlier than Sophia.

Cecily's situation had seemed to be a hopeless one, and for Sophia to hear of such news, she could almost believe that anything was possible.

THE SOLICITORS, upon obtaining confirmation of Sophia's condition, advised Dev that he ought to insist a physician be in attendance, at the least, to witness the birth of his niece or nephew.

They advised him that it would benefit Lady Harold to give birth to a son, and that he knew of one occurrence, anyhow, where an infant boy had been substituted intentionally, so that the title was not transferred to another relative.

Dev assured them that Lady Harold could be trusted implicitly. He did not tell them he intended to attend the birth himself when the time came. It would be unusual, he knew. But he refused to allow her to go through childbirth without him by her side. He would do what he could to comfort her, if she allowed it, that was.

He could not imagine lazing in the library, drinking

brandy, listening to her cries of pain from a distance. He wondered how Sophia would react when he told her this.

What with the duchess' blessing, her desire for Dev to marry Sophia, he relaxed the distance he'd kept from Sophia earlier. In fact, on a daily basis now, he walked with her outside for a half an hour. He often took tea with her and the duchess.

Spending even a small amount of time with Sophia openly, alone, was balm to his soul. They chatted about all the things they'd not had time to discover about one another before. He told her of his childhood, his travels, and some of the trials he was having over the dukedom, and she, in turn, confided stories about her friends, the relationship she had with her mother, and fears she had of childbirth. They were coming to know each other in a much different way than they had before.

Dev was proud of Sophia for hiring a new lady's maid. She was finding her place — discovering her own strength.

The duchess had been slightly cooler than usual for a few days after that but had warmed up again quickly enough. It went without saying that his aunt was overjoyed at the prospect of a grandchild.

The duchess — and everyone else, of course — believed the child to be Harold's.

Despite the horrible tragedies they'd endured that summer, hope had crept into the house again, with the expectancy of a new life.

Cooler weather was just around the corner, with a hint of frost covering the landscape in the early mornings now.

The leaves turned from green to reds and yellow and before long had all fallen to the ground.

On the first day of October, Dev was perusing a few reports on various harvests throughout the dukedom when he finally came across the letter he'd been watching for.

He recognized Harold's handwriting right off.

Feeling as though he held a bomb in his hands, he tore open the seal and methodically deciphered the code he'd taught Harold so many weeks ago.

The wording was awkward, but it took only a moment for the meaning of the letter to become apparent.

RECEIVED YOUR LETTER BEFORE SAILING. *Distraught hearing of the tragedy but sailed anyway. I cannot return. Please understand and support my decision. Happiness at last within my grasp. You were born for this. More a brother to me than the Saint. Be happy with her. No turning back. A free man at last.*

JOY AND SATISFACTION assailed Dev at the news.

Harold was alive.

He was happy.

And with Harold's happiness, Dev knew what he must do.

Pulling the bell pull, he sent Mr. Evans to request that the duchess and Lady Harold join him in the library.

If he and Sophia were to have a future together, free of deceit and guilt, the truth must be told. He'd considered this conversation for weeks now. At last the time had come.

The ladies arrived together. He rose from his chair and bowed when they entered.

Waving at him to sit, the duchess smiled benevolently. "Evans said you wished to speak to us."

Sophia found a wing-backed chair off to the side, and the duchess sat in her usual place.

Dev cleared his throat and, despite having rehearsed his words a thousand times in his mind, suddenly had no idea where to begin.

"You poor dear…" His aunt was in a gracious mood today. "…I know you did not anticipate any of this falling upon you. But you must know you've handled everything wonderfully. I don't know what Sophia or I would have done without you these past weeks. Do you, Sophia?"

Sophia must have sensed that he had something of importance to discuss. She merely smiled timidly and agreed. "I do not, your grace."

"Aunt," Dev began, "I must confess something to you. Before I explain, please understand that the blame ought to rightfully be placed upon me. I could have stopped the events of what I am to tell you at any time, but I did not."

Sophia sat up straighter at his words.

Her grace's brows furrowed at his statement. "What is it, Dev?"

"Before Harold and Sophia married, before they traveled to Priory Point, you must have known that Harold's life was in grave danger, as was Stewart's." At the mention of Harold's lover's name, the duchess looked away from

Dev and pinched her lips together. "My father," Dev continued, "informed me at the time that Prescott had received some threats, as had Harold. Did you know of any of this?"

"Vile creatures." She surprised him with her answer. "Blackmailers and hypocrites, the lot of them."

Dev nodded and then forced himself to continue. "Harold did not wish to marry Sophia but conceded in order to protect you –– and Stewart –– in order to protect the family from scandal."

The duchess blinked away tears. "Why are you bringing all of this up now?" She shifted her eyes in Sophia's direction, obviously not wanting to share such skeletons with her daughter-in-law. She had no way of knowing that Sophia had learned of Harold's proclivities firsthand. And, of course, no one was happy to discuss such matters openly. "None of it matters any longer, after all."

"Ah, aunt, but it does. Because Harold devised an alternative solution, one where he and Sophia would not be required to live out their lives as man and wife, one where he could live openly with the person he loved." He then handed Harold's letter, with his own translation scrawled in the margins, across the desk to the duchess.

"This is gibberish," she said at first. And then realizing the carefully written letters were familiar somehow, she set to examining both the handwriting and the decoded words.

"It came in the mail today." He would divulge all. "Harold faked his death. The jump was planned and executed in a way that it would appear he could not survive." He went on to explain about the cave, the getaway, the planning they'd all put into it.

As the duchess gradually comprehended what he was saying, tears began to fall unheeded. "He is not returning, though?" she asked, waving the paper in the air. "What about Sophia and the baby? He loved Sophia! Penny told me!"

What he had to confess now was even more difficult. But Sophia spoke up first. "Penny was wrong."

"But that cannot be so! Sophia, dear, you are with child! Dev is mistaken on this. Oh, Harold must return to you, Sophia. He must take up his rightful position!"

"He was unhappy here, your grace." Sophia spoke softly but with great conviction.

"The rumors were becoming dangerous," Dev interjected. "You know this. Read the letter again, Aunt Loretta. Harold has done all of this so that he can live his life in his own way."

She read it through again and then blew her nose into a handkerchief. "But what of the baby?"

Dev had already decided to tell his aunt everything… well nearly everything. Looking across the room into eyes as blue as the sky, Dev held back nothing. "I love Sophia. I've loved her since the day we met. The child she carries is mine."

Barely able to tug his gaze away from the woman he loved, Dev faced his aunt once again. Would the duchess lash out at him? Would she blame him for the other tragic events of the summer? Would she hate him forever?

No, she merely shook her head sadly. Dev handed her a

new handkerchief. "It was too good to be true, wasn't it?" She smiled wanly at Sophia but did not break down sobbing. This woman hadn't lived most of her adult life a duchess for nothing. She raised her chin and glanced between the two of them. "But Harold lives? My son is alive?"

"He is," Dev confirmed.

Over the next thirty minutes or so, Dev answered every question the duchess could think of pertaining to the summer's events. She was surprisingly agreeable, even acquiescing to the decision they'd made to keep Dudley's demise from the Scofields.

And then, at last, she had just one question left.

"What do we do now?"

EPILOGUE

$\mathcal{T}$he sun shone bright, exactly six months to the day since Sophia's first wedding day.

Whereas the dress, the cathedral, the large congregation had made her first wedding seem like every girl's dream, it was her future husband who'd put the sparkle in her eyes today. It was the groom who caused the bride to glow.

For the bridal gown was a simple lavender muslin, the church a small family chapel, and the congregation made up of only the closest of family and friends.

The groom's side of the church held the duchess and a handful of her sisters and cousins. On the bride's side sat Mr. and Mrs. Scofield, Rhoda and her mother and two sisters, Emily and her aunt, and Mr. and Mrs. Stephen Nottingham. Behind them, Gilly sat in a pew and held tightly to Peaches, who had a silk ribbon tied around her neck in honor of the occasion.

No one complained of the bride's stepbrother's absence.

Cecily glowed. Emily was her normal studious self, and Rhoda, although obviously pleased for Sophia, seemed unusually quiet.

But nothing could subdue Sophia's joy that morning.

For she and Dev would finally be wed. And they would be wed without any hovering clouds of deceit. Their future would hold only the promise of love and new life to come.

After confessing all to the duchess, the three of them had discussed what would be best.

Harold would not be returning to London, and so they would continue perpetuating the story of his death for all intents and purposes.

The duchess had cried tears of relief as well, knowing that he lived. Perhaps, someday, she would be able to go to him, to see the son she'd once believed dead. But not for some time. It was difficult for her to give up her hope that he would turn out to be a *normal* boy, like St. John had been. But she would always love him. Of course, she would always love him!

When Dev had announced his plans to marry Sophia, he had begged the duchess for forgiveness, and she'd granted it to both of them.

And then she'd surprised them.

She'd apologized to Sophia for her part in manipulating the marriage in the first place.

She'd asked Sophia for forgiveness.

After more tears and hugs even. She'd asked Sophia to call her by her given name, Loretta. "But not Lettie, please, dear," she'd clarified. "Reminds me too much of the days before I married."

And so, they'd begun planning another wedding.

This time, Sophia had done things her way.

She had refused to be given away. Not by Mr. Scofield, not by Peaches, not by anyone.

Now, as the music played, Sophia proceeded confidently down the aisle alone, a free woman, willing to give herself to only one man. The man she loved.

At first he'd been her hero, and then her lover. He was soon to be her husband.

He awaited her at the altar, most solemnly –– her Dev. His attire was simple, yet elegant. He'd finally hired himself a valet, and the man had done himself proud.

When she arrived, Dev took her hand, raised it to his lips, and then turned them so they both faced the vicar.

Dev's cousin, Mr. White had been more than happy to perform the ceremony for them. And this time, as the age-old vows were recited, Sophia concentrated intently upon them. She repeated the words earnestly to her equally sincere groom.

And in the end, when the vicar pronounced them husband and wife, Dev tilted her head back and placed a chaste-but-loving kiss upon her lips. It held the promise of a lifetime of love.

Peaches took that moment to escape from Gilly and rush to the altar with a series of celebratory barks. At first, a few gasps broke the silence, but when Mr. White bent down, picked the dog up, and got a wet kiss on his face for his troubles, laughter erupted.

For there was a time to mourn and a time to dance.

There was a time to weep and a time to laugh. And of course, there was finally a time to love.

At last, it was time.

** The End **

Emily Goodnight's story comes next.
Turn the page for Chapter 1 from
Hell's Belle

CHAPTER ONE
Infatuation

Marcus Roberts, the Earl of Blakely, leaned against the brocaded wall, arms crossed. The gorgeous fellow seemed completely unaware that his good looks drew the gaze of nearly every wallflower present.

Miss Emily Goodnight was no exception.

Of course, she'd never confess her infatuation to anyone, especially her closest friends. They assumed Emily was immune to such nonsense. She'd gone out of her way, in fact, to perpetuate the opinion. She'd quite intentionally developed her reputation as a practical, rational miss to protect herself from the sting of rejection she'd surely experience otherwise. When she found herself forlornly seated while the comelier ladies danced, she wouldn't feel so pathetic.

She pushed her glasses up the bridge of her nose and

pretended to watch the dancers in his vicinity. In truth, she secretly watched *him*.

His appeal wasn't only in his looks but something else, something nearly unidentifiable. He slouched slightly, as he leaned, not bothering to adhere to what was considered appropriate behavior, and his slightly hooded eyes perused the room lazily. He lifted his broad shoulders, stretching them up and back, drawing Emily's attention to his abdomen, flat and firm looking.

When he tilted his head to one side, a lock of thick chestnut hair fell across his forehead, partially covering one eye.

Emily looked away before he caught her staring.

Surely, he would not remain alone for long.

Ah, yes, she was quite right.

Mrs. Cromwell, a newly widowed beauty, promenaded past several other ladies to reach him before "accidentally" dropping her handkerchief at his feet.

His bored eyes flicked up and down the woman knowingly before he bent to retrieve the effective wisp of fabric. With a flourish, he bowed and presented it to the raven-haired beauty. A subtle twinkle in his smoky gray eyes revealed his interest in what the widow offered.

Emily hated him at that moment.

Nearly as much as she hated herself for feeling sentimental emotions for such a rake in the first place.

Since their first meeting at a formal dinner party, when Emily had stuck her foot in her mouth more than once, she'd never failed to devolve into a graceless idiot in his presence. Not that she was graceful to begin with... but she floundered with unusual flare on such occasions.

Why continue torturing herself? Emily glanced down at her dance card. A few gentlemen who'd approached her friend Rhoda had charitably scribbled their names beside some of the livelier dances on her own. Those sets would not come up until much later in the evening.

Mrs. Cromwell tilted her head back in laughter and then gazed at him from beneath fluttering eyelashes.

How did ladybirds do it? What gave them the confidence to flirt so outrageously?

Emily peeked from beneath her lashes in the direction of the couple. Lord Blakely was smiling roguishly at the daring woman. He lifted Mrs. Cromwell's hand and pressed his lips to the back of it for longer than was appropriate. As the voluptuous woman giggled and looked away, he turned his face slightly toward Emily. As though he knew her every thought, he dropped one eyelid in an insolent wink.

Oh, the rotter!

Heat crawled up Emily's neck and into her face. Of course, now she would appear blotched and bothered. Drat, the swine.

She turned her legs firmly and stared intently in the opposite direction.

She missed Cecily and Sophia.

Cecily had married a bounder but then managed to find true love after all, and how could any man not have fallen in love with sweet, blond, lovely Sophia? Good heavens,

Sophia was a duchess now, of all things! Of the four wall-flowers, Emily and Rhoda remained unattached.

Normally Rhoda would be sitting beside her.

Rhoda, with her chestnut hair, sultry eyes, and complete lack of nervousness around gentlemen. Surely, Rhoda would be the next to become betrothed. In fact, last summer she'd practically landed an eminently eligible husband… the heir to a duke. But it had not been meant to be. The heir had died in a tragic accident.

Poor Rhoda.

Poor Rhoda indeed! Every single dance on her card had been claimed this evening. Seeing her squired about by a marquess last Season had apparently opened the eyes of the fickle gentlemen of the *ton*. Tonight, at the first ball of the Season, she seemed the most sought-after lady of them all.

The sudden onslaught of attention was uncanny, really.

"Sitting alone this evening, Miss Goodnight?" Emily's heart jumped at Lord Blakely's voice. At the same time, his cock-sure attitude set her teeth on edge. "Has Miss Mossant abandoned you?" If he requested a dance, Emily thought she might scream. She refused to accept charity in any form.

"She is quite popular this evening, my lord." Emily stared at his neck cloth. If she stared into his eyes, her brain would cease to function. He would test her, however, by dropping into an exaggerated bow, one foot pointed in her direction.

"Have you been claimed for this set, or will you make me the happiest of men and allow me the pleasure?" A pang shot through her at the words. They almost sounded like a proposal.

Idiot. Fool!

She glanced around, making certain he was, in fact, asking her before rising somewhat haltingly. So much for her pride.

"I will dance with you, my lord, if that is what you are asking." She continued to avoid his gaze and in doing so caught Mrs. Cromwell watching the two of them with a snide expression.

Had he told the lady he would dance with poor Miss Goodnight, a lowly wallflower, in order to prove his gallantry? "Unless you'd prefer to dance with Mrs. Cromwell again. It's really not necessary, you know, dancing with me, just because we are both well acquainted with Mr. and Mrs. Nottingham..."

Was she to make a cake of herself, after all?

She sounded as bitter as she felt.

At last, she forced herself to meet his gaze. He'd raised one brow but extended his arm for her to take, nonetheless.

"You should know by now that I lack such manners, Miss Goodnight. Have you not considered I might be seeking your conversation to liven my evening? If I remember correctly, you have a habit of... saying the most fascinating things."

Oh, so *not* charity. He sought to be entertained by her unfortunate habit of failing to maintain her dignity in most social situations. "Very well." What else could she say? He was an earl, after all. And Cecily's husband's closest friend.

Pretending this wasn't the Earl of Blakely, *her* Earl of Blakely, she tucked her hand into his arm and allowed him to lead her onto the floor. Oh, but the other dancers weren't lining up for a country dance.

It was to be a waltz!

She gulped.

Her stomach did a quick flip as he placed one hand upon her waist. "So, I'm fascinating." She snorted. "Ought I to be flattered?"

Her hand shook as she placed it on his shoulder. Surely, he would feel her trembling when he clasped her other hand in his. If he held her even half as inappropriately as he'd held Mrs. Cromwell, he'd feel... everything.

"Absolutely." The music began, and he stepped boldly into the dance.

Backward, she was to go backward. She struggled to match her feet to his until he paused. "Don't watch your feet." He released her side for a moment and tipped her chin up to look at him. "I promise I won't dance you into a table or a plant." His eyes laughed. At least he wasn't condescending. If he'd been condescending, she would have abandoned him then and there.

Although she'd learned to waltz years ago, she didn't get much practice.

Oh, but now she had the perfect excuse to lose herself in his eyes.

His hand once again settled upon her side, exerting just the right amount of pressure for her to know which foot to move.

And then they were dancing.

"You see?" he teased. "I've only run down a few other couples."

In addition to being extraordinarily good looking, mysterious, and heroic, he also had a delightful sense of humor.

No wonder she'd fallen in love with him!

"I must say," she admitted without thinking, "I was surprised to see you in attendance. Your father is here, you know. As are Lord and Lady Hartley. Have you reconciled with the duke then?"

His jaw had tightened at the mention of his father. He and the Duke of Waters had been estranged for nearly ten years. Rumor was that Lord Blakely had refused to honor a betrothal made by the duke when Lord Blakely was much younger. In an effort to bring him up to snuff, the duke had cut him off. Luckily for the earl, he'd experienced success in trade... although members of the *ton* did not speak of such. The funds he'd amassed, however, kept Lord Blakely from having to kowtow to his father's wishes.

According to Cecily's letters, Lord Blakely was far from destitute.

"I won't be chased away from anything by my father." A steely edge crept into his voice.

"Ah, so you have not reconciled then."

He spun her and then pulled her back into his arms. "No."

"What of your sister? And your mother? Do you speak to them?"

She kept herself from flinching as his grip tightened on her hand. "They have been instructed to steer themselves well clear of my rebellious ways." Did he not realize he was nearly breaking her poor fingers with his tightening grip?

"So, you remain steadfast in your refusal of the girl, then?" Emily knew this was not something she ought to have brought up, but somehow, her mouth voiced the words of its own accord. Was this what he meant by her fascinating conversation? Perhaps it was fascinating when some other poor soul stood in her crosshairs... but not nearly as fascinating when he was the subject of her ineptness.

At least no one else could overhear their discussion.

"How do you know so much of my personal affairs?" And then he shook his head. "Your dear friend Cecily must have shared them with you."

"Well, of course. Do you think ladies don't speak of such matters?" Her fingers had grown numb by now. "And you haven't answered my question."

"I suppose this interrogation is my own fault, eh, Miss Goodnight? You are showing me exactly how entertaining you can be?"

His comment surprised her. She wished she'd thought of the idea herself. "I'm merely curious. That is all, my lord."

His eyes no longer danced. She'd made him angry. Why couldn't she find something light and pleasing to converse about? What sort of topics would be pleasing, anyhow? "Er... did you have your hair shorn recently?" She could have groaned. Did men ever talk about their hair? And with ladies, no less?"

He threw his head back and laughed. Perhaps it was her

368

awkwardness he found fascinating. She scowled at the thought.

"As a matter of fact, I have. Do you think I've left the sideburns long enough, Miss Goodnight? Ought my valet utilize more pomade?"

Oh, no. "They're perfect enough, my lord." And then his grip on her fingers lightened. She nearly stumbled and thought to look down at her feet. She forced herself to look into his gaze instead.

"As usual, you have not disappointed."

"So, it is my social incompetence you find fascinating." She made the statement dully. It felt rather like something of a set down.

"Would you not rather be considered fascinating than a veritable bore? If I were to dance with any other debutante here, I would most certainly find myself subject to the same conversation repeatedly. The weather... the food... the latest styles... I much prefer your forthright manner, as provoking as it can be at times." His smile was warm.

Much as a man might bestow upon his sister or a much younger niece...

The music came to an end, and most of the couples stepped apart. Another dance would begin momentarily, as most sets contained at least three.

He did not release her.

"I do not intend to provoke, my lord," Emily said softly. Although a good deal of chatter rose up around them, she did not wish to be overheard.

He leaned down. "Pardon?" His ear was only inches from her mouth. He smelled of some subtly exotic spice

369

and cigar. It was not unpleasant. She cleared her throat before speaking around the lump that had suddenly formed there. "I do not intend to provoke, my lord."

He chuckled. "You would not be my dear Miss Goodnight if you acted any differently." And then the second dance began. She determined to keep her mouth clamped firmly shut throughout this one. She'd already provided him with enough entertainment.

"I will not make good on my father's promise," he said out of nowhere. "If he wishes to remain the obstinate fool that he is, then so be it." It was almost as though he were speaking to himself. His eyes were pinned upon something behind her. When they spun around, she could see he'd been watching the Duke and Duchess of Waters as well as his sister, Lady Hartley. A few others mingled around the lofty family, including the girl Emily was certain had caused the falling out.

"She is beautiful," Emily stated baldly.

"She is," he agreed. "But she is not my choice."

Emily snorted again. Lovely sound, really. It was no wonder all the men didn't drop to one knee and propose to her on the spot.

"You think I ought not to have an opinion regarding whom I might marry?" Most men would be annoyed that a lady had laughed at them. He didn't sound indignant, merely curious.

"I think you have refused to allow yourself to form an opinion of the girl. I think you are finding fault with her to thwart your father."

Again, he turned her and then twirled her. The sensation was dizzying in more than one way. Physically, as the spinning affected her balance, but in her heart as well. When he led her around the floor so confidently, she felt feminine... and pretty. Despite her dull brown hair. Despite her plain figure.

Despite her blasted spectacles.

"Perhaps there is some truth in your words." He smiled down at her. "Do you hope to heal the wound between Waters and myself? Is that it? You will convince me that I ought to woo her? Court her?" He laughed. He was teasing her once again.

"You must marry eventually," she pointed out.

Which was not something one ever told Lord Blakely. "Not so, Miss Goodnight, not so." He was smiling but a cold hard look returned to his eyes. "I'd as soon marry you as I will do my father's bidding."

She stumbled. Gosh darn it! All those feminine feelings that had come over her just a moment before transformed into a heightened awareness of her own insignificance. "Such the flatterer, you are."

And upon hearing her words, he seemed to catch himself. "Ah, do not take offense. I'd as soon marry anyone rather than give in to my father's wishes."

She wished she understood. What had caused such bitterness?

The dance came to an end. Rather than await the third piece to begin, Emily curtseyed and excused herself. Perhaps she could escape to the library until her other promised sets began.

Such an arrogant and selfish man! She'd tell him where to go if he ever asked her to marry him!

She nearly sobbed at the thought.

Fool, Emily! You fool!

Click here to Read more! Hell's Belle

ALSO BY ANNABELLE ANDERS

The Devilish Debutantes Series

Available in e-book, paperback and audible

Hell Hath No Fury

Hell in a Hand Basket

Hell Hath Frozen Over (Novella)

Hell's Belle

Hell of a Lady

To Hell and Back (Novella)

Not So Saintly Sisters Series

The Perfect Debutante (Louella Rose)

The Perfect Spinster (Olivia)

The Perfect Christmas (With Bonus Material) (Eliza)

Lord Love a Lady Series

Nobody's Lady

A Lady's Prerogative

Lady Saves the Duke

Lady at Last

Lady be Good

Lady and the Rake

I love keeping in touch with readers and would be thrilled to hear from you! Join or follow me at any (or all!) of the social media links below!

Amazon

Bookbub

Website

Goodreads

Facebook Author Page

Facebook Reader Group: A Regency House Party

Twitter

www.annabelleanders.com

ABOUT THE AUTHOR

Married to the same man for over 25 years, I am a mother to three children and two Miniature Wiener dogs. After owning a business and experiencing considerable success, my husband and I got caught in the financial crisis and lost everything; our business, our home, even our car.

At this point, I put my B.A. in Poly Sci to use and took work as a waitress and bartender. Unwilling to give up on a professional life, I simultaneously went back to college and obtained a degree in Energy Management. And then the energy market dropped off.

And then my dog died. I can only be grateful for this series of unfortunate events, for, with nothing to lose and completely demoralized, I sat down and began to write the romance novels which had until then, existed only my imagination. I am happy to have found my place in life. Finally.

Thank you so much for taking the time to read my stories!

Love,
Annabelle Anders

Ms. Anders loves to hear from readers! Please contact her at:

AndersAnnabelle@gmail.com

facebook.com/HappyWritingGirl

www.AnnabelleAnders.com

twitter.com/AnnabellReadLuv

amazon.com/-/e/B073ZLRB3F

The Regency House Party: Annabelle's Facebook Reader Group:

facebook.com/groups/AnnabellesReaderGroup

Made in the USA
Middletown, DE
24 March 2020